THE MAGELLANIC COLLISION

BY

MARVIN E. FOX

© Feb. 27,2012 Registration Number TXu 1-798-371
ISBN 13:9780989690539

THE MAGELLANIC COLLISION

TABLE OF CONTENTS

MARVIN E. FOX

1
MAGELLANIC COLLISION

The collision between the Milky Way and the Magellanic Cloud galaxies began long before we began recording our history. We learned about the collision as our society progressed scientifically and began looking into deep space. We didn't care about it. The collision was occurring on the other side of the galaxy. We couldn't do anything about it. Galactic collisions occur very slowly. The best guess of the occasional scientist, who gave it any thought, was hundreds of thousands of years before we had to deal with any problems caused by it, or so we thought.

Naturally, Jeonk and Shok were the one's who discovered the problems the galactic collision was pushing into Argan lives. Jeonk is, Jeonk Shap, King of a nation of Arga on the planet Okron. Shok is an Argan Fleet Admiral born in the Republic of the United States on planet Earth. His birth name is Kevin Kelly. He and Jeonk met years ago when Jeonk became interested enough in the electronic transmissions from Earth to see what the people on the planet were doing.

Jeonk met Shok on Earth at that time. They became friends, business partners, and battle buddies. Everything they tried in business seemed to come up roses. They worked side by side in more dangerous situations than most people could get into in a few life times. They were famous as warriors because of their many battles, and the fact that they were the last ones standing when the battle was done.

The Argans began using the name, Shok, for Kevin Kelly while he was traveling with Jeonk on his first trip to Arga. The name means 'quick,' and he has lived up to the name. He has a quick mind, makes decisions rapidly, acts as quickly as he can form a plan, and he is fast with a variety of weapons.

Shok and Jeonk are the wrong people for the galaxies worst people to hassle. The more intelligent bad guys know that, and they either try to steer clear of them or kill them first. So far, both ways have been disastrous for a variety of thieves, murderers, pirates, and a few royal tyrants trying to take their turn at ruling the galaxy.

The first sign that the Magellanic Cloud galaxy was about to be a problem surfaced at a family gathering in King Plask's castle. Plask didn't like being the king so he pushed the king business off on his son, Jeonk, as soon as Jeonk became old enough and had the experience he needed to handle the job.

Plask's castle is a huge, ancient looking stone megalith in Arga's Lersta Mountains. The old castle stands near a waterfall fed by a lake that makes up one boundary of the castle grounds. The lake overflow cascades down a cliff to form the Shap River below. The old castle has been the Shap family's ancestral home for more than seven hundred years.

Jeonk and his wife Aslain were at the castle. Shok and his wife Alice were there. Plask thought of Shok as another son and treated Alice like the daughter he never had. Anyone who makes Alice unhappy is in big trouble. Sitak Rakoup, the oldest family friend and long considered by the family to be one of their own, was there with his wife Iliaska.

Fleet Admiral Karst Doskel and his wife Teenskalee were at the castle. Fleet Admiral Zesho Brak and his wife Obrana came for the meeting. All of them were at Plask's castle on serious business but it was also an informal weekend gathering of family and close friends.

The dinner was delicious. Everyone regretted getting so full they couldn't eat any more. The Lersta castle family dinners are sometimes a mixture of Argan and Cajun dishes. Shok loves Cajun dishes, especially grilled alligator, and he introduced the family to it. The family and most of their friends like Cajun dishes almost as much as Shok.

The nation of Arga established an embassy on Earth in the city of New Orleans, Louisiana. They put the embassy in New Orleans, at Plask's insistence, because that is where Plask buys his food, beer and cigars. They also have diplomatic relations with a place called Vatican City, but they can't get Cajun food from there. Plask and Sitak Rakoup have food, quarts of beer and cigars sent to the castle from Louisiana at regular intervals. Beer and cigars are an after dessert treat for the men, usually on the rear verandah of Plask's castle.

The overstuffed dinner guests retired to the castle's back verandah. Plask handed out the beer and cigars to the men, most of the women don't like beer. The men bite off one end of the cigars and spit them somewhere before they light the cigars. The women look away when the men do that, even Alice and she's from Earth, somewhere named Decatur, Illinois.

The men sat around a big table and all of them stretched out their legs and put their feet on it, except Shok. He's too short. Six feet is tall for an Earthman but the Argans are two feet taller than Shok.

Jeonk had something on his mind and that was why the serious business was mixed into the family gathering. Jeonk blew a smoke ring. He then put his cigar close to his ear and rolled it between his fingers as if he was listening to it before he spoke, "Shok and I have discovered a problem that involves the family and Arga. As you know, the fleets have been updated with the technology we took from the Dragon Spit Corsairs we captured in our war with the planets Tuplej and Kashtool. We cured the Spit's problems that caused them to lose the war and our engineers found a way to make our cruisers faster than the corsairs.

"The late King of Pishtup, Sot Pah, of the planet Tuplej, and the late Emperor Astol, of Kashtool, used the older Spit technology to manufacture their corsairs. We have known for a long time that someone else gave them the technology, but we don't know who. We did discover that the technology came from the other side of the galaxy.

"Shok's Office of Special Military Projects has discovered four planets on the other side of this galaxy that have become very concerned with the collision of the Milky Way and the Magellanic Cloud Galaxies. Those four planets joined together to put a large space station near the collision to observe its affects. The space station is in the area we think the Dragon Spit technology came from.

"Shok, I and our military analyst have concluded that the Dragon Spit technology wasn't their best technology. No one gives people like Astol and Sot Pah their best technology. We also concluded that anyone willing to give a dangerous technology to two rotten people like Astol and Sot Pah are no better than they were. Sooner or later we'll have to deal with them. Shok has a plan to check them out and he will tell you about that now."

The most powerful and the best of the military might of Arga attended the dinner. The two kings, Jeonk and Plask were now, and previously, in command of Arga's military might. The Fleet Admirals were as high as they could go in military rank. Only the King outranked them.

Each of the Admirals had his own fleet of sixteen cruisers and each cruiser carried fifteen fighters. Each of the Admirals, present for the meeting, at sometime in the past had faced the military might of an entire planet with only his fleet of sixteen cruisers. Those who chose to fight it out with them lost.

Shok is the tactical genius that planned a large part of those winning strategies. Jeonk and Shok beat the Astolian Empire with fourteen cruisers. They destroyed thousands of Dragon Spit Corsairs and captured several hundred. Shok and Jeonk fought the first Dragon Spit they saw and fought in every Argan battle with the Spits after that time.

Dragon Spits Corsair is the name the Argans gave to that particular spacecraft, which is much smaller than the Argan cruisers. The Spits carry a crew of from four to ten. The Argans called them Dragon Spits because they light up just before they reach maximum speed. One vocal Argan thought the corsair looked like the spit from a dragon traveling a fiery course through space, and the name stuck.

The Dragon Spit war planners depend on its great speed and large numbers to win a battle. They are cheap to build and were a formidable enemy on the planet Tuplej before the Argans captured many of them and improved on their technology. The Argans found a way to beat them during the Tuplej war, and exceeded the Dragon Spit tactics and technology. The war with Kashtool proved the Dragon Spits in any number were no longer a threat to Argan cruisers.

The other Admirals at the meeting have galactic reputations and they are just as dangerous in a battle. Rakoup is the oldest and the most feared. Rakoup's battle philosophy is, go in hot, hit hard enough and fast enough to reduce the enemy to ashes on the first strike. Doskel is as much of a genius on the technical side of the planning as Shok is on the tactical side. Doskel used his technical genius to shut down every important electrical system on the planet Krex before he made his attack on that planet. Brak designed Arga's space armament systems for Arga's forty fleets of cruisers, and only fools in this part of the galaxy go up against Arga's cruisers. Brak's fleet orbited the planet Iklug and held the Iklug's at bay until they surrendered rather than fight it out.

Shok was among friends, but his plan wasn't going to be heard by cheerleaders. These men had been honed to a sharp edge by many battles. They would cut any plan to the bone if it didn't sound right. A plan heard by this group was either good or gone, no matter whose plan it was.

Shok began, "The Problem of a possible enemy with a superior technology has bothered all of us for a long time. We had to wait until our fleets were upgraded and capable of producing the best protection for Arga before we could address the problem. All of us have had our fleets trained to use the new technology. We are faster, better armed and more prepared than any of us would have dreamed we could be only a few years ago. The time has come to be deadly serious about taking control of, and solving the problem.

"We think the Dragon Spit technology came from the other side of the galaxy. It certainly didn't come from this side. Tuplej and Kashtool, who originally used it in our galaxy, are toward the center of the galaxy. We don't know where they got the technology. We must find where it came from and discover how far the original designers have developed the technology.

"We assumed the original owners gave the Spit technology to Astol and Sot Pah in the hope of clandestinely checking out its effectiveness during their drive to control our part of the galaxy. If the two tyrants could have pulled off a takeover using the Spit technology, the original designers had a better technology available to destroy Astol and Sot Pah if they refused to give up control of the conquered planets. Astol and Sot Pah were nothing more than unwitting errand boys for the real tyrants.

"For the past few years Argan space probes have been crisscrossing the galaxy looking for signs of the Dragon Spit Corsair technology. We haven't found it with the probes. We did discover something very interesting that might be related. We know our galaxy is colliding with a part of the Magellanic Cloud galaxy. That didn't bother us, but our probes have discovered inhabited planets near the collision, and those planets will be bothered by the collision sometime in the near future. It appears they know that, and they are preparing to do something about it. A very large space station has been constructed near the collision area to observe its affects.

"The plan I have to conduct the search, for whoever gave the two rats the Spits, is dangerous and it involves some danger to the family as well as the fleets. The space station used to observe the effects of the galactic collision gives us the excuse we need to be in the area to conduct the search. The plan involves the Royal Cruiser, the Royal Family, and four of our fleets. The four fleets commanded by the Admirals at this dinner are the most powerful, best trained and the most diverse among all of our fleets.

"We want to take the Royal Cruiser with a one fleet escort to that space station. The space station has a huge viewing section and a very large holographic display to keep tabs on the collision.

"The people on the other side of our galaxy are worried that the collision has gotten close enough to their planets to begin affecting the orbital paths of the inhabited planets in their area, and the time of the effect is near. If they are correct, they will have to move their populations somewhere else because their planets will be destroyed.

"Our worry is that they intend to move from their side of the galaxy to this side to cure that problem. We think they may intend to conquer the inhabited planets on this side of the galaxy to support that move. We think they will use the best technology they have to assure themselves success in that conquest.

"All of us at this meeting will be in the Royal Cruiser. Our vice Admirals will be in charge of our fleets unless we go on board and take charge. We need the most technically experienced battle savvy people to do the up close observations and information gathering. While we have specialists in all fields who know more about their specialized fields than we do, we have no one but ourselves who are as well versed in all of their fields as we are. We need the expertise that only we have to make the broad based critical judgments that must be made.

"While the Royal Cruiser and its escorting fleet is near the space station, the other three fleets will be scanning everything on the nearby planetary systems for every piece of information they can get. Only our four fleets are equipped with the specialized equipment and crews necessary to get the information we need.

"We don't expect the space station to have the technology we're after. It's stationary and doesn't need it. The space station is the starting point where we inform the planets in the area that a foreign king has come to observe the galactic collision. When we arrive at the space station and the station announces the presence of a foreign king in that area, it should get us invitations from the planetary leaders. That's when our search will get serious. We'll have a chance to visit those planets.

"This is also the point where the fleets are endangered. Our supposed enemy will have an opportunity to view our technology. Our technology will either give him second thoughts or help him to decide that he can win a war with us. The danger to the Royal Family will begin with those invitations. He will know he has the most formidable protectors of our part of the galaxy in his part of the galaxy. Does anyone have any comments?"

Brak was the first to comment, "We must assume that the battles on Tuplej and Kashtool were observed by the people we are trying to identify. The Royal family and the leading Admirals were on Tuplej during and after the war. Our assumed enemy will be able to identify us, on sight, from the information given to him by his spies on Tuplej. The battle on Kashtool was even more devastating to his technology, and he will have identified you and Jeonk from that battle. If our enemy knows who we are, he will also know we are the core of our defenses. Why won't he just kill all of us and make it easy for himself?"

Jeonk explained, "It took sixty four cruisers to beat the Dragon Spit technology on Tuplej. We lost several cruisers and many of our fighters. We faced a much larger force on Kashtool with only fourteen cruisers. We had no losses on Kashtool, cruisers or fighters, and we destroyed over thirty percent more of his technology than we did on Tuplej.

"Whoever the enemy is, he already knows we upgrade our technology and tactics very quickly. He will have some idea about the increased capabilities of our spacecraft from the exterior appearances of our cruisers and fighters but he won't be able to evaluate his own ability to beat us from that source of information alone. The information about us is as critical to him as the information about him is to us. He won't try to kill anyone until he gets it. At least, that's our assumption."

Rakoup gave them his dissenting thoughts, "If he must discover our capabilities before he attacks us, why can't we wait for him to send probes or spacecraft to us, bring them down and see what he has? That costs nothing and there is no danger to anyone?"

"If we were going to do the same kind of research on his battle capabilities," Shok replied, "we would send the most inconspicuous spacecraft we have and it wouldn't tell anyone anything if it was lost or brought down. All we would know after we brought his down is that someone is looking at us. We already know they are looking at us but we don't know where they are getting their information. They certainly have spies on Tuplej and Kashtool. We must assume they have spies on Prssk and they could have probes in space that we haven't found."

Doskel questioned, "Have you considered that we have the best technology we have ever had and we can not expect to upgrade it for years to come? We have no one at this time that can engineer a more sophisticated upgrade. We may be risking the best we have against someone who has just as good or better."

Jeonk responded to Doskel's criticism, "We have made technological advances in our spacecraft that far exceed what we learned from the Dragon Spits. We are assuming that our advances are equal to what they have. If that is correct, we cannot hide those advances from a technically sophisticated enemy for long even though we keep our technology at its highest security classification.

"We are also assuming that they have had this technology for much longer than we have. They will be closer to their ability to upgrade than we are, but how many months or years closer is unknown. If we wait, we may be giving an unknown enemy the time he needs to discover our capabilities and exceed them. If we have to go to war after that time, we may lose the war because of the time we gave the enemy to upgrade his technology."

The men sat back to think the plan over. They didn't like it but they understood the logic. After a few minutes of consideration Plask made his objection, "If there is so close a possibility of going to war, why are we taking our women with us?"

Jeonk looked to where Shok was smoking his cigar and said, "Why don't you explain that Shok. You can do a better job on that than I can."

The women turned toward Shok to hear what he would say. Alice winked at him. She knew Jeonk frequently asked Shok to explain things Jeonk didn't like to explain himself. Shok reached for a quart of Plask's Louisiana beer, took a drink and said, "Aslain, Alice, and Iliaska have more diplomatic experience than anyone we could possible take with us. Their experiences on the planets Iklug and Egrin taught them important things we military men miss. They have dealt with more different races of people at the personal and diplomatic level than anyone we know of from here or any other planet. We need them for the insight they bring to our dealings with the new races we expect to meet. That insight will be missing, entirely, without them.

"This is not a war mission. We are spying. We want to give the impression of rich, self satisfied, well-protected royalty who go wherever they want to amuse themselves and their friends. Our planet hopping royal outing can't be complete without our lovely wives on our arms. With them, we are a rich and lazy group out for a jaunt around the galaxy. Without them, we are a bunch of suspicious looking military people out for who knows what."

Plask retorted, "The enemy you and Jeonk describe won't believe we're just a bunch of royal lay-abouts out for a little fun."

Jeonk felt he had to give Shok more support in the discussion, "The real enemy will know were not there for fun but the real enemy won't give us any information. The scanners of the three roaming fleets will pin point the location and technology of the real enemy. We have no plan to drop into a trap. That's why we need the best we have for this mission. We will have to do our spying while we visit the neighboring planets. It will be great luck, and great danger, if we get an invitation from the real enemy. We will not accept his invitation to a meeting on one of his planets."

Plask didn't like the plan and he had no qualms about saying so, "This time, I think you two are farther out on a limb than I have ever seen you. Everyone here is trying to think up a better plan to get you off of the limb, but you've done your homework on this one. I want two weeks for us to come up with a better plan. If we can't think of one we'll probably go along with yours. If we do go along with your plan, we'll be doing everything we can to keep someone from sawing off the limb your putting us so far out on.

"I think your right about the enemy and his technology. Somehow, we must discover who he is, what his real intentions are, what his best shot at us is, and if he is efficiently belligerent enough to take his best shot. I hope he is some weak minded nut who was flimflammed out of his technology by Astol and Sot Pah, but I don't think so."

The best military minds came up with many plans during the next two weeks, but none of their plans filled in the empty spaces that had to be filled for their safety and the safety of Arga. The women came up with a pretty good plan but it was militarily too difficult to use.

They wanted to bring in the fleets from the Galactic Forum nations. Eight hundred fleets from ten planets would be impressive but it would take months of diplomatic discussions to put it together. In addition, the Forum fleets could no longer match the speed of the Argan fleets and the Forum fleets would take too long to reach the other side of the galaxy. There was one more consideration; if an attack occurred while the most powerful Argan fleets were gone, the Forum fleets would be needed for the defense of their own nations.

As always, Arga was the nation the enemy must beat and Arga had to be the one who prepared to defeat a strong enemy. Arga was the only nation strong enough to take the chance of being the first with the most to meet the new threat.

2
THE VIEW OF ARMAGEDDON

The Argan cruisers' Light Infused Thrust Technology worked beyond their expectations for crossing the galaxy. People think the speed of light, 186,000 miles per second, is the maximum speed for light and nothing can change it. That is incorrect; light traveling through a vacuum can arrive on the other side of the vacuum at the same time it left. Space is a vacuum and light takes no time to cross it if the light is full spectrum light.

The fleets used their standard thrusters to lift off of Arga and accelerate to light speed. That was very quick. When they reached light speed, they switched the thrust mode to Full Spectrum Acceleration. The ships' outer hulls were constructed of a newly designed fulgent metal that could be totally infused with light. The Full Spectrum Accelerators cast a beam of light from the rear hull of the cruisers and ahead of the cruisers with the same width and height as the cruiser. The accelerators, installed in the aft of the ship, flooded and infused the hulls of the ships with the same full spectrum light that was cast ahead of the ship.

The infused light, passing through the hull of the spacecraft already accelerating beyond light speed, kept the ship accelerating to maintain the same speed as the light the accelerators projected forward. It can't do that instantly because the inside of the ship is not full spectrum light. The Argan cruiser, however, is very light in space and its weight is only a small factor in the speed equation. The ship's hull effectively becomes a part of the projected beam of light. The thrust of the spacecraft constantly accelerates until it reaches the speed of the projected light. The Argan cruisers continue the acceleration mode until the cruisers reach the speed of the full spectrum light it generates. There is no beam of light that can be cast forward of the bow of the ship after that time.

Light, at its maximum speed, takes zero time to cross a vacuum. The Argan cruiser's speed is controlled to whatever lower speed the crew wants it to travel by controlling the Full Spectrum Accelerator so it will generate the necessary portion of its full spectrum for the desired speed.

The Argan spacecraft have the standard plasma thrusters, gravity thrusters, armament systems and maneuvering capability they had before they were redesigned with Light Infused Thrust technology, but in deep space the LIT is the choice to accelerate speed.

The Argans jumped their fleets into deep space on a course that would take their nation to the brink of total defeat. They were about to discover a very interesting enemy who was equal to their battle technology--an enemy who was, in no way, more interesting than the Argans themselves.

The three fleets assigned to do the spying from deep space, separated from the Royal Cruiser and its escort fleet light years from the space station. They fanned out in search of the inhabited planets they expected to be hiding their most dangerous enemy. Each ship proceeding to its separate assigned search area, but would remain in contact with the other ships to share whatever data their search produced.

As the Royal Cruiser and its escort fleet neared the space station, they slowed and opened the Royal Cruiser's view ports for a more personal look at the station than they had seen on the command deck holoscanner. Shok was the first to speak, "The holograph showed it to be more than two miles in diameter but actually seeing it gives a real sense of its immensity. These people are very serious about tracking the affects of the collision."

The collision of the two galaxies was not evident from the Royal Cruiser's view ports. The stars of the Milky Way galaxy appeared to mix easily and naturally with the stars of the Magellanic Cloud. There were no fiery collisions, and what was occurring seemed to be normal galactic activity. The dangers of the collision were too subtle for the naked eye.

The gravity fields of the two galaxies had begun to interact and that interaction made the collision dangerous. As the collision progressed, if the galaxies were passing through each other, the paths of the solar systems from one galaxy would be affected by the gravity of the other galaxy. The resulting orbital changes would destroy all life on the inhabited planets whose orbits were warped by the force of two different giant gravity fields pulling them in opposite directions.

"We have contact with them," Admiral Brak reported, "They have been informed of who we are and of our intentions to go on board to view the collision. They have given us permission to launch a shuttle and they will open a shuttle bay directly in front of us as soon as we launch. The admiral in charge of the station will meet us in the shuttle bay. He is Admiral Keet Nonazk of the planet Ker."

Admiral Nonazk was no shock to people used to meeting people of other races. His uniform was ordinary and the signs of his rank were cloth markings on his left chest. He was clearly wearing a working admiral's uniform. He stood seven feet tall and had gold colored skin. He appeared to be a pleasant man as he approached the incoming party of strangers.

After the usual introductory pleasantries, the Admiral helped them into a travel vehicle that operated on the familiar anti-gravity principle. They quickly proceeded to a central compartment that was approximately one kilometer in diameter. The inside space of the compartment was filled with a gigantic holographic display showing the colliding portions of the two galaxies. Viewing the display from short distances was best done in movable viewing vehicles that could be positioned over any target of concern within the display area. The royal party was asked, but declined the closer view of the collision. Their spying mission didn't need close up views. Admiral Nonazk, and his guests, viewed the entire display from a balcony around the circumference of the display.

Admiral Nonazk explained the dynamics of the display. "This display represents the data bank from more than a million probes positioned uniformly in the path of the collision. What we see here is constantly updated by the input from those probes. The sensors on board the probes are also giving us data we can't see here. We have computers taking data from those sensors and they give us information about the strength of the gravitational shifts on the leading edge of the collision. The gravitational shifts are the major danger to us, and to the galaxy.

"We have come to an understanding that the people living on the inhabited planets in this area must go somewhere else. The inhabited planets are the ones with the special lighting. As you can see, we have four of them we know of but there could be more inhabited planets in the broader regions of the danger area that we don't know about.

"Less than one hundred years from now, our planetary orbits will be seriously affected by the gravitational pull of the attacking galaxy. We think, in a thousand years, the nucleuses of the two galaxies may begin a cataclysmic interaction. We believe, eventually, life in this galaxy will be extinct because of that interaction. If the nucleuses collide, the explosion will destroy all life in both galaxies. If they do not collide but only interact, there is a possibility of some life surviving in the galaxy but that isn't certain.

"We believe the attacking galaxy is slowly slipping below our galaxy. We don't know if the two nucleuses will pass each other or be drawn into each other. Our scientists like both theories but they can't decide which is right. The Event Dynamics are too complicated for them to be positive about either. We have no intention of waiting to find out who is right. In either case we will be dead or gone when it happens."

Jeonk asked, "Admiral Nonazk, where do you intend to go to save your people from this disaster?"

The Admiral answered, "We don't know. The attacking Galaxy is in two parts. The smaller of the two is interacting with us. The next closest galaxy is also doomed to eventually collide with ours. The nearest safe galaxy is too far away for us to reach with our present technology.

"It will take more time than we have to develop a technology capable of reaching that galaxy and transporting our populations to it. We are hoping to find uninhabited planets or friendly planets to live on until we can develop a new technology. We can add one thousand years to our time schedule by finding places to live on the other side of either galaxy.

"We have recently heard of a race of people on the other side of this galaxy. They are said to be a highly developed technical people. We were told they are a race of blue giants who are both fierce and friendly. We have one of our fastest ships going to their planet, called Okron, to ask them for help. You probably passed our ship on your way here. I recognized you as those people when your ship identified you and asked for entry instructions for your shuttle. I, and all of our people, will be delighted that the fierce, friendly Argans are here."

Shok, with the suspicion that these people had neither the technology nor the temperament to wage the war he was expecting, said, "Have your probes recorded spacecraft activity from the other galaxy or from unfamiliar planets in this galaxy?"

The Admiral replied, "We have noticed some activity from the Attack Galaxy. The Attack Galaxy is the name we have used for the intruding galaxy since this space station was first installed. Their spacecraft have caused us no trouble but they appeared as an anomaly in the data from our probes. Our probes aren't the type used for spacecraft surveillance, so we didn't have a very clear picture of them.

"They have appeared so persistently in certain areas that we became curious. We put spacecraft surveillance probes in those areas. Their technology, whoever they are, is better than ours. Their ships are very fast. We think they may be fast enough for intergalactic travel and intergalactic travel is of great interest to us. At a minimum, their technology represents a quantum leap above ours and would help in our search for galactic exit technology.

"We have tried many times to contact them but with no success. We have sent communications probes to them at frequent intervals. The probes stopped transmitting after entering the area of the Attack Galaxy where we think their planets are. We also sent a spacecraft with diplomats on board several years ago. We have heard nothing from them. We know our spacecraft has had time to reach them and return.

"I have a small holograph in my office. I'll access a data bank of information we have about their ships and put it on the display for you as soon as we are finished here."

The Admiral continued talking for two and a half hours longer about his most interesting intergalactic mission. He finally asked, "Do you have any questions?" All of them were too numb to ask questions. The party retired to the Admirals office to see the display they were intensely interested in, and wouldn't become numb from watching.

The Admiral accessed his data bank to show the various types of spacecraft his team had seen with its surveillance probes. The first spacecraft was a Dragon Spit Corsair. The second was a spacecraft about the same size as an Argan cruiser. The third was a real powerhouse, the size of ten Argan cruisers combined. It had a crescent shaped upper structure. The bottom was rather flat with geometric patterned protrusions across the broad base of the ship. It's bottom and sides were covered with what appeared to be pulse cannons and lasers. Its smooth upper surface was indented with shapes that could be hatches for elevators used to raise large particle beam weapons.

Admiral Nonazk informed them, "The big one is the one we think is probably intergalactic. We can track the others for short distances. We can't track this on at all. We made this record when it was sitting still, looking for or waiting for something in space. It didn't leave the area like a spaceship it just, disappeared. Most spaceships disappear when someone is looking at them with their eyes but this one disappeared while a spacecraft surveillance probe was looking at it. That's a good trick."

"Did you get any information on its electronic emissions?" Doskel asked.

Brak added, "What about its armament capability?"

"Have you been able to track the course of any of these ships into--our--inner galaxy?" Shok asked.

The admiral responded to all of the questions with one answer, "No, we aren't set up to for that type of surveillance. We are interested of course but they don't seem to care about what we are doing. We think they know what we know about the collision and they will be affected as much as we will. We believe they have a different plan to handle the problem and we don't think we are a consideration in that plan. If they wanted to attack us they could have done it long ago. Our four planets would not have been able to resist their technology."

"Do you have a name for these, Attack Galaxy, people?" Shok asked.

The Admiral replied, "We have had no direct contact with them and we don't know the name they prefer for themselves. We think they are powerful and that there are many of them. Our name for them is, the Horde.

The Admiral had announced the fleet's arrival to his many planetary superiors before the Argans first came on board the space station. The discussion with Admiral Nonazk was interrupted by requests from the closest planet, Hika, to the space station.

The governments of the four planets were in close cooperation in their interplanetary fight against death, and they were requesting a meeting with the Argan King and his party. The eager leaders were willing to come to the space station for that meeting, or they would be glad to entertain the royal party on the planet Hika. Leaders from many of the governments were already on their way to Hika, either for a meeting there or to leave from Hika to meet on the space station.

Jeonk decided it would be more informative for the meeting to be on Hika. That would give his escort fleet's crews a better shot at close scanning of the planets they had come to spy on. Admiral Nonazk said a pleasant goodbye to them in the shuttle bay. He then returned to a spacecraft surveillance console to watch them leave for Hika. The Argan fleet made its exit. It just disappeared from the space station surveillance scan.

The Admiral turned to his chief aide who was watching the departure with him and said, "I think there is going to be one hell-of-a war. I think we'll be able to see it from here. If you ever prayed for anything in your life, pray that those Argans win it. Right now, they're our best hope for escaping this galactic planet grinder."

3

THE HIKA PLANETS

The discussions on the Royal Cruiser were mixed. No one knew how much trust could be put in Admiral Nonazk's information. There was a feeling that Nonazk was honest but there was too much at stake to believe him without knowing for certain. Nonazk's people were in a terrible bind. They believed they had to move or die. They weren't powerful enough to move without allies to help and they had no certainty of help. What they were willing to do, or who they were willing to do it to, to resolve their deadly dilemma was anybody's guess.

The Argans knew their supposed enemy was no longer supposed but real. The Dragon Spit technology had obviously been supplied by a source in the Magellanic Cloud galaxy. The enemy who supplied the Dragon Spits to Tuplej and Kashtool was in as much of a bind as Nonazk's people, and were preparing to move into the Milky Way galaxy.

The intergalactic population transfer wasn't going to be a friendly move. The new enemy had contacted and supplied interplanetary troublemakers in the inner galaxy with some of their technology. They would certainly have contacted people on the planets nearer the galactic collision. Who and how the contacts were made and what agreements were reached were unknown ingredients in the stew of war. The stew of war was about to be stirred with vigor by people who were good at the practice.

Plask was never silent for long when he had something on his mind and he said what they were all thinking, "We need to be very careful during the diplomatic contacts. Whatever we say will be reported to the Horde by someone we meet."

Alice offered, "I think we five women should concentrate on the women at the meetings. You men don't pay enough attention to the women and you underestimate how much they know about dangerous situations. We may be able to get critical information from the women that even their husbands might not know the women have. The information we get from them could be more critical than the information their husbands are willing to share with you."

"That's a good idea," Jeonk agreed. "I hope your notebook diplomacy will be as effective on Hika as it was at the Galactic Forum."

Doskel's wife, Teenskalee asked, "What's notebook diplomacy?"

Aslain answered, "Alice and I used notebooks instead of recorders when we were working with the Galactic Forum nations. We found the many different races in the Forum were willing to discuss their lives in more intimate detail if we used notebooks to make a record of what they said. Voice recorders put people's comments on permanent records in their own voices forever. People are more cautious about what they say when a voice record is made. Notebook diplomacy may work as well on Hika as it did at the Forum."

Brak brought the conversation back to the main danger, "We're close to a very powerful enemy with very little protection. We have three fleets spread around four solar systems and one fleet at ground zero. If the Horde decides we are here for serious business, they could attack us to reduce our numbers in a future attack. I think we should regroup the fleets and bring them to Hika with us."

"You have a point," Jeonk replied, "but regrouping may allow the Horde an opportunity to kill off four fleets instead of one. If they are as powerful as Admiral Nonazk thinks they are, they could destroy our four fleets with ease. What do you think Shok?"

"I agree with both of you," Shok answered, "and this is what I think we should do. We can't send a message across the galaxy as quickly as we can send cruisers. We need to send two cruisers back home. One should go to Arga to inform the Admiralty that the enemy is real. We need to order the Admiralty to send twenty fleets to stand off between Arga and the Horde, far enough so they can remain unnoticed but close enough to assist if the fleets here are attacked by the Horde. I think ten light years should do that.

"The second cruiser will go to the Galactic Forum with our assessment of the situation. If we go to war, and I think we will, the war will start soon. We should request the Galactic Forum nations to position their spacecraft for battle. The Forum fleets will take longer to get here. By the time they arrive, the battle will probably be in progress. If it isn't, they should position themselves no further from the galactic collision than Admiral Nonazk's space station. The Forum spacecraft shouldn't try to hit the Horde head on. We will have to take the brunt of the attack. The Forum nations should concentrate on flanking attacks to take the pressure off of our frontal attack.

"Our three fleets should finish their scan runs and then return to us but they should remain out of the scan range of Hika and the space station. We don't want the Horde spies in this group to be able to report the amount of fleet activity we have in the area. So far, we have detected no scan activity from the Attack Galaxy but they could be scanning us with some means we can't detect.

"I think we must assume the Horde know we are here. Unless they were prepared to go to battle before we arrived, it will take them as much time to prepare as it does us. Our four fleets were battle ready when we left Arga but four fleets aren't enough. There is no indication the Horde intended to go to war at this time and I suspect they intended to bring their war to the inner galaxy in a surprise attack. They expected Tuplej and Kashtool to chop us down to easy victory size but that didn't happen. I think their present war preparations will be more cautious and caution is usually slower. We should make the maximum effort to strengthen every fleet we, and the Galactic Forum have, to a new level for military survival."

"Do you think war is unavoidable and that it must be here?" asked Admiral Doskel.

"No I don't," Shok replied, "and no plan should be that solid. We can't predict the precise activities of an enemy we expect to attack us. The activities of war should always be considered fluid and include a means of avoiding war when it is reasonable to do so. I think the war will probably occur, and it will probably occur here. It's better for it to occur here, rather than in the inner galaxy.

"An inner galaxy war will give them large populations to attack. If they attack the inner galaxy planets and their attacks give them inner galaxy bases, we will have to attack friendly nations to beat them. We will cause major losses among our own people in a war of that kind. Here, there are only four planets and they will probably not be in the war. The Horde has no interest in them and those planets may not help us.

"If we force the Horde into population centers for their own protection, the population centers best suited for their protection are Horde population centers. The Horde will, hopefully, go for the maximum protection of their own territory."

Plask interjected, "We need a voice of authority at home to speak to the Admiralty. I'll be that voice. After I've spoken to the Admiralty, I can bring the twenty fleets to the position Shok suggested. We also need a powerful voice to address the Galactic Forum and get their fleets involved. The Galactic forum fleets have to act as one fleet when the Horde attacks. That old Paracan space warrior, Chosteel, is probably the best they have. I may be able to get them to put him in charge of their fleets.

"You tell the people on Hika that this old man became ill and had to return home. They'll believe that, old kings get sick all of the time. It will give them a reason for a couple of our cruisers to be missing from the fleet.

"I think it will be best to have five of our home fleets giving close cover to Arga. Three more fleets should be in deep space monitoring the possible activity of the Horde on our side of the galaxy. The eight unassigned fleets can be put in space to back up the twenty-four fleets waiting for the Horde attack to begin. We should consider a three-wave defense. Your four fleets here will be the first wave. The twenty I'll be bringing is the second wave. The eight home fleets, joined by the three monitoring fleets will be the third wave. If we add the Forum fleets from more than eight hundred nations under the command of Chosteel, the Horde will have to be pretty tough to beat us."

"All right father," Jeonk agreed, "it sounds like a go to me unless someone has something to add. We'll slow the fleet to give you time to get to a cruiser. As soon as you're on your way home, we'll take the fleet to Hika."

Everyone in the room was familiar with hard decisions and fast actions. There were no additions or discussion. The plan, as far as it went, was acceptable to all of them. King Plask was quickly on his way.

They continued following the Hika beacon being transmitted to bring them to the interplanetary meeting. The fleet fanned out in a protective umbrella as the Royal Cruiser came to a halt over Hika. The landing party made its final descent in the ships shuttle, leaving the Royal Cruiser two hundred miles off of the surface of the planet Hika.

As the shuttle neared the beacon location, Iliaska remarked, "The building for the meeting is large enough to be a sports arena on the bottom but it has eighty floors."

Admiral Brak's wife Obrana added, "It's probably the main meeting place for the diplomats of the four planets. The diplomats must have a large number of assistants."

The beacon brought them to a landing pad near a large entrance. There were ten civilians and several rows of honor guards waiting as they left the shuttle. The first of the strangers to walk forward and greet the party was President Ak Tontz of the nation of

Pintz. Pintz was the most powerful nation on the planet Hika.

The introductions were made. President Tontz ushered the Argans inside, to a large room used as a formal meeting hall. The applause as they entered was polite and friendly. As President Tontz ushered them to a long table at the head of the room, he apologized for the lack of a dinner for the guests. He had no knowledge of the type of food they might find pleasing and didn't want to force their acceptance of possibly unacceptable food for the sake of being polite.

During President Tontz's introduction of the guests to the main body of the planetary leaders, he made many references to the strong and friendly nation of Arga, its gallant king and the wonderful giving nature of the Argan people. He explained the nature of their problem with the galactic collision in stark detail and asked, on the part of all of their peoples, if Arga could help them resolve that problem.

Jeonk's response was cautious. He couldn't tell them he expected to go to war with the Horde, and any help Arga could give would have to be determined after the war. He knew it was possible that Arga might not be in a position to help if it lost the war. He began, "We came to your area to see the affects of the galactic collision on this area and its affects on the people who are here. We didn't expect the dangerous situation you are in. I know of no uninhabited planets you can move to in our galaxy. The help you receive must be from friendly planets that are already inhabited. There are several possibilities in that group.

I cannot speak for them but there is an organization called The Galactic Forum and most of those planets' nations belong to it. The central offices of the Galactic Forum are on a planet called Veolsh. Arga is a member, and I will give you introductions and the navigational coordinates to reach the Forum. I'm certain they will be glad to help you find locations to transfer your endangered populations.

We have discovered the galactic collision will be of major importance in the lives of our own Argan people. Admiral Nonazk has told us that the entire galaxy may eventually be destroyed by it. If that is true, we will all have the same concerns you are now having.

We have also discovered a people in the galaxy you have named the Attack Galaxy. Your name for them is, Horde. They are sending their spacecraft into our galaxy but they appear to make no contacts when they arrive. We were told their planets are threatened, as are yours; yet, they ask for no help from you or us. In order for them to move into this galaxy, they must find living space on the same planets you must go to for your survival.

It would be helpful for us to know how they intend to do that. We are curious about them and we will appreciate any information you have about them. If any of you have information about the Horde, please contact us after this meeting. If any of you have questions, I or my friends will be glad to answer them."

The questions lasted for hours and were mostly about the types of planets available to them on the other side of the galaxy. There wasn't one question asked, or one piece of information given to the Argans about the Horde, or how they and the Horde might share the limited resources of friendly planets at the same time. If one believed the contents of their questions, the entire assembly of Hikan diplomats was unaware of a possible war that would probably occur over galactic real estate. No one came forward later with information about the Horde. The Argans left the meeting with more questions than they arrived with and some very uneasy feelings about their new acquaintances.

The first action the Argans took after returning to the Royal Cruiser was to regroup their fleets and move them into deep space. They spread the fleets in a wide battle formation and ordered constant scanning of the hostile area on the Magellanic side of the collision. After the business of fleet protection was completed, they settled in for the discussion of the Hika meeting and their impressions of those they had just met.

Admiral Brak began first, "The Hika people either think the Horde are just tourists in this galaxy or they are someone else's problem."

Alice remarked, "They can't really believe their counterparts across that intergalactic valley of death are just going to wait to die without doing anything about it."

"They're afraid of the Horde," Admiral Doskel suggested, "and any recognition of the Horde outside of their own group will force them to make a commitment. They are afraid to take any position that might make themselves vulnerable to a Horde attack."

"People who are afraid to make a commitment that is necessary for their survival aren't much of a people," Iliaska added. "We should think twice before inviting them to live on our home planets."

Obrana was more charitable, "They are so worried about their survival that they can't think of anything else. If they get involved in a war, they might not have enough spacecraft left to get them to the friendly planets even if they win the war."

Rakoup was more direct, "If we don't win the war, they will have no planets to move to. The Horde will own them and the Horde are not their friends."

"Shok has been too quiet," Aslain reported. "When he's quiet, it's because he's sifting things to get them right. Shok, as soon as you quit sifting, tell us what you think."

"It will be a long time before I finish sifting this situation," Shok replied, "but I'll tell you what I think so far. The first problem is why the Hika call the people, across Alice's valley of death, the Horde. They don't seem to know anything about them but the word, Horde, suggests a large number of people. Admiral Nonazk showed us three of their ships but he didn't say how often or how many others he had seen. Are the Horde called the Horde because of their large population or because of their large number of spacecraft. Remember, Nonazk said they were unable to make contact after many tries. All he knew about them was what he saw from the probes he placed on this side of the collision. I think he saw a horde of spacecraft and used that name to describe what he saw.

"The Hika diplomats and the diplomats we talked with from other planets certainly do know there will be a war. They aren't fools. They don't want to enter the war on either side for strategic reasons. Two enemies, both having great power and similar technology are about to go to war. If we lose we will not be able to help them, but both we, and the Horde may destroy each others potential to resist the Hika's move to other planets.

"The Horde may be hurt so seriously they will find it impossible to move into our galaxy even if they win the war with us. We may be hurt so seriously we can't help the Hikans move even though we win the war. But, the Hikans don't need our help to move. All they need is a place to move to. They know we are going to protect the only places where they can move. They will be able to keep their fleets intact and battle ready if they don't enter the war. The fleets of four planets may be enough to enforce their own choice of the planets they want for their new home. They may have a very large force for badly damaged space fleets to defend against, and ours may be badly damaged. I think the Hika politicians want us to win but just barely; otherwise, they can only move with our permission."

Jeonk looked at Shok before he remarked, "If you're right and the logic is on your side, the Hika politicians are doing some very poor planning. They could make the difference between success and failure in a war with the Horde. If they were the ones who made that difference, every planet on our side of the galaxy would welcome them with open arms. If they don't help to keep their new homes secure, they will be tolerated until we can get rid of them and that will be done as fast as we can."

"Politicians have never been known as good battle planners," Shok responded. "Anyone who insists on losing a battle can have a politician plan it. They see themselves as wise leaders, and great statesmen, for reasons I have never understood."

Shok's general assessment of politicians was interrupted by information from the command deck, "Battle formations are coming at us from the other side of the galactic collision."

4

THE SKIRMISH WITH THE HORDE

Shok was the first to reach the command deck. He rushed to the global holoscanner for a first look at the incoming spacecraft. Jeonk and the other Admirals followed right behind him. All watched the holograph as the enemy spacecraft approached. Jeonk asked the deck officer, "How many are there and what's there speed. Give me an ETA for maximum pulse cannon range."

There are four thousand of what appear to be Dragon Spit Corsairs. They are stacked in four waves of one thousand each. Each wave is one hundred ships wide. Their approach puts each wave thirty seconds apart. The first formation will be in our maximum range in nineteen minutes but..."

Jeonk interrupted him, "Admirals get to your own command decks. I'll brief you on the way. Shok you remain here. Your fleet is the closest to the battle and you can command it from here."

As the Admirals hurried off the deck, the deck officer finished his report, "There are twenty cruisers in stationary positions behind the corsairs and there is a very large ship above the twenty cruisers. It appears to be about equal in size to ten of our cruisers and it's presently holding a stationary position."

Shok ordered the fleets to pull in close to his fleet, stacked and spread for a sweep of the first formation. A sweep was being formed to put the laser and pulse cannon fire of the sixty-three Argan cruisers into a blanket of fire covering the first formation of corsairs. The first wave of corsairs advanced with one hundred Dragon Spits across and ten rows deep. The Argan sweep had to work with deadly precision to protect the fleet.

Jeonk reported the Admirals had reached their command decks and were briefed just before the first formation came into maximum firing range. Shok waited another thirty seconds to allow the corsairs to get deeply into the pocket of fire. He gave the order for his sixty-three cruisers to begin their synchronized fire as the second wave of corsair entered the maximum firing range of the Argan cruisers.

The blue and green fire of the Argan armada ripped space between the cruisers and the corsairs. The corsairs had not yet reached their maximum firing range when the fire from the Argan cruiser tore into their hulls. The first wave formation and the forward ships of the second wave caught the brunt of the sweep. The hulls of the first formation of corsairs glowed with heat before they began exploding from the intense temperature melting their outer skins. The survivors of the second wave of corsairs broke formation and dived to the left and right to avoid a second sweep. The third and fourth waves of corsairs began a wheeling maneuver to retreat from the attack. The Horde fighter pilots would quickly learned the Argans were not easy to avoid in a battle.

Jeonk ordered, "Rakoup, get your fleet under the corsairs. Brak, take your fleet above them. Doskel, split your fleet and swing it to both sides, Shok's fleet will charge through the center. We'll sandwich them between us and cut off their retreat across the collision area."

Shok pushed his fleet directly into the center of the fleeing corsairs. His charging spacecraft split their formation and forced the retreating corsairs toward the other three Argan fleets. Shok's gunners pummeled the corsairs with deadly accuracy as they advanced.

Jeonk asked, "What do you think they are doing Shok? This is one strange battle. The big ship and the cruisers haven't moved to help the corsairs."

Shok replied, "They are testing their equipment and tactics against our equipment and tactics. I'll get on a fleet channel and tell the others not to use the Super Pulse Cannons unless they must. We don't need to give them that information. As soon as we work our way through the corsairs, we're going after their cruisers and that big ship. We'll do some testing of their tactics and equipment."

"It's your fleet, go for it," Jeonk encouraged.

Shok responded, "I'm commanding your Royal Cruiser and I didn't want to take it into the battle without telling you."

Jeonk laughed and said, "It's the fastest and toughest ship we've got. The ladies won't mind the excitement. They're always griping about not being allowed to go into battle. They wouldn't like it if they thought we didn't do it because of them."

The Argans had fought the same type of corsairs in their war with Pishtup on the planet Tuplej and in their war with the planet Kashtool. The corsairs were too slow and weak to stand up to Argan cruisers unless there were tens of thousands of them in the battle. The maximum firing range of the Dragon Spits was the optimum firing range for the Argan cruisers. The four-wave formation the corsairs were in was a doomed formation. The Horde must have known that from their spies on Kashtool and Tuplej. They were sacrificing a corsair fleet and its crews to observe Arga's battle tactics.

The Argans developed a Super Pulse Cannon that supplied itself with power from the direct hits by an attacker's pulse cannon fire on the Argan cruisers' hulls. It proved to be a very effective weapon in their battle arsenal. Argan cruisers could be destroyed by lasers and pulse cannons, but the attacking armament had to be very large to do it. The Horde corsairs had no lasers and their pulse cannons were too weak to destroy Argan cruisers without making repeated hits in the same place on the cruisers' hulls.

Shok sped his fleet through the retreating corsairs, allowing his gunners to hit targets of opportunity as his fleet fought to advance beyond the corsairs toward the Horde cruisers and the big ship. Rakoup, Doskel and Brak would take care of the mopping up action.

Doskel had already pulled his fleet ahead of the Dragon Spit Corsairs and was spreading his fleet in a broad circle above, below and on each side of their oncoming formation. The corsairs would be forced to fly between Doskel's cruisers to make their retreat and only a few would make it.

Jeonk and Shok watched the command deck holograph as the corsairs approached Doskel's fleet. Rakoup and Brak constantly pounded the Dragon Spits on the outside edges of their formation to force the retreating Spits to fly between Doskel's ships. The corsairs were being torn apart by pulse cannons and lasers from both sides and by Shok's fleet hurrying through the center of their formation. Doskel chewed holes in the Dragon Spits with his lasers and pulse cannons as they frantically dodged to avoid the surrounding fire.

Few of the corsairs managed to maneuver into firing position. If they left the formation, an Argan cruiser on their outer perimeter hit them. If they stayed in the formation, Doskel's gunners destroyed them as they approached his fleet's position. For the corsairs, space had become green balls of explosive energy and blue bars of hull melting hell. Few corsairs escaped the grinding energy of the Argan response to their attack.

Shok ordered flank speed as his fleet threaded its way between Doskel's cruisers. Admirals Rakoup and Brak saw what Shok intended to do. Instead of mopping up the remaining corsairs, they ignored them and pushed their fleets to flank speed to move in behind Shok's fleet. Doskel told his second in command, "To hell with the Corsairs, We'll follow Jeonk and Shok." He wheeled his fleet and ordered flank speed.

The bigger Horde ship and its twenty cruisers recognized the danger coming at them. They spun their spacecraft, and pushed to flank speed to make their retreat.

Shok said, "I'm calling the big ship a destroyer from now on. It's too big to be called a cruiser." They gained on the twenty cruisers and the destroyer for several hours without catching them. As the Argan fleets began closing on them, the Horde ships veered to the left, and set the Horde fleet course for a planet on the edge of the Argan's scanning range.

Jeonk observed, "They have no one coming to help them and we're in their home ports. They've had plenty of time to arouse some sympathy for their plight. I think we're going into a trap."

Shok responded, "Ask Doskel to scan the planet they're headed for. I'll bet there are some big ground batteries there or a fleet of destroyers." The four fleets continued on until they were in good scanning range, then Shok brought the fleets to a halt. Doskel reported the planet was generally uninhabited but it was choked with large ground batteries. The Horde ships came to a halt near the surface of the planet and remained there, hoping the Argan fleets would be foolish enough to face the planets ground batteries.

The Argans learned little from the battle. They learned the Dragon Spits they destroyed were no better than the ones they had destroyed in their other wars against them. They realized the enemy was willing to lose a large number of people and spacecraft to discover a tactical advantage. They learned the enemy could fly at almost the speed of their Argan cruisers, if the enemy wasn't flying slower to bring them into the trap.

The Argans felt, in the final analysis, they had a slight speed advantage on the Horde spacecraft. That was a very important point, but the battle taught them nothing of the battle capabilities of the enemy cruiser and destroyer. The Argans were disappointed that they couldn't battle the larger Horde spacecraft. The information they didn't get from the battle was far more important than the information they gained.

The Horde learned more from the battle with the Argans. They learned something of Argan battle tactics and something of the firepower the Argans could bring to a battle against an enemies weaker spacecraft. They learned a battle to destroy the Argans on their homeland wasn't going to be easy or cheap.

The Horde's choice of fighting for the survival of the people on the Horde planets, by taking the lives of people on the Forum planets, put the enemy in the position of fighting two desperate battles. One battle was for the time it would take them to move from their galaxy to the Milky Way. The Horde's other desperate battle was to beat the Argans, a people who had no intention of giving up their lives to the Horde.

Jeonk ordered the fleets to retreat. The Argans were not interested in fighting over real estate that was doomed to go into a galactic planet grinder. Shok stated, "I think we should move the fleets closer to home. That will force their next attack to be far from their home planets and allow our Galactic Forum fleets to enter into the battle more quickly. It will also allow our fleets guarding the home planet to enter the battle if they are needed."

"Won't that endanger our home planets if the battle is closer to them?" Alice asked.

"Yes it will," Jeonk replied, "but they are in even more danger if we bring our fleets to the collision area and lose there. We may be fighting an enemy with such power that we have to retreat to the home planets to survive. We may not be able to defeat them in a fleet-to-fleet battle in space. We may need the firepower of our own ground batteries to win. Shok is right; we have to make them come to us."

"Before we leave the area," Shok suggested, "I want to have a personal discussion with Admiral Nonazk at the space station, just me and him. He's an old soldier and he may open up and tell me everything he has seen if he knows his words are only for the ears of another old soldier."

They brought the fleet to a halt near the station. Shok landed one of the fighters in a station bay and was greeted by Admiral Nonazk. The Admiral said, "I told my aid there would be one hell-of-a war and we would be able to see it from the station. So far, I was right."

Shok replied, "That was only a skirmish to test our ability to fight. The real war will be somewhere else."

The Admiral responded, "We had the action on our scanners from beginning to end. I thought you were finished when four thousand of their ships attacked your sixty-three cruisers but you lost nothing in the battle. You have great tactics and great ships."

Shok took a long look at the Admiral and said, "We do, indeed, and great crews to man them. What are the politicians saying about the battle? Have you heard anything from the Hika bunch?"

"You and I need some privacy for that discussion," The Admiral replied. "Do you have time for some private words in my office?"

Shok nodded his assent and they proceeded to the Admirals office. After closing the door, Admiral Nonazk stated, "The politicians are pissing in their pants. When you arrived they thought you had no chance to beat the Horde. I transmitted the battle scan pictures to them as soon as the battle was over. The whole crew of politicians was still at Hika discussing your meeting with them. They were shown the entire battle on large monitors and every one of them stayed to see it. Within minutes after they saw it, arguments began about our planets entering the battle on your side or staying out of it to wait for the results. The generals and admirals are telling the politicians, 'If we stay out of it and the Argans win, they will have no reason to help a bunch of self serving cowards.'

"Most of the politicians are saying, 'The Argans are a strong and gallant people, surely they will understand our position and help us--if they win.' What do you and the Argans say?"

Shok answered, "We think the Horde are extremely strong and as desperate as you are. They must win to survive. We think they will throw everything they have at us in one big effort to win. We think every person in the battle on our side will contribute to our winning it and those who help will be repaid for their help. We think we know very little about the Horde and the type of battle tactics we must use to win and we think you are probably the one who knows the most about them. If you have information we can use; now will probably be the only time you have to give it to us. Do you have more information than you gave us at our last meeting?"

The Admiral had some serious thoughts before he answered but finally he said, "The information you are asking for is highly classified, but I believe there is a time in some military men's lives when they must balance the destruction of their careers against what they know for certain is more important. For me, this is that time.

"There was a time several years ago when the Horde massed a formation on our side of the galactic collision near our planets. I believe they displayed their fleet as a show of their power and superior technology to our four planets. The politicians and military people took that lesson to heart. I saved a personal copy of one of the scan records from that time. What the Horde wanted us to see is on those scans. It's the reason we call them the Horde. The Horde fleet was not only massive, it was far beyond our technology; none of us had ever seen anything like it. I will give you my personal copy of those classified scans.

"If we can get that copy to your fighter without anyone knowing about it, my career may survive at least until someone discovers I gave it to you. Everything I know about the Horde is in that copy."

The Admiral gave Shok the data pack and hurried him to his fighter. The last words he said as Shok entered his space fighter were, "We need you to win this war as much as you do. I think you can win, but it will be a very tough fight. My prayers will be with you. If there is anything I can do to bring the four Hika planets into it on your side, I'll do whatever it takes."

Shok turned to him and replied, "Old soldiers know the desperation of war and why we have to win them to survive. Politicians think war is about hurting an enemy bad enough to force him to negotiate. That's why politicians never end a war. You and I know this war is a win or die for both sides. Thank you, Admiral Nonazk, for your help. It is badly needed. If we win, the Argan debt to you and your people will be richly repaid."

5
THE HORDE SCANS

Shok returned to the Royal Cruiser with more information than he thought he could get from a fellow old soldier. He hoped it would be enough to find the combination for winning the war. Rakoup, Doskel and Brak had returned to the Royal Cruiser for their personal assessment of whatever Shok returned with. After some technical assistance from one of Doskel's fleet technicians, Admiral Nonazk's scan record was displayed on the Royal Cruiser's global holograph.

The scans turned out to be a power shock to the Argans. The scan record displayed a super fleet of the three types of spacecraft they had previously seen and it was stacked and spread for battle. Forty destroyers, the Argans considered the destroyers to be equal to ten of their cruisers, was at the top of the stack, spread so they could protect all elements of the fleet from their position above it. Below the destroyers were six hundred cruisers spread in squadrons of ten. Fifty cruiser lengths separated each cruiser squadron. Below the cruisers were ten thousand Dragon Spit Corsairs in squadrons of one hundred. The Dragon Spit squadrons' separation was the same as the cruisers. Two thousand additional Dragon Spits were positioned at the two upper levels of the fleet in squadrons of one hundred, protectively surrounding the battle perimeter of the destroyers and cruisers.

Suddenly, the formation changed with quick fluid maneuvers to different positions. Each battle squadron quickly maneuvered to a higher or lower position with only the destroyers remaining fixed in their original positions. The position changes continued until each squadron had taken many new positions and then returned to its original position. After a few moments, while the giant fleet held a static position, the destroyers disappeared briefly and then reappeared in a different position on the outside of the fleet. They disappeared and reappeared five times. Suddenly, the entire fleet wheeled and disappeared from view. Admiral Nonazk's scan record ended at that point.

There was no immediate discussion as each of the viewers sat back to consider what they had just witnessed. Jeonk's wife, Aslain, was the first to speak, "If that's all they have, we can beat them but it may take everything we have to do it."

"That isn't all they have," Jeonk assured her. "That was no more than a show and tell demonstration to frighten a lesser enemy. We can have their corsairs for lunch, but we'll need to have our military analysts make an expanded assessment of their cruiser and destroyer capabilities to find their weak spots, if they have weak spots."

"We have six hundred and forty cruisers total," Rakoup stated. "Their show and tell fleet of cruisers was six hundred. If we count ten cruisers for each of their destroyers, that count means four hundred more cruisers.

"The thousands of Horde corsairs are nothing in a battle with our cruisers, but they can count for plenty anywhere else. Their show and tell was more powerful than our entire space force. We are going to need as many allies as we can get in this war with the Horde. Shok was right, the closer we are to our home planets when we fight them, the better our chances to win."

Doskel suggested, "We need something to knock their cruisers and destroyers firing systems off line at a crucial point in the battle. I am thinking of the Gravity Disrupter Jeonk and Shok used in their reconnaissance mission to the Veolsh planet. It knocked out the navigation and armament systems on the Veolsh cruisers and I hope it will work on these."

Admiral Brak objected, "We, and they, are using light based systems, a strong gravity pulse won't disrupt our system, why should it disrupt theirs?"

Admiral Doskel replied, "Gravity bends light, our navigation systems are affected by it but our computers constantly update our systems to compensate for the weak gravity pull we receive in flight. An unexpected strong pulse from a Gravity Disrupter, say a force twenty, can cause an earthquake on a planet. It might give us the edge we need in the battle with their destroyers and cruisers. A pulse that strong will probably destroy their corsairs and maybe their cruisers at close range. We can check that out with the corsairs we have if anyone thinks it's important."

Jeonk asked, "Shok, do you have some kind of a plan we can all argue about? We are badly in need of the tactics to beat the Horde."

"First," Shok replied, "Doskel's observation is good and I think his plan for disrupting their navigation and fire control systems may work. We can't know for certain until we try, but we should try. The problem with it is this, we only have one ship equipped with the Gravity Disrupter and we may not have time to build more and install them in our other cruisers. We should have one of our scientific teams begin building them immediately and fit Doskel's fleet with them if we have enough time.

"I think we have some time but I don't know how much. The Horde knows us as chargers who are unafraid of the odds. We came to them and we followed them to their home ground. They will want to do battle with us on their own terms in their own territory if they can. We aren't going to do that. It will take them time to figure out that they must come to us. When they have that figured out and are ready to do battle, they'll be coming with everything they have.

"Their attack will probably bring them between Tuplej and Kashtool. That course is in a direct line between the Horde and Arga. They know those two planets are still recovering from war and are very weak. They will ignore both and continue on toward Arga. We need space probes in that area to tell us of their advance. We'll need more probes and better detection than we had in the Veolsh War. The Horde spacecraft are very fast; and because of the speed, they may choose a different route than the one I favor for them. We need to be able to detect them no matter which route they attack from and we need that protection in every direction around our home planets. In a war with people as well organized as the Horde, our first mistake might be our last.

"Admiral Nonazk said their probes stopped operating after entering Horde territory. The Horde probably detected and destroyed the Hika probes and they may be able to detect ours. Our only warning may be the fact that our probes have stooped operating.

"Our defenses must be constant and as massive as they can be. It is absolutely necessary for us to get the Galactic Forum fleets in this battle. All of their military spacecraft are adequate to fight the Horde's corsairs. We are the only nation with the ability to, possibly, beat the Horde destroyers and cruisers.

"We can't stack and spread to sweep their corsairs as we have done in the past. Wherever the Horde attack comes from, their corsairs will lead it. If we use the tactic we showed them in the area of the galactic collision, their destroyers will pick us off before the corsairs come into our range. The Horde will probably expect us to use that tactic. Our fleets must ignore the corsairs and let the Galactic Forum fleets do the best they can with them. We have to destroy enough Horde destroyers and cruisers to force them to break off the space battle and retreat. After they retreat, we can turn our attention to the Galactic Forum's battle with the corsairs.

"That's my thoughts on how we fight. The specific tactics for the destroyers and cruisers will have to be formulated after we have Admiral Nonazk's scan data analyzed. Everything we do, including the analysis, must be done at top speed. I think we have very little time to organize a defense of this size and the clock is ticking faster than we have ever experienced."

"You didn't leave us very much to argue about Shok," Rakoup argued. "If I think of something you haven't already thought of, I'll let you know."

Jeonk went to work on the problem at once, stating, "I'll have several copies of Nonazk's scans made. One will go to the Admiralty for analysis. One will go to my father's fleet coming to meet us. One will go to the Galactic Forum for the members to see and I'll send a personal copy to Chosteel on Paraca. He will probably be their choice for Fleet Commander. I'll give every diplomatic and military help I can to make sure he's the one in charge.

"I'll send a voice recording of everything we've said here with each copy. Shok's opinions are respected on every friendly planet. When they hear what Shok has said about the war, every clock on every allied planet will be ticking as fast as it can go. The Horde would be fools to give us the time to prepare our nations for battle. We need every minute of time we have. I think we will be lucky if they aren't following us with some type of a harassing force now. It will be lucky if we can warn all of our nations. If Chosteel has the time to put their fleets together before the Horde attack, this will be an easier war to win. If the fleets can be put together, he's the one man who can do it.

"One of our cruisers will be making flank speed to deliver each of the data packs except the one we're taking to the Admiralty. The Royal Cruiser will be making flank speed to deliver that one. Rakoup, you take your flagship and stop my father's advance. Get his fleet turned around and in position to protect Arga."

"I'll take my fleet with me," Rakoup stated. "You won't need it, but we might."

"Sure," Jeonk replied, "take Admiral Brak and his fleet with you. Shok and Doskel's fleets will stay with me."

Jeonk turned to the ladies and said, "Ladies, you're going to have a quick trip home. We'll be at flank speed all the way."

6
THE HORDE BATTLE PLAN

The Argan battle planners on the Royal Cruiser were unaware of a similar, but larger, war-planning meeting at the heart of Horde power on the planet Turt.

The Emperor listened with great interest to the Horde commanders who viewed the battle against the Argans from the command deck of the Imperial Fortress; the Argans call the Horde Imperial Fortress, a destroyer.

After the lesser Commanders gave their assessments of the Argan fleet, Chief Commander Grol, the supreme commander in charge of the Horde space and ground forces spoke, "Your Majesty, the battle was a failure. The Argan fleet destroyed our fighters as though they were something to build fires with. They were so sure of their tactics they didn't bother to launch their fighter spacecraft. They had no loss of life and no damage to their fleet in the battle. We cannot win a war with them based on a massive numbers of our fighters sent to attack their solar systems.

"The Argans have eight allied planets who are capable of helping them in a war. They have three more allies who cannot help. One cannot fight, that is the planet Nordic. They have two allies who are too weak to be of any help, those are the planets Tuplej and Kashtool. The Argans are in control of two more planets, Krex and Mog, who would willingly fight against them but both are too weak to fight against the Argans, or to be of any help to us.

"We know the Argans share their battle tactics and technology with their allies. Their allies on the eight battle capable planets will be a strong factor in this war. They too are able to destroy our fighter spacecraft. Our fighters will only be helpful in keeping the Argan's friends busy while we destroy the Argan cruisers. We will lose most of the fighters we send against the Argan allied forces.

"Our Imperial Fortresses and our Honor Guard class ships will have to carry the battle to the Argans. We learned something else about the Argan spacecraft; they call cruisers, which are about the same size as our Honor Guard class ships. They are faster than our spacecraft.

"Our friends on the planets Gamac and Prssk, who have refused to fight the Argans on our side, have informed us that the Argans are using the fighter technology we gave to the planets Tuplej and Kashtool. The Argans have become more than just capable of using the technology; they have improved on the technology and used it to upgrade their space fleets. That improved technology is what we could not outdistance in our Imperial Fortress and Honor Guard spacecraft. The Argan fleet would have caught our most advanced spacecraft if we had allowed them to follow us long enough.

"Our own scientists have found no way to improve "our" technology for "us". This technology is so new to the Argans that they are probably unaware of its intergalactic capabilities. We must capture that advanced technology in the war with the Argans. The small difference in technology has prevented our spacecraft from being intergalactic."

Emperor Sinleek interrupted Chief Commander Grol, "Chief Commander, we have the power of eighteen planets to bring against Arga and its seven allies. We have one hundred twenty of our mighty Imperial Fortresses and each has the power of many Argan cruisers. We have one thousand five hundred Honor Guard's and each Honor Guard is equal to one Argan cruiser. We outnumber the Argan fleets by more than four to one in major firepower. Plus, we have so many fighters that I have never bothered to keep track of the number. I think your pessimistic attitude does no credit to your judgment. Our friends on Gamac and Prssk assure us that the Argans are pathological about hunting down their enemies and destroying them in battle.

"Added to our overpowering advantage in spacecraft will be our overpowering advantage in our ground based systems used to destroy spacecraft. We have nothing to fear. We can stay where we are, and wait for the Argans to exercise their pathological habit of quickly destroying their enemies. They will come to us like cattle to the slaughter. We will destroy them when they do. Do you have anything you would like to add, Chief Commander?"

The Chief Commander looked back at his Emperor and stated, "The Argans will not come here to attack us. If we don't take the battle to them, and quickly, we may lose the war."

The council Chamber was large and it was filled with war commanders from eighteen planets. Many of them respected their Chief Commanders opinions. Emperor Sinleek felt he had an obligation to repudiate the Chief Commanders last statement, "Our populations are too numerous for us to share the planets we are about to conquer with our enemies' populations. Our only choice is to conquer and destroy them for the sake of our own people. We have discovered only fifteen planets, including Gamac and Prssk, suitable for the population of our eighteen planets. We have time to fight a patient, wise and deadly war to save ourselves and keep our Empire intact. All things belonging to the Argans and their allies will fall like ripe fruit into our hands when we win. Their inter-galactic technology will be the sweetest fruit of all.

"Our informants from the planets Gamac and Prssk have told us the Argans have only two people who do the planning for all of their battles. Their King, named Jeonk Shap, and an Admiral called Shok. Admiral Shok is not an Argan. He is from a different planet called Earth. Earth is capable of supporting our people but conquering it must wait until we have finished with Arga.

"Two men cannot, possibly, plan a war of this size and succeed in winning that war. Our problem in this war is how to preserve our spacecraft from destruction. We need to protect the spacecraft we will be using to move our populations from our eighteen planets. We will fight a war whose first priority is to have the patience to bring the Argan's spacecraft to our planets for destruction.

"We will not fight a war which puts our spacecraft in maximum danger of destruction near the Argan's planet and the planets of their allies. The power of our great Empire will win this war for our people and the safety of the Empire. Our Imperial leadership is greater than the leadership of any one king and his lone advisor."

The council chamber remained quiet after the Emperors proclamation of the greatness of his personal leadership. The objections any of them may have dared to make against his battle plan would have to be made to trusted aides in the privacy of that trust. The Horde battle plan was set. None of them could change it, except the Emperor himself.

Chief Commander Grol had a trusted aide who asked him privately, after the war-planning meeting, "Do you think the Argan's King, Jeonk, and Admiral Shok do all of the planning for their battles?"

Grol answered him, "Of course not, I watched their fleet in action. Each of their Admirals commanded his fleet with military brilliance. Each cruiser Commander knew how to control his ship to win the battle. They used the finest battle maneuvers I've ever seen.

'They obviously have strong leadership, but that leadership didn't plan that battle. We planned 'that battle' as a surprise attack to force them to show us their tactics. Every one of their ships worked like a finger on the same hand. Every one of them knew what the other was doing and when the battle shifted the entire fleet shifted with it. The shift was so quick no one had time to give orders. Those people know each other, they agree with each other, they trust each other, they plan with each other, and they damn well know how to fight"

The aide asked, "What do you think of the Emperors plan to kill all of the people on their planets to save ours? He worked that into the discussion as though it was a part of the original plan, but hearing his words in the meeting was the first time I've heard that part of the plan. Is killing the people on their planets a part of the original plan?"

Chief Commander Grol replied, "No, the original plan was for us to destroy their space fleets and then force them to accept us and the Empire as rulers. We had no plan to kill entire populations. The plan I originally gave to you was the, only, original plan. The Emperor has given us an entirely new plan.

"If the Emperor gives the Argans enough time to marshal their forces, we may lose the war even though we win the space battle. Our loses in space might put us in a position where our air cover isn't able to protect the ground troops we need to conquer the surfaces of their planets. The Argans are going to be tough to beat in space. We can't expect them to be easy to beat on the ground."

The Aide asked one more question, "Is there any way we can save our population and theirs at the same time?"

Grol responded, "There was an easy way but I didn't know about it until it was too late. We could have gone to the Argan's, told them our problem and received their cooperation in solving it. I didn't know they had the technology to help us until their ships began closing on ours after the battle--we started--ended.

"Their spacecraft have the technology ours need to be intergalactic and we have already destroyed the only opportunity we had to ask them for help. They now know we are the ones who supplied Tuplej and Kashtool with fighters to conquer their galaxy. The Argans will never trust us enough to share their technology with us. The only way for us to get it is to take it by conquest, if we can. We should be above their planets now--right now. If our fleets had followed them home--we would be certain of winning."

Chief Commanders Grol's dilemma wasn't new in the annals of soldiering. He was a brilliant commander faced with fighting a war he must, for the people he loved, against a people he didn't know, and his Imperial Commander was a fool.

The Argans were more fortunate. They had brilliant commanders faced with fighting a war they must, for the people they loved, against a people they didn't know, and their brilliant King and his most trusted military leaders were the first warriors in the battle.

7
THE ARGAN ADMIRALTY

The final Admiralty meeting at Arga had blossomed beyond anything its Admirals had experienced. General Sokeasel, commander of all Argan ground forces, and his leading generals were there. Admiral Chosteel, who had been put in charge of the Galactic Forum space fleets, was present. Admirals and Generals from each of the Galactic Forum nations were in attendance. The Galactic Forum nations combined their armies and space fleets on each planet to support the planetary and interplanetary efforts to win the war against the Horde. They only lacked the details of a war plan.

Jeonk started the meeting by showing the interplanetary military leaders the video footage of the corsair battle at the galactic collision area. Following that was the showing of the Horde scans given to Admiral Shok by Admiral Nonazk. The room was quiet during the viewing, and remained quiet after it. There was an expectant wait for Jeonk to begin his address concerning the many problems of the war.

Jeonk stood at the podium with obvious seriousness and began to speak, "This will be the toughest test our Galactic Forum nations have ever faced. Arga has the only spacecraft with any chance of winning against the Horde's major spacecraft.

"In the first video, you saw four of our Argan fleets destroying a fleet of four thousand Dragon Spit Corsairs. That video ended with our fleets chasing one destroyer and twenty cruisers to a well-armed planet. The Horde spacecraft flew slightly slower than our cruisers but we think they were trying to lead us into a trap. After careful consideration, we can no longer expect their spacecraft to be slower than ours. We have found no way to increase the speed of our fleets. The speed we have is the speed we must go into battle with.

"In the second video, you saw six hundred cruisers, forty larger destroyer and twelve thousand Dragon Spit Corsairs. The Horde was making a show of superior strength to the four Hika planets. We can anticipate that their entire battle fleet is much larger than the fleet they were willing to show to the Hika.

"The Horde must win the space battle first to win the war. Our Admiralty analysts have given us a forty percent chance of winning if their fleet is only twice as large as the one we have already seen. We think they may have three or four times the number shown in the scan report. We have launched probes to check that out but we aren't sure where their planets are. We hope for, but don't expect, new information from that source.

"Admiral Doskel is working on a weapon to use against them. If he has time to manufacture it and get it installed on our cruisers, our chances of winning may possibly increase dramatically.

"Admiral Shok and Admiral Brak are working on another weapon that is so bizarre only Shok could have imagined it. Shok and Brak think it will work, but we must have time to make it work and none of us think they will give us that much time. The only reasonable choice for them is to hit us as quickly as they can. Our estimate is one month. Every day after that will give us one day more to increase our preparations to defeat them. They must certainly realize we are preparing to win and they are the ones with the most power in this war. They will delay at their own folly.

"Now, we must prepare our battle tactics. The Galactic Forum fleets must destroy as many of their Dragon Spit Corsairs as they can possibly destroy. The Forum fleets must keep the Dragon Spits away from the Argan cruisers so our cruisers can carry the battle to their larger spacecraft. All of us must use our fleets for maximum battle ability in close cooperation with all of the other elements in the war.

"As I have said, there is a good chance our Argan fleets will be destroyed in the space battle. After our fleets are destroyed, the Horde must fight on the ground to secure their victory. The only victory they can hope for is to defeat our planets and occupy them with their own populations. They must kill our citizens to make a place for their own.

"Our ground armies must be ready to repel the Horde with every soldier and every piece of battle equipment we have. Every citizen must be armed and trained for a house-to-house war of resistance against the Horde invaders. I suggest that all of our nations call up every old soldier who can still carry a weapon and every new soldier who can be trained quickly.

"The Horde will have to bring their troops onto our planets' surfaces slowly. We expect they will try to conquer our planets one at a time for the most effective use of their ground troops. We expect them to attack Arga first, but that isn't certain. They could attack any of us first.

"We will have no way to support each other in the ground war if we lose the space war. We must kill as many of their ground troops and destroy as much of their equipment as we possibly can in every battle. We must expect no quarter and give no quarter. The more of them we destroy on one planet, the fewer troops and equipment they will have to fight on the next.

"Our Generals must hope to destroy, and expect to lose, massive numbers of troops in this war. We hope to make the Horde suffer enough losses in the space war to fatally wound their efforts to support their troops in the ground war. I think we can do that much.

"I and our military analysts don't think the Horde can win a ground war against all of our planets. All of us have large standing armies and ground batteries dug in against attacks from space. Our ground troops have fighting experience that our military analysts say the Horde Empire, or any empire, is unlikely to have met before.

"An older Empire is more likely to have troops trained to fight conventional battles against weak or inexperienced enemies. We are not weak and we are not inexperienced. Our generals are experienced generals who fight well and train well. Our battle experiences are real and recent. The Horde's battle experiences may be limited to technical discussions of how past battles were won.

"Arga has had ground battle experience with most of the generals who are here from other planets. We have been amazed by the bravery of your troops, their fighting abilities, equipment and tactics. As a result of those shared war experiences, we have incorporated much of your equipment and tactics into our own tactics. You have shared our experiences and incorporated our tactics and equipment into your armies.

"We do not envy the enemy who decides to attack you on your home planets. Still, we know our enemy is fighting to destroy all of our people. Our major problems will occur when we battle the unfamiliar equipment of an unknown enemy who can field the large number of reinforcements we expect the Horde to bring to the ground war. Neither problem can be endless. Sooner or later they will run out of enough of both. It will become apparent to them that they have lost their main objective, to conquer and inhabit our planets. At that point, they will withdraw and we will have won the war to save our planets.

"This war will not be won easily. Our cheers for the courageous will be silenced by the sorrows for our dead. Many of us and our loved ones will have to wait for the call of God to meet again. We must honor our citizen heroes by arming them and training them to fight this war well enough for the maximum number of them to survive. I know the citizens of your planets are, as are our Argans, being armed and trained as I speak. Our position is desperate. Our strategies are dangerous, and we will win whatever the cost.

"We will now take our places in the assigned groups with each planet represented in each group. Space commands and surface commands must devise strategies and coordinate their efforts carefully for maximum battle effectiveness. General Sokeasel and his Generals, Admiral Shok, the other Admirals and I will be available to combine our, and your counsel on the battle strategies to be used during the war. Your ideas to win it are crucial to success. If there is anything Arga can do to help you prepare your battle strategies, every Argan will be glad to help.

8
THE HORDE BATTLE CONFERENCE

The Horde battle conference was not called for individual input. The space and ground commanders were there to hear the Emperors new battle plan, which would include his newly made decision to kill the population of the Galactic Forum planets in the Milky Way galaxy. He had decided, without consultation, that there wouldn't be enough room and facilities on the planets to support the Galactic Forum population and the Horde population at the same time. The Emperor concluded that, "In order to assure the population of his Empire a place to live, the other populations must die."

There was one other concern the Emperor had that he didn't bother to mention to anyone. The Empire, with himself as the Emperor, would most easily be held together without the interference of contaminating ideas from people who were not the subjects of an Empire. He further feared the same contaminated people, who had so recently defeated the empire ruling most of their planets, were in no mood for another empire or emperor no matter who ruled it. If he didn't have them killed, he feared he would be saddled with the constant war they would certainly wage to be rid of his Empire; they might even try to kill the Emperor--himself!

A hush fell on the assembled war planners before the Emperor spoke. He appeared impressive with his chalk white face above his light gray military uniform bedecked with the medals he had awarded to himself for unnoticed valor. He spoke with imperial ease, a slight smile on his face, "After a thorough re-assessment of our military position and in consultations with our highest military leaders, we have decided to wait within Our Imperial area of control for the Argan space fleets to attack us here. We can more easily defeat them here than attacking them on their own planets.

"Our intelligence efforts, based on planets near to them, and familiar with their leadership, have given us a psychological profile of the Argan nature. They are brave, excellent fighters and have very good spacecraft. But! The Argans have a fatal character flaw. They are pathological about solving problems quickly and with finality.

"In the past they have consistently and brashly gone forward, at great risks, to face problems they believe to be dangers to themselves. Whether the problems were commercial or military made no difference to them. We intend to exploit that character flaw and reduce the risks we face in conquering the Argans, including their neighboring planets.

"Here is my plan for the final conquest of all of their planets. Our Imperial fleet and our ground batteries are to remain on high alert in preparation for the Argan attack. We expect to destroy most of their spacecraft in that battle. A few of their spacecraft may escape but the few will not be a later problem. We may be fortunate enough to destroy many of the battle craft in what they call the Galactic Forum nations.

"As I have said, the Argans are excellent fighters and they certainly realize we are not a weak enemy they can dispose of with their usual brashness. We expect them to bring their allies to that battle. It is best for us that they do.

"It may take them months to cross the galaxy. The speed of the Argan battle fleets will be controlled by the addition of the slower Galactic Forum spacecraft. The Galactic Forum fleets are much slower than the Argan battle cruisers. We must be patient. Whether they are early or late, alone or with others, Our Imperial fleet and our ground batteries will dispose of them with routine ease.

"After we destroy their spacecraft, we must begin the ground war on their planets. We expect the ground war to be the most difficult part of the conquest. The ground war will be difficult because of the experience level of the Argan and Galactic Forum inhabitants. Our informants tell us the Argans and the Galactic Forum nations have engaged in many ground battles on neighboring planets. They have won every battle. Our ground troops are, unfortunately, not as experienced, but they will be given massive air support to insure their victory.

"Our Imperial fleet will arrive on their planets and destroy the spacecraft they will have reserved for their ground defensive efforts. When we are certain of our superiority in space, we will bring our ground troops into the conquest.

"First, we must secure the planet Nordic for our ground invasion of the other planets. This will be an easy task. Nordic is thinly populated. We consider it to be uninhabited. We will use Nordic for our staging area to attack Arga. It's very close to Arga in the terms of the speed of our spacecraft.

"There are three planets we must keep under constant pressure during our ground attack of Arga. Those planets are Paraca, Oglak and Veolsh. In every battle the Argans have fought, those three planets have come to their aid and assured their success. It is unfortunate that two of the planets, Oglak and Veolsh, are not suitable for our population. Veolsh is a nearly waterless, sand blown wasteland but its people are numerous and can be expected to aid the Argans The Veolsh will fight to the last man in Arga's defense. We must nullify Veolsh.

"The planet Oglak is peopled with a population who live underground. Oglak is a dark, cloudy planet and their people are also numerous. They are ugly, fierce, strong, excellent fighters and they are dedicated to keeping King Jeonk's principal advisor, Admiral Shok, alive. They protect him as though he is their own child. They will help in Arga's defense because of Admiral Shok. We must, totally, control the air space of the planet Oglak in our conquest of Arga. Since they are underground dwellers, it is my belief we can occupy their surface areas with ease in the initial control effort.

"The planet Paraca has a more normal topography and atmosphere. The Paracans can also be depended on to aid the Argans in the defense of their home planet. They have also been present in all of Arga's adventures off of their own planet. We see Paraca as the most difficult of the three to conquer. Their population is spread over the total surface of their planet while the other two are gathered in small areas, so our intelligence tells us. We will need a much larger number of our ground troops to gain control of the broad areas of Paraca.

"We have two hundred million ground troops. We are recruiting more as we proceed to the culmination of our conquest. We can move as many as two million ground troops a day. That number should allow us to establish a large area of control on the surface of each of those three planets.

"We will bring in enough reinforcements to expand our areas of control and complete the destruction of the population of the three planets. We expect to lose hundreds of thousands of our ground troops in this war to bring safety to our people. Only our desperation to leave our present homeland planets makes those losses acceptable.

"We must begin our ground attacks on four planets, Arga, Veolsh, Oglak and Paraca at the same time. Some of my military advisors have cautioned me that I have too much of an optimistic view of our success in attacking four major planets in the early part of our conquest. I disagree, we either have enough to beat them or we do not. We can either overpower them with Our Imperial power or lose.

"It is unthinkable that this group, calling themselves the Galactic Forum, and using a weak organization for interplanetary nations to discuss their mutual problems, could band together to defeat this Empire of eighteen planets. This is especially true when their most important leaders are reckless warriors who are locked into the pathology of their own attack first philosophy. We will win and we will win because we are better strategists, better fighters and we have more, and superior equipment, to fight with. Are there any questions?"

There were no questions of importance. The Imperial military leaders understood the Emperors plan very well. They knew the logistics and the finer details of implementing the Emperor's strategy would have to be worked out at their level of planning, and questions would solve none of those problems. Most of them thought the Emperor's strategy to be very reasonable. If there were problems with it, the problems would be overpowered by the large volume of equipment and the massive number of troops they would bring into the war.

Chief Commander Grol was the exception. He had serious doubts about the plan. He felt his silence was necessary to keep him in a position that would allow him to rescue the Empire. The Chief Commander believed that, when, was more probable than, if, for the failure of the plan. Grol's chief aide sensed his discomfort with the Emperor's strategy and asked, "Do you think moving two million ground troops a day onto the surface of the four planets is a sufficient number to conquer the four planets?"

Grol gave his bitter reply, "It probably is if we can keep moving them for enough days. We have enough troops in the advance party and our reinforcements to conquer those four planets, but there are things we don't know about them. Our informants from Prssk and Gamac have never visited three of those planets. The only planet they visited and have first hand knowledge of is Paraca. I think we have a good description of it. Paraca is also the one we think we'll have the most trouble with, other than Arga. If we have miscalculated the military power of the Veolsh and Oglak planets, we will be in trouble.

"There is one more problem the Emperor didn't address. Two million a day is the maximum number of troops we can plan to move. Our transports carry thirty thousand troops each. Every time we lose a transport, our maximum troop delivery rate decreases by thirty thousand per day. Our enemies on those four planets will be shooting at those transports.

"We are going to lose transports each time we land troops on any of the targeted planets until the enemy can no longer use their ground batteries. We can't win a battle against enemy armies on the ground from space and we can't move our troops into a hard fought battle with transports we no longer have. If they destroy enough of our transports, we will lose the ground war. If we lose the ground war--we lose everything.

"The Emperors plan is all or nothing. He expects a hard fought but quick first wave win on the Forum's four major planets. He wants to use that win as a springboard to what he considers to be easy victories on the other planets. The people on the other planets may not be willing to die just because we killed all of their friends. If their leaders have assumed that our purpose is to kill all of them, and they have armed their populations for self protection; the quick, first victory could cause us to lose enough of our ground troops to prevent our conquest of the other planets.

"Further, all of this quick conquest depends on our enemy being stupid enough to attack us on our home planets, while they leave their home planets undefended instead of using the time--we are giving them--to organize their home defenses.

"The Argans--will--not--attack. They are at home preparing their fleets, hardening their ground defenses against space attacks, and preparing the ground troops on every planet in the Galactic Forum for total war. I'm certain we can beat their planets right now with the massive amount of firepower we have available.

"If we give them six months, or a year to prepare, maybe we can beat them and maybe not. The only good thing about the Emperor's plan to wait out the Argans and the Galactic Forum fleets is that his plan is going to fail, and be put in the trash where it belongs, and a different strategy will be used for the war."

9

THE FRANTIC WAIT

Waiting wasn't the word for what the Argan side of the war was doing. They knew the Horde attack was coming at them. Every waiting moment was snatched from time to be used to the ultimate. Every planet was busy training and shaping every able bodied man for its fighting units. Putting massive numbers of mines in likely landing sights for enemy troops was a constantly expanding effort. Building new, and strengthening older underground bunkers to keep the troops safe from space attacks was a high priority. Hardening the surface batteries to fire on incoming space vehicles was an emergency project.

When annihilation is in the air, there are no petty discussions. Cooperation is as sweet as any flower at the fullness of its bloom.

Battle hardened veterans began training well-armed citizens for house-to-house warfare. Each nation's factories increased the manufacture of hand held assault weapons and ammunition to supply the individual citizens. Each planet taught its noncombatant citizens combat strategies, and taught the planets' populations what to expect during a war of annihilation.

There wasn't a square foot of outer space in any direction that wasn't constantly in the view of a surveillance probe. Admiral Doskel worked feverishly on his Gravity Pulse weapon and within two months installed the first on its first cruisers. He would have all of his cruisers fitted with the new weapon within six months from the beginning of the project.

Admirals Shok and Brak were just as feverish in their efforts. They were in constant contact with the team of scientists, who kept telling them, "If this works at all, it will probably kill everyone who uses it."

They always gave the same reply to the scientists, "If we don't use it, we will all die anyway. Get it done now and make it as safe as you can. We'll take it from there."

Admiral Chosteel of Paraca made it his first priority to train his Galactic Forum pilots and crews. The crews worked every second of time they could stand without becoming totally exhausted. Chosteel's job was to keep the Horde fighters away from the Argan cruisers. The space battle needed enough survivors to return to their home planets and defend against the attacks they expected to follow Arga's defeat. The crews understood the dangers of total war, and there were no slackers among Chosteel's crews.

The religious leaders on all of the planets prayed to God for time. God and time was their best friend. Both were being called on to provide the maximum advantage. The churches were better attended than they had been in many years.

The Horde didn't bother praying for victory, except for Chief Commander Grol and a few of his close associates. The bulk of the Horde military leaders were certain of victory. The Emperor announced to the people of His eighteen planets, "I have found new homes for you on the planets in the unfriendly galaxy that is destroying ours, and the homes are suitable for all of our citizens. In a few more months we will begin the evacuation.

We have found it necessary to go to war with the stubborn and fierce people who will not cooperate with our desire to survive. We, and Our military forces will prevail against them. As soon as we force them into submission, using our Imperial plan, we will begin moving all of you to your new homes."

Six months went by with no Argan attack. Quiet, respectful, questions began arising about the possibility that the Emperor might have been wrong about the brashness of the Argan leadership. The Emperor heard of these quiet questions and decided to enlighten those who were beginning to question his planning ability. He called a special meeting of the high command of the Horde space and ground forces.

The Emperor explained to his assembled military heads, "It has come to my attention that there have been a small amount of criticism of our plan to allow the Argans to bring their fleets to our planets for destruction. This, unwarranted, criticism stems from the fact that they have not arrived as quickly as some of my critics thought they should. The critics are ill informed concerning the time it takes the Argans to twice travel across the diameter of their own galaxy, enter ours and make their attack.

"Our military analysts have advised me that the Argan's minimum time of travel for that distance cannot be less than four months. We cannot expect them to attack alone. They will certainly bring fleets from their Galactic Forum allies with them. My analysts have advised me that it will take at least two months for them to organize the Galactic Forum to bring those fleets. None of the Galactic Forum spacecraft are as fast as the Argan spacecraft. The Argan's return time, accompanied by those allied fleets, is undetermined.

"Our informants from that part of their galaxy have told us the Forum spacecraft have been modified for faster travel but they have no information on how fast they are. My military analysts have concluded that the Argans and their allies will arrive here in no less than nine months or more than one year after their original contact with our spacecraft.

"Our home defense teams have been on high alert and will remain on high alert until the arrival of the enemy fleets. We must be patient. Our best hope for total conquest is to destroy the fleets that are, at this very moment, on their way to fall within the grasp of my Imperial Fleet. I feel your impatience. I know how anxious you are to free the Galactic Forum planets for the occupation of our Imperial subjects. All of you must remain alert and hold your subordinates to the very highest level of readiness in anticipation of the moment of freedom for your people.

"Unless there are questions, that concludes the information I had for you." The Emperor, with a wave of his hand, proclaimed, "All commanders may return to their units."

The year of high readiness passed slowly for the Horde. It ended with the Emperor cast in the throes of deep disappointment because of the Argan's inability to follow the course of their pathological brashness. Everything Chief Commander Grol had predicted about them seemed to have come true. There was still some possibility of a last minute

Argan attack to uplift the spirits of the despondent Emperor, but revision of the Imperial battle plan could no longer wait for that happy event. The Emperor called another meeting of his high command. This time, Chief Commander Grol would do most of the talking.

The Emperor made his peace with the high command in the following manner, "It seems our military prowess has frightened the bold spirit from the Argans and their allies. Unless it is taking them even longer to traverse the galaxy than our analysts anticipated, they are not coming. We find ourselves forced, by their cowardice, into the necessity of taking a more difficult road to their destruction. You must take our mighty Imperial Fleet and our superior Army to their planets for the sake of your people. Your victory over their planets will be more difficult but no less certain. Chief Commander Grol has formulated a plan of attack and he will offer that to you at this time. Chief Commander Grol, please begin."

Chief Commander Grol stood firmly and frowned at the assembled High Command before he spoke, "This will be the most difficult test our strategy, military equipment, and men have ever faced. Our supply lines will be long and the only reinforcements we can count on will be from the spacecraft we leave here to protect our home planets. We are leaving one-third of our space command here. If we must use that one-third in the war, our home planets will be principally defended by our ground based laser, pulse cannon and particle beam weapons.

"Prior to the space attack, we will move fifty million mobile ground troops to a planet called Nordic. Nordic has a moderate climate and many open areas for landing and bivouac sites. Our pre-invasion staging areas will be on an uninhabited continent that is far from Nordic's small population.

"In addition to our troops on Nordic, we will have two million ground assault troops following the Imperial Fleet. They will be far enough behind the fleet to keep them secure from an attack by the Argan cruisers. The ground troops following the fleet will attack the nation of Arga at the earliest possible moment, on my orders. As quickly as we can land those troops, our transports will fly to Nordic for additional support troops and return to land them on Arga.

"The primary factor in our mission is the destruction of the Argan fleets. Our intelligence tells us Arga has forty fleets and each of their cruisers carry fifteen fighters. That means they have six hundred forty battle cruisers and nine thousand six hundred fleet based fighters. We know they will have more fighters that are not fleet based but our intelligence doesn't give us an estimate of how many more.

"Our four man fighters must not engage the Argan cruisers. Their cruisers destroy our fighters with ease. Our fighters will be totally engaged with keeping the Galactic Forum spacecraft from attacking our main fleet and our transports.

"The Imperial fleet must engage and destroy the Argan cruisers before any of our ground transports are allowed to enter the area. Our attack fleet has three times the firepower the Argans have and there are no other spacecraft in the Galactic Forum that can hope to match us.

"After the Argan fleets are destroyed, the space battle and the sky are ours. The Imperial Fleet can then concentrate on supporting our ground troops. After Arga is defeated in space and on the ground, we will have a solid base from which to attack and defeat the other planets."

One of the fleet's commanders asked, "How will we approach this battle? Will our fleet be flying in a self protecting envelope of power or will we be dispersed for better control of a broad area of space?"

Grol replied, "You will receive orders prior to the battle with course coordinates and target information. You and the other fleet commanders have done this many times. You will follow those orders."

One of the army generals asked, "Do we have information on the size of the Argan army and its battle capabilities?"

Grol answered, "We do not, Arga is a closed society except for its friends and our intelligence sources are not their friends. Our informants were not allowed to approach their planet. One thing is certain, if our battle capabilities aren't better than theirs, we will lose this war. We have an overwhelming number of men to bring to the battle, but an overwhelming number of troops can lose to overwhelming tactics and weapons. We must not offer ourselves the luxury of--one thought--that we can win easily."

A fighter Fleet Commander brought his criticism to the group, "We have seventy thousand fighters. It's unlikely we will meet half that many fighters on the other side. Wouldn't it be wise to use some of our fighters to protect the transports and make an earlier ground assault on Arga? We in fighter Command might hasten the end of the battle by getting our troops on the ground earlier. Our ground troops will then be able to attack the Argan ground based space batteries."

Grol responded, "I admire your willingness to commit to the battle, but there are a few holes in your suggestion. We don't know where those batteries are, and they will be the best-protected installations the Argans have. There is an even more impressive hole in your strategy; the Argans don't give a damn about your fighters. If they bother to kill them instead of just ignore them, you will die for nothing. If we bring transports in with only your fighters to protect them, the Argans will ignore the fighters and kill the transports. Every lost transport means a daily loss of thirty thousand troops we cannot bring to the battle. Thank you for your comment but sit down."

Chief Commander Grol answered many questions during that meeting but he gave very few details of his plan. It was his conviction that the battle plan was so simple and so devastating that it could be understood and carried out without fault, by his master military organization, with the orders they would receive en route. His other fear was that the master military organization that criticized the Emperor's plan might be faster and more willing to criticize his. Grol thought the Imperial forces had a ninety-five percent chance for success before the Emperor pissed away the time needed to insure that success. Now, he considered their chance of winning to be fifty percent. He felt every passing day brought them closer to defeat and he was unwilling to suffer even one more day of delay in useless discussion.

Grol had one final order for all to hear, "We have identified the voices of King Jeonk and Admiral Shok from the Argan fleet transmissions with the help of our informants from the planets Gamac and Prssk. We now have voiceprints we can use to identify them and the cruiser they will be flying. In battle, they always fly on the same cruiser. Our ship's computers have been programmed to identify them. I have been told that we can insure our victory if we kill those two leaders. The two leaders will become a special target for whoever identifies them. A two tier promotion will be given to the crew who destroys them and their cruiser."

The Argans passed the year in hectic preparation, giving thanks for every new day that allowed them a better chance for survival. Admiral Doskel's fleet was fitted with the Gravity Pulse equipment and he was eager to see if his idea would be decisive in the coming space battle.

Admirals Shok and Brak were still working to perfect their new weapon. They knew they had little time left, but Jeonk had become more confident in their eventual success. He ordered them to take their scientists and the project to the planet Nordic where they would be safe from the first wave attack. If they couldn't complete upgrading their fleets with the new weapon system for the initial battle, a later completion time would give Arga two battle ready fleets with some possibility of defeating the Horde while the ground war was still in progress.

The two fleets proceeded to Nordic and descended to the floor of a valley between high mountains, thousands of miles from the Nordic settlements. They immediately camouflaged their fleets and scientific work area to prevent overhead detection. Their work was feverish but the scientist seemed to have finally worked out the problems. It was now a matter of the difficult job of combining dangerous metal pellets, smaller than a grain of sand, and the tedious work of installing them in the firing systems. Both Fleet Admirals thought they might make it to the first battle if the Horde held back long enough.

10
THE HORDE ATTACK

The Horde didn't hold back long enough for the two Argan fleets on Nordic to get into the first battle, but they didn't surprise the Argans as they had hoped. The Horde hadn't detected the Argan space probes. The horde thought their fleet armada was catching the Argans by surprise. The Argan and Galactic Forum fleets launched into space at the first warning from their deep space probes. They were as ready for the Horde attack as their fleets and crews could make them.

The massive Horde fighter fleet came in between the Argan and the Forum planets, effectively doing what each side wanted the other to do. The Horde fighter fleet kept the Forum spacecraft from attacking the Horde Imperial Fortress and Honor Guard class ships. With the same action, the Horde fighters stayed far from the Argan cruisers the Horde destroyers were vectoring to destroy.

The Horde Imperial Fortresses and the Honor Guards vectored into Argan space with their fleet split into three wings. Each wing approached Arga from a different planetary quadrant. The Horde fleet was surprised by the absence of a counterattacking fleet rising from the planet to meet it. The Horde surprise ended when its commanders realized the Argan fleets were coming down on them very fast from their position in the roof of the galaxy. The Horde scanners had concentrated on detecting the Argan fleets coming at them from the planet's surface. Only when it was obvious to the Horde that the Argan counterattack was overdue did they make a deep space search and detected the Argan fleets.

The Argans attacked the rear echelon of the three Horde wings with one hundred thirty-five cruisers attacking each of the three horde wings. The first wave of Argan cruisers concentrated their attack on the Horde destroyers protecting the Horde cruisers like a hen with its chicks under its wings.

The second wave Argan attack cruisers bypassed the Horde fortresses to destroy the Horde cruisers. The Argans hoped their rear echelon attack would force the three Horde wings closer to the planets surface where the Argan ground batteries would be able to destroy many of them. Two Argan fleets were kept above the battle and out of the initial assault to attack where the battle became the most dangerous. The two fleets would attempt to reinforce the most damaged Argan fleets.

Arga's second wave assault was very effective. They came in high, and then dived below the destroyers to attack the cruisers, hoping their cruisers attacking the destroyers would keep the destroyers busy enough for them to kill a large number of Horde cruisers.

The Argans launched drones as they closed to firing range. The drones appeared to be more Argan cruisers and fighters to the Horde scanners. Immediately after the drone launches, they launched their missiles.

The Horde commanders had two choices, to shoot at the missiles coming at them or the drone cruisers and fighters coming at them. As soon as the Argan missiles were on their way, the Argan cruisers launched their fighters to enter the Horde fleet while it was defending itself from the missiles and drones.

The Horde commanders made many mistakes. They didn't know what to shoot at. They couldn't tell the real spacecraft from the drones. Horde scanners blossomed with real and false dangers. The Horde lost many cruisers because of their indecision. The Argan fleets lost few cruisers as their short-range missiles blasted their way through the Horde cruiser hulls and then exploded inside the cruisers. The Argan cruisers followed their fighters to the outer perimeter of the Horde wings, blasting Horde cruisers into fiery death traps with pulse cannon and laser fire.

The Horde Destroyers immediately dived into the battle to save their cruisers. Argan cruisers began breaking up as the destroyers' larger pulse cannon and particle beam weapons hit them.

The Horde cruiser losses slowed after their destroyers came into the battle. Many more Horde cruisers were lost than Argans but the Argan cruiser fleets were more seriously damaged. The Argans had fewer cruisers and couldn't afford the losses as well as the Horde.

The Argans killed nine of the Horde destroyers and did serious damage to five others but the combined attack cost the Argan's sixty-eight of the attacking cruisers. That kill rate told the Argans they couldn't go after the Horde Destroyers and hope for any of their fleet to survive.

Admiral Doskel's Gravity Disrupter worked with great effect on the Horde cruisers but his fleet was among those who attacked the destroyers. His fleet took very few shots at the cruisers. The destroyers survived being hit with the Gravity Disrupters and recovered quickly enough to remain in the battle. Doskel's Disrupters aided in the destruction of several Horde cruisers but Doskel lost most of his fleet in the battle. If they had been able to arm all of the Argan cruisers with Gravity Disrupters it might have been a different story; but, unfortunately, the Gravity Disrupters weren't decisive in the battle.

Jeonk's cruiser was one of the first to go into battle and was one of the first to be hit. His cruiser had to disengage and limp back to Arga. He and the surviving crewmembers managed to get out of the cruiser safely but they were forced to leave it in the open where it landed.

The ship had suffered too much damage for them to move it to a safe place for repairs. The crew knew it would be destroyed when the battle came close to Arga. Jeonk grabbed the first command plak to approach the damaged ship and flew it to Arga's Space Command bunker.

The news he received at Space Command wasn't good. The Argans had already lost half of their cruisers. The Galactic Forum fleets were killing Horde fighters by the hundreds but the Horde fighters outnumbered them by the thousands and they were faster than the Forum spacecraft. Admiral Chosteel informed Jeonk that the Forum fleets were losing the space battle.

Jeonk ordered the Argan cruisers to break away from the battle with the destroyers above Arga. The ground batteries would have to do the best they could against the Horde main fleet. He ordered the Argan cruisers to set a course for the Forum battle and destroy the Dragon Spit Corsairs the Horde called fighters.

Jeonk wanted to save the Forum fleets and the remainder of his Argan cruisers until Shok and his two fleets came in from Nordic. If Shok's two fleets could get into the battle, they might still have a chance to damage the Horde fleet enough to save themselves.

Chief Commander Grol thought the Argan cruiser Commanders had panicked and were running from the battle out of fear, giving the Horde supremacy in Argan Space. Instead of following them and destroying them, he turned his attention to the Argan surface.

Chief Commander Grol had insisted on personally commanding one of the Horde wings. One of Grol's chief aides was in command of the second wing. The Emperor's most trusted Commander was in charge of the third. The Emperor was in orbit, a safe distance from the battle, in his personal Imperial Fortress with a guard of fifty Horde cruisers.

The Emperor, with a poor view of the battle from his safe position and thinking the battle was over, ordered the entire Horde fleet to attack the Argan population centers. Neither Grol nor his aide, the Commander of the second fleet, followed that order because it was obviously foolhardy. The Emperor's man in command of the third wing of the fleet began his attack on the planets population as soon as he heard the Emperor's order.

Grol immediately tried to stop the third wing from attacking the Argan surface. He understood the Argans had left the Horde in command of Argan space, temporarily, but the war wasn't over. Grol needed to conserve his spacecraft to win the war. There was also a nagging question in his mind. His Vice Commander had informed him that two of the Argan fleets consisting of thirty-two cruisers hadn't been in the battle. Where were they, and why hadn't they fought in the battle? That was a major problem. Grol thought this battle was too important to the Argans for two of their fleets to be missing from it.

Grol shouted into his inter-fleet communicator, "Commander Varst, Break off your attack! Keep your fleet away from the surface! Retreat immediately!"

Commander Varst retorted, "We are following the Emperors orders, Chief Commander, not yours. We are continuing our attack."

Grol watched with dismay as the third wing neared the surface and sent its missiles into the Argan capital of Poshalla. Commander Varst's third wing followed its missiles speeding toward the city and began pummeling the neighborhoods of Poshalla with its lasers and pulse cannons. Arga's smaller ground batteries opened up on the missiles and destroyed many of them in the air; many others hit the capital city neighborhoods. As the third Horde fleet neared the surface, Arga's larger ground batteries opened up on it with lasers, pulse cannons and particle beam weapons.

Varst realized the gross nature of his error when he couldn't find a safe direction to swing his fleet away from the incoming fire. He did the only thing he could, he

THE MAGELLANIC COLLISION

ordered his fleet to reverse direction and climb straight up out of the field of fire. While they were wheeling at max thrust for safety, he lost seven of his destroyers and fifty-two cruisers to the lethal bursts of super heated energy burning its way through his fleet's hulls.

After Commander Varst's fleet was safely out of range of the Argan defense network, Chief Commander Grol ordered Commander Varst to report to his flagship. As Varst entered the command deck, Grol demanded, "What are your losses?"

Varst nervously replied, "Seven Imperial Fortresses and fifty-two Honor Guards."

Grol looked at him with steely-eyed disgust and demanded, "The damage to the rest of your ships?"

Varst's humiliating reply was, "Eleven damaged Imperial Fortresses and ninety-three damaged Honor Guards--but my damaged spacecraft are still capable of fully supporting my Emperor's mission."

Grol said nothing about Varst's fully supportive role for his Emperor. He jerked Varst's laser out of its holster and burned a hole in Varst's heart with it. Chief Commander Grol assigned one of his own command deck officers to replace Commander Varst. Grol said to him as he left for his new duties, "I suggest you follow, my orders."

Commander Grol went one step further. He flew to the Emperors safe haven and spoke with the Emperor about reinforcements, "Your Majesty, We have just lost seven more Imperials and fifty two Honor Guards in that senseless attack on the Argan surface. Eleven more of the Imperial Fortresses and ninety-three Honor Guards were damaged. We have also discovered the massive amount of protection Arga can bring to the battle from its ground batteries. We need half of the fleet we left to guard the Empire and we need them quickly. I suggest you order them here."

The Emperor didn't like Grol's depiction of the attack the Emperor, himself, had ordered, as senseless but he couldn't use the results to argue against its logic. The Emperor considered what he thought was Grol's overly cautious nature and his past pessimism as the source of his request for reinforcements. The Emperor was also afraid the brash Argans might have broken off their attack on the fleet to attack the Empire. The Argans might believe they were facing all of the Imperial spacecraft, and hoped to find the Empire unguarded. The Emperor also wanted to prove to Chief Commander Grol that the Emperor was still in charge, in Spite of Commander Skursk's tactical errors.

The Emperor stated, "We can not leave the Empire so lightly defended. We are in good shape and in good spirits. We have destroyed half of the Argan fleet with little loss to ourselves. The other half of the Argan fleet ran to hide until we are gone.

"We will not be defeated by our minor losses. We, who are here now, shall remain here and destroy the other half of their fleet, while we conquer their planet. We have all of the power we need to do that, and it is all here with us."

The Emperor added, "Will you send Commander Varst to me? I intend to give him a medal and a promotion for his bravery for following my orders."

Chief Commander Grol smiled and said, "Your Majesty, I'll be very pleased to send Commander Varst to you."

MARVIN E. FOX

The Emperor's refusal put Grol on the razor's edge of a tactical dilemma. He needed more spacecraft to attack Arga's ground batteries and be certain of victory. The Emperor controlled the reinforcements but the Emperor was certain of victory with what they had in place.

Grol couldn't bring the Horde fleet close to the Argan surface batteries without his fleet being destroyed. Yet, he must take Arga quickly. He had to destroy the ground batteries without destroying his fleet in the process. Grol turned his fleet's scanner on the nation of Arga and found it peppered with ground batteries except in some remote coastal areas.

Grol developed a plan to put his two million ground troops in those, largely undefended, coastal areas and have them move inland to destroy the ground batteries. If the Argans hadn't prepared a trap, the Horde transports could unload their troops and set a course for the planet Nordic to pick up more troops to reinforce the Horde beachheads.

With the Argan cruisers out of the battle the Horde fighters could support the ground invasion. Grol ordered fifty percent of the fighters battling the Galactic Forum fleets to return and protect the landing troops and their transports.

Grol's destroyers would hold their positions unless the Argan fleets returned and attacked the Horde transports. In that event, he would be forced to lower his fleet nearer to the surface, take his losses from the Argan ground batteries, and fight the Argan fleets to support the landing.

The retreating Argan cruisers were well on their way to help the Galactic Forum fleet when Grol gave the order to his Fighter Command for half of the fighters to break off their attack and set their course for Arga. The Horde fighters covered a broad area of space as they flew their course for Arga. The Argan cruisers, on the other hand, were still in their battle formation when they met the Horde fighters heading for Arga.

The Argans chewed through the approaching Horde fighters with unusual ferocity. The Argans destroyed several hundred of the Horde fighters as they passed through the fleet but did not abort their mission to help the Galactic Forum fleets fight off the remainder of the Horde fighters. Several hundred are not very many when several thousands are considered.

The Argan fleet advanced unharmed. The several hundred fighters loss didn't do an appreciable amount of harm to the Horde fighter mission. Both sides continued on their missions after their brief battle in space.

The Horde Fighter Commander reported his fleet's encounter with the Argan cruisers to Grol. Grol knew the Argan cruisers would destroy most of the Horde fighters as soon as they reached the battle raging between the Horde fighters and Galactic Forum's outnumbered fleets.

Grol, very carefully, balanced the tactical loss of his fighters to his plan for a ground attack to conquer the Argan's planet. He knew he would lose half of his Fighter Command if he didn't send enough of his Imperial Fortresses after the Argan cruisers to protect the fighters.

He knew he would lose the war if he lost Arga. Grol could not relieve himself of the nagging fear of what Arga's two missing fleets were doing. His computer had identified King Jeonk's voice in the battle with the Argan fleets but not Admiral Shok's. He was told they were always together on the same command deck in every battle, but they weren't together on the same command deck for this battle.

Where in the hell were Shok and those two fleets? If Grol could take and hold the nation of Arga, the two fleets would mean nothing. If he couldn't, the two fleets might mean everything was lost. He decided to continue on with his plan for a ground offensive to insure the Horde a rapid conquest of Arga. The fighters battling the Forum spacecraft would have to be sacrificed. He could see not other way.

The Horde landing was routine, fighter cover for the landing was massive and the Horde troops had no problems after the landing. But the Argan fighters had penetrated the Horde fighter cover and destroyed four inbound transports with one hundred twenty thousand troops on board.

The Horde ground troops found that the Argan coastal towns in the area had been evacuated. Horde troops formed up and moved quickly through the Argan countryside and they initially received no resistance in their march inland toward the targeted ground batteries. Grol considered himself very fortunate not to have lost more of his troop transports.

The Horde fighters covering Grol's ground troops hung listlessly over the Horde troop formations until the Argan fighters attacked. The battlefield immediately became a chaotic jumble of low-level dog fights. Burning fighters from both sides slammed into the massed troops, spreading the aerial chaos to the ground troops fleeing the explosive crash sites.

In the chaos, one lone Argan Black Hole fighter was followed by one of Arga's captured Dragon Spit Corsairs, the mirror image of a Horde fighter, off of the battle damaged surface of Arga.

The Black Hole fighter burst into space with the Dragon Spit in close pursuit. The Dragon Spit fired at the space bound fighter repeatedly but missed. The fighter headed for deep space with the Dragon Spit close behind, firing at it often enough to make the Horde think it was a serious encounter between one of their own and a fleeing Argan fighter.

11
THE BATTLE OF THE TWO FLEETS

The Horde missed the importance of that false battle. Jeonk Shap, king of Arga, piloted the Dragon Spit. He was on a course for Nordic to see why his two fleets were late for the battle, and to get them into it as quickly as possible.

The two ships maintained their hunted and hunter formation from Arga to the planet Nordic just in case they encountered more of the Horde armada along the way and needed to renew their space act.

Jeonk had guessed that Nordic was likely to be the staging area for the Horde ground troop buildup but he didn't know the staging area location. He discovered the location when the Black Hole Fighter and his Dragon Spit descended on the planet in plain view of the massive buildup. Jeonk renewed his false firing act with the Black Hole fighter as they crossed the huge encampment. They continued on, far beyond the troop buildup before the Dragon Spit was near enough to the two Argan fleets to drop down to Jeonk's meeting with Shok and Brak.

The Black Hole Fighter was supposed to follow the Dragon Spit to the ground but its pilot decided, due to their passing in view of the Horde troop buildup, it would give the Dragon Spit better cover if he returned and made them think he had shot the Dragon Spit down. He turned his fighter and retraced his course. He reached the Horde encampment without trouble and began strafing runs on the Horde troops. The fighter fired on and destroyed a communications center, destroyed two Horde troop transports and strafed a troop bivouac area.

Before the pilot was satisfied he had done as much damage as he could, A Horde destroyer, ten Horde fighters and four supply ships appeared on his scanner, new arrivals from the Horde Empire. He knew he was in a bind. He could stay ahead of the Horde fighters but there were the four big fat supply ships he wanted to kill, with a Horde destroyer protecting them. He couldn't escape from, or beat, the Horde destroyer in a battle. He knew he was a dead man.

The Black Hole Fighter pilot made a quick decision. He maneuvered to put one of the supply ships between him and the Destroyer. He made several hits on the supply ship as he closed on it. With the crippled supply ship yawing out of control, he skimmed the surface of the dying supply ship and set his powerful thrusters to one hundred percent. He set his armament control system for continuous fire and aimed his Black Hole Fighter for the center of the destroyer. No matter how hard the Destroyer hit his fighter, it would hit the destroyer at his fighter's maximum speed.

The Horde commander saw the Black Hole fighter blasting his destroyer. He knew he was about to be rammed. He had no time to maneuver out of its way to prevent the collision. The only thing he could do was put a massive amount of firepower into the fighter coming directly at this ship. His pulse cannons stopped the fighter's thrusters and killed the pilot, but the fighter's debris couldn't be totally destroyed. The fighter's debris slammed into the Horde destroyer, it made several holes in its outside hull and penetrated through seven of the destroyers inside compartments before it stopped just short of the command deck.

The commander thought that, under the circumstances, he had lucked out. He would be able to regain control and save his ship. His propulsion system was intact. He had lost a few weapons but he could still fight. He lost a few dozen of his crew in the impact, but most of the destroyer's crew had survived. He had those few seconds to gain back his confidence before strange things began happening to his ship. Everything on his ship that could move was moving toward some of the smaller parts of the fighter debris.

The Black Hole Fighter was so named because it uses a rare metal, called black hole metal from an exploded black hole, for its interstellar propulsion system. Black hole metal is extremely dangerous to work with. It must be shielded by Anti-Gravity Screens and controlled by Gravity Modulators to be used in spacecraft.

When the Black Hole Fighter was hit, and crashed into the destroyer, its Anti-Gravity Screens and Gravity Modulators were destroyed. The black hole metal used in space travel is too old and weak to become another black hole, but it is still strong enough for even the smallest amount of it to disrupt everything around it for miles.

The Imperial Fortress Commander had no idea what was happening to his ship. He had no experience with, nor had he ever heard of black hole metal. He knew all of his systems were beginning to shut down. He could see parts of the destroyed fighter attached to the floor and bulkheads of the ships compartments. He watched helplessly as his inner bulkheads began bending toward the fighter parts. He couldn't ask for damage reports from the other parts of his ship because his inter-ship communications had gone off line. Some of his dead crewmen had been drawn to the, running wild, black hole gravity components in the fighter's damaged parts. His live crewmembers near the damaged compartments were having trouble walking to safety and the ones who were even closer were being pulled helplessly to the bulkheads nearest the debris.

The Imperial Fortress Commander realized his ship was dying. He ordered all of the crew he could speak with to go to the fighter bays and use the ship's fighters to abandon ship. He added more of his crew to the escape party as they hurried to the fighter bays. They boarded the fighters and prepared to take off but the Horde fighters' space propulsion systems wouldn't come on line. They reset their propulsion systems time after time without success.

Strong gravity disrupts light and the Horde fighters used Light Accelerators as their propulsion system in space. The gravity pull from the Black Hole fighter's debris had disabled the destroyers systems as the Argan fighter's dead pilot had intended.

Panic raged as the desperate crew felt the increasing pull of gravity inside the fighters. The Horde fighter pilots, in last-ditch desperation, tried to use their standard thrusters to leave the ship, but the fighters' thrusters were too weak to win the fight against death. The thrusters were only used for the initial thrust needed to escape the normal gravity pull of their planets' surfaces. By the time the Horde pilots tried their thrusters, the black hole metal was affecting all of the parts of the ship. The Horde fighters no longer had enough thrust to break the ships' landing pods loose from the gravity pull infecting the destroyer.

The Argan fighter pilot had lost his life but he had won his battle. The crew of the destroyer couldn't call for help and no one could have helped them if they did. They couldn't leave the dying ship. All the crew could do was silently experience the crushing death of too much gravity. The Horde destroyer, its dead crew and its fighters would drift through space forever unless it crashed on the surface of some unfortunate planet. If there were inhabitants on the planet, they would quickly learn to stay many miles from the strange wreck for many millennia.

Jeonk's landing was safer and less dramatic. The fighter pilot had successfully completed his mission of delivering Jeonk to Nordic. The Horde assumed that such an aggressive fighter pilot had downed their fighter before he returned to die in battle over their encampment. The Horde had no time to search for one downed fighter, and what was happening to the destroyer was beyond their comprehension. The Argan Nordic operation's two fleets were still safe but their mission wasn't yet ready to go.

Shok's assessment of a time of completion was one more month. The firing mechanisms on the cruisers had been perfected and were ready to go. The cruisers' crews had been trained and were ready for the mission shortly after their arrival. The remaining problem was the black hole pellets they intended firing into the Horde destroyers and cruisers. The scientists had to surround the pellets with a very light but strong insulation to keep the pellets from attaching themselves directly to the firing mechanisms. They used jury rigged anti gravity screens to control the operation and their scientific equipment was causing them trouble. As soon as the scientists delivered enough black hole pellets, the mission was a go. They expected that operation to take as much as a month but it might be sooner if they were lucky.

Jeonk asked, "Are you aware of the camp the Horde have set up for their ground troops?"

"We are aware of it," Shok responded, "and we could destroy it but if we destroy them, they will destroy our two fleets and bring in fresh troops. We'll be handing them the victory we are supposed to be taking away from them. How does General Sokeasel see the ground assault on Arga going?"

"Sokeasel has twenty five million troops," Jeonk replied. "He called up every veteran who can still fight but he's afraid that isn't enough. Sokeasel thinks he can handle a forty or fifty million troop invasion unless they all land at once. The Horde were landing and making beachheads in the areas Sokeasel left open to them just before I left. The fighting old bastard thinks he still has things under control. He's usually right; I hope he's right this time.

You know the rim country. You and I hunted there a few times. There are about three hundred miles of cliffs ranging from fifty feet high to four hundred feet high in sloping mountain country. Sokeasel has that entire rim filled with high explosives deep in the rock. He drilled into the rock from the high side where it wouldn't be seen. Below the rim are broad expanses of gently sloping terrain that is ideal for troop staging areas. Sokeasel hopes the Horde will land in that area and use it for a troops' jump off positions to attack the other areas. If they do, he says he can detonate his explosives and take out about fifty percent of everything they put there for the entire three hundred miles. He left the place almost wide open for them.

"The Horde troop transports are big, Shok remarked. "We figure they hold about thirty thousand troops each, and they are leaving and returning at regular intervals. Sokeasel will have his work cut out for him if it takes us the entire month to finish. The scientists are doing the best they can. I can't push them any more than I have already. If I push any harder, I might be causing more of a delay instead of shortening the delay we already have."

12
THE GROUND WAR

The ground war wasn't going well for the Horde. Grol realized the error after it was too late for him to pull them back. Grol had allowed his troops to walk blindly into an Argan trap. Grol's army was fighting battle-hardened troops the Horde hadn't been prepared to fight. The Argans used a large variety of weapons and every trick one army can play on another. Grol thought he could win if he could get a kill rate of one for one from his troops. He didn't know the actual kill rate, so far, but it was obviously pathetic.

Grol had no first hand knowledge of the ground battle and he needed to know precisely what the troops were up against. He had one of his ground commanders brought to him, a commander who was close to the actual fighting. "Tell me exactly what you are up against?" Grol demanded.

"We're in a trap the Argans set for us," The commander reported, "And they use the terrain itself like a weapon. We can't use our heavy weapons because we don't see the enemy until they begin shooting.

"The weapon our troops fear the most isn't the one doing most of the killing. The one our troops fear the most is a rapid-fire weapon that fires an explosive metal projectile. It makes a loud bup-bup-bup noise when it's fired. Our troops have never heard anything like it before. The Argans use that weapon to frighten our troops and force them to retreat into a position where the Argans can use the more lethal weapon.

"The loud weapon causes an ugly death but the real killer is silent. It fires a finger length piece of very fine wire through some kind of a magnetic accelerator. We think it fires seven or eight thousand rounds per minute and it is certainly a high velocity weapon. The thin wire whips through a body like a whirling scalpel every time it hits.

"A platoon getting hit with it looks like they belong on the counter of a butcher shop. The Argans are so damn big; the smallest of them can carry a day's supply of ammunition for either weapon. We can't capture the ground batteries you targeted for us with the two million troops we have."

The Argans gained the upper hand time after time by staging retreats to trap Grol's army into canyons, valleys and meadows filled with buried land mines or explosives. Whatever triggered the trap caused chain explosions, or segments of canyon walls to explode and bury the Horde troops. The Horde troops would advance along an Argan line of retreat until the Argans were clear of the area, then the whole damned area blew up in the faces of the Horde troops. The Horde lost thousands of troops to that battle maneuver.

Grol's troops came into the battle expecting to be up against hand carried lasers and pulse cannons. There was some hope of surviving the burns of less than a direct hit with them. The unfamiliar weapons used by the Argans killed everyone they hit, whenever they hit, and that was often.

Grol had no hope of retraining his army to face new weapons while they were in the field, and he didn't dare to take them out of the field. He didn't believe the transports taking them out would survive if he did. Grol needed the transports if he was to have any hope of beating the Argans.

Grol ordered his commanders give their troops whatever information they could on the unfamiliar tactics and weapons. Grol really wanted a staging area for a massive attack the Argans weren't prepared for and couldn't repel.

His scans of the Argan surface showed one area he thought would serve his purpose. It was a few hundred miles from the capital of Poshalla in mountain country. Thousands of square miles of absolutely nothing of any importance stood open and mostly uninhabited. There were three hundred miles of vertical cliffs forming a wall on one side and gently sloping valleys from the cliffs to the next mountain range. If he could get his troop transports into the cliff area, they could set up defenses for troop bivouacs, and they wouldn't be exposed to the Argan ground batteries.

Grol thought he could move millions of troops and their ground support fighters into that area. With their backs to the cliffs, they could make a massive move against the Argan ground troops with comparative ease, no matter what kind of weapons the Argans used. The valleys sloping toward the Argan capital from the cliffs were accessible from a sparsely settled forest area that spread to the Argan coast.

Grol decided to use six of his Honor Guard spacecraft to test the feasibility of bringing troop transports over the safe appearing Argan forest. He would bring his Honor Guard ships down to the planets surface over one of Arga's neighboring nations. The Horde had received no ground salvos from them and the planets curvature would protect his test fleet from the Argan scanners' detection and ground batteries.

Grol thought the area seemed safe enough to take the chance. If his Honor Guards made it to the surface of the planet, they would remain at low level as they crossed the sea to the forest. Following the dense forest and sparsely inhabited land to the area Grol wanted to use as a troop staging area was the dangerous part.

The six Horde spacecraft made it to the surface without problems. True to plan, they skimmed the water and lifted slightly for their cross-country run. They skirted the small coastal cities and entered the forest. Halfway to their target they received pulse cannon and laser fire from four small ground batteries. The flight of Honor Guards lost two of their six ships before they silenced the ground batteries.

Grol ordered the remaining four ships to continue to the target. They arrived at the target with no further losses and were not fired upon during their return over their entry route. Grol was so pleased with the ground situation he momentarily forgot his fear about Admiral Shock and the two missing fleet.

Grol immediately ordered fifty of his Honor Guards to protect the route. He wanted the route and the area kept secure for the troop transports. Grol felt victory was in his grasp. He had found a place safe from the Argan ground batteries that he could use to introduce millions of ground troops into the war. He ordered his troop transports to begin bringing in the fifty million troops from Nordic. He needed thirty-two days to bring in all of his troops. He needed the extra time because of the loss of some of his transports in his first assault attempt.

General Sokeasel kept a watchful eye on the troop buildup in the rim country. The Horde troops cleared and leveled land as bivouacs for troops and landing pads for their fighters. They liked having the three hundred mile rim close to their backs. They kept their encampments as close to it as they could. The Horde Army set up guard posts on the mountaintops behind the cliffs. It would be very difficult for them to be attacked without warning. Day after day they packed the rim area with more troops, equipment and fighters.

Jeonk and Shok were fit to be tied with worry, but battle logic kept them in hiding. They knew the Horde troops on Nordic were leaving for Arga. They had confidence in General Sokeasel, but he was outnumbered two to one and had no air cover. The Horde had more air cover than they needed. Jeonk knew the ground offensive against Arga would begin in earnest when the last troops left Nordic. He had no idea where the Horde was landing its troops on Arga. He was afraid the beachhead they were trying to establish when he left had been successful. If that was true, Arga could be overrun.

He was faced with two equally unpleasant options. He would have to refuse air support for the Argan ground troops or order his damaged fleets back into the conflict to provide the ground support. If he used the remainder of his fleets to support the ground troops, they would be destroyed but they might turn the ground battle in Arga's favor before the Horde destroyed the fleets. If he saved the fleets and his two Nordic fleets entered the battle with their new weapons; that could, possibly, destroy the Horde air support and he could win the ground battle with the air support he had left to give to his ground troops. Both options were dangerous and neither was certain to be decisive. He decided to put his hopes on Shok being able to bring the two fleets into the battle with their new armament systems working as planned. If that didn't happen, Arga would lose the war.

13
THE EMPEROR'S BATTLE AGAINST OGLAK

The Emperor became ecstatic when Grol reported he beginning of the ground battle. He even forgave Grol for shooting Varst, the Emperor's favorite Commander. As soon as Grol told the Emperor about his good luck in finding a safe staging area for millions of Horde troops, The Emperor began his own private military action.

Before Grol ordered his first troops to Arga, the Emperor ordered an air, and ground attack on the planet Iklug. He didn't bother to communicate his plan to Grol. Emperors have no need to consult their underlings in all areas of command, and the Emperor wanted Iklug to be, entirely, his own victory. The Emperor ordered the attack to be made by the same home guard units Grol had asked to be used for reinforcements.

The Emperor envisioned a simultaneous air and ground invasion of devastating proportions that would drive the Iklugs to surrender before the Argans were forced to their knees. The Emperor wanted to be the first to conquer one of the Horde's new home planets--not Grol. His subjects would love him for freeing them from the impending disaster of the galactic collision, and for being the primary warrior whose bravery provided them with new homes.

The Emperor made one small error in his orders to the home fleet. He ordered their attack be made on the planet Oglak instead of the planet Iklug. It was a simple mistake! The overly anxious Emperor gave the incorrect planetary coordinates to the Home Fleet Commander, who was unfamiliar with the planets. Anyone could make a mistake like that.

The Iklugs are a decent people, very friendly, and not exceptionally brave, but not cowards either. It would have been a hard fight but the Emperor's new Fleet could have beaten the Iklugs in a simultaneous air and ground assault with the force he ordered from the home planet, and the ground troops the Emperor intended to take from Grol's invasion of the nation of Arga on the planet Okron. Iklug is a lovely planet of soft breezes and lush vegetation. Any planet load of people faced with the necessity of finding a new home would want to live there.

The Oglaks and their planet are very different from the Iklugs and their planet, even though both are in the same general area of the galaxy. The Oglak planet is completely covered with a thick cloudy atmosphere. Sunlight filters through the dark clouds with only a hint of brightening the planets surface. The surface of Oglak is soggy, stark, and difficult to move across. Oglak's main living plants are large, tough, deep-rooted vines of various types. The vines grow into everything one tries to build. The vines make it very difficult to build permanent structures on the surface. That's why most of the Oglaks live in underground cities.

The Oglaks have a long history of helping their neighbors against unwelcome intruders. The Oglaks are friendly, tough and they love to fight for a good cause. They would be on Okron helping the Argans defend themselves if they hadn't been advised to fortify their planet against the Horde invasion, and they fortified it with a vengeance.

MARVIN E. FOX

The Oglaks are somewhat the size of Earth people but usually just a little taller. They have a thick, dark green skin for protection against planet Oglak's miserable ecology. They have two long bony heat sensors on the top of their head for when the planet is even too dark for their eyes. Oglak eyes are one of their most striking features, very large, and each eye has eight segments. The Oglaks can see very well in what most of us think of as total darkness. They can also see in regular daylight but they don't like it. They wear heavy darkened lenses over their eyes when they fight alongside the Argans, or their other friends on planets flooded with the discomfort of ordinary sunlight.

The Oglaks have a great respect for, and a strong friendship with the Argans. They have a special respect for King Jeonk and his old friend Shok, who they fought beside many times. They had argued among themselves often in the last few days about going to help Arga in its war with the Horde. They held back for only one reason. Jeonk and Shok, both, told them, "If we fail, you must fight to save your own planet. The Horde cannot win if they must fight for every inch of ground on every planet. When the Horde lose, we will rebuild all of our planets."

The Horde Emperor remained in his safe position to be near the defeat of the Argans. Only the Home Guard Fleet Commander knew the Emperor remained in personal command of his personal triumph, victory on the planet he thought was Iklug.

The Emperor thought twenty of his reserve Imperial Fortresses and two hundred fifty Honor Guards would be more than enough air power to take Iklug. He would flesh out his Iklug ground force by diverting the last two million troops from Nordic for his battle on Iklug.

The Emperor decided Chief Commander Grol, certainly, would be able to take Arga with a few less troops. The Emperor's reserve transports from home would bring five hundred thousand Imperial troops to the Iklug battle from his reserve army. His five hundred thousand ground troops along with the two million form Grol's army would secure the victory on what he thought was a weak planet.

The Emperor expected to polish off Iklug long before Grol was victorious against Arga. The Emperor felt this first victorious conquest was a done deal and he eagerly awaited his chance to finesse Grol out of the first victory. The Emperor's first victory would also save some of the face he lost when Grol changed his brilliant four planets offensive to Grol's meager one planet attack.

The Imperial home fleet arrived over Oglak, true to the Emperor's prediction, days before the transfer of troops from Nordic to Arga was finished. The Horde Fortresses' fighters descended through the cloudy gloom of Oglak's atmosphere to test the resolve of their enemy. They found no enemy and few people on the surface of the planet. Their ship's scanners were their only eyes in the Oglak murk and their scanners were battle scanners not planet scanners. The fighter pilots reported no defensive activity on the planets surface.

The Oglaks detected the Horde arrival long before the Horde fleet came to a halt above the Oglak atmosphere. The Oglaks had been prepared to do battle with the Horde for several months, and were glad for the opportunity to stop fuming and start fighting.

The Horde, wanting a safe place to bring their troops, decided to land in the area the fighter pilots said was almost empty. The Oglaks didn't want them to land there because they didn't have troops in that area, and they didn't want their troops traveling long distances across the unfriendly planets surface to engage the Horde. The Horde was obviously planning to put its buildup area in a place that was not an advantage to the Oglak planetary defense plans.

The Oglaks also knew the Oglak spacecraft were slower than the Horde's, and the longer flying distances would allow the Horde's spacecraft a better chance to destroy the Oglak ships. Oglak troops would have to slog through the planets silt filled bogs and tough plant life to get to the battle and that put them in danger from the Horde air cover.

The Oglaks troops, or maybe the Paracans, were the best guerrilla fighters in the galaxy. Suckering an enemy out of a good position and into a poor one to fight from was part of their basic battle strategy. Before the Horde could land the ground troops, the Oglaks brought one of its ground army units to the surface near one of their three city complexes. The army unit was large enough to entice the Horde but not large enough to give them any deep concern. The army unit used enough lights to make sure the sight challenged Horde would see it, and it was well enough armed so the Horde would think the unit was serious about going to war.

A few nearby but small Oglak ground batteries began firing at the Horde fighter spacecraft, which were assigned to keep the area secure for the Horde troop landings. The Oglaks ground batteries fired from a rather long distance, too far away to do the Horde any serious harm. The Oglak army unit was just close enough to get the Horde more seriously interested in the war.

The Horde Commanders scanned the lighted area and found they had discovered a city and one Oglak Army unit to fight. The Horde Commanders considered the position of the Oglak ground unit and began to formulate a new plan. One Horde cruiser lowered into the atmosphere as much as it dared, and with better scanners than the fighters, located the three entrances to the Oglak underground cities. The cities were in the area where the ineffective Oglak ground fire and the well-lighted Oglak unit was still waiting. The Horde decided to change their landing site and surround the three cities with their five hundred thousand troops. After landing their troops, they would call for the Emperor's promised two million reinforcements.

The Horde Commander, Skursk, believed the underground cities could be easily destroyed with his Imperial Fortresses' pulse cannons and lasers from high above the atmosphere. The plan was for the Fortresses to fill entire cities with deadly heat by constantly hitting their open entrances with the Hordes most powerful weapons. The super heated cities would be death traps for their inhabitants.

Skursk's only worry was the expected Oglak counteroffensive against the Horde ground troops. That worry was muted by the paltry defensive effort the Oglaks had mounted thus far. Commander Skursk decided the Horde would be able to kill most of the Oglak ground troops while the Oglaks defended their cities from the surface surrounding the cities' entrances.

The Horde took the Oglak bait, landed their ground troops in a broad circle around the three Oglak cities and began their march through the boggy land toward the cities in an ever-thickening circle of troops. Like hunters, they would surround the prey, frighten it, and force the enemy into a group at the center of the closing circle, and destroy it. Destroying the weak Oglak army would establish a Horde ground base in the three destroyed cities that would shelter the incoming two million Imperial troops.

The Oglaks hadn't fired a shot at the encircling Horde troops up to this point. The Horde destroyers and cruisers began their aerial bombardment of the Oglak cities with pulse cannons, lasers and particle beam weapons from above the Oglaks cloud cover. The thick layers of the Oglak atmosphere dissipated the Horde pulse cannons, lasers and particle beam weapons. None of the Horde weapons could damage the city entrances from high altitude. The Horde bombardment from above the Oglak atmosphere looked more like flash lightening than weapons fire. By the time it reached the surface of the planet, it couldn't light a candle.

The Oglaks only used similar weapons for close in targets in their own atmosphere because they don't work very well at long range. The Oglak standard weapon for ground combat is a really nasty machine-gun. Its bullet splinters when it hits a body. The Oglak machine-gun was the frightening weapon used by the Argans against the Horde. The Oglaks also favor a weapon that fires a two-inch piece of magnetically propelled wire, eight thousand rounds a minute. Both weapons make it difficult for a wounded man to survive. The Oglaks shared the technology of the two weapons with the Argans many years ago.

The Horde encirclement continuously closed through the vine-covered bogs until it had passed inside the outer perimeter of the Oglak version of foxholes. An Oglak foxhole is a patch of mud or a bog hiding one or more Oglaks with self contained breathing gear, and their weapons.

The Oglaks began rising out of the security of their bogs, killing a few of the Horde with their machine-guns or magnetic wire Gatling guns, then re-entered their protective camouflage. The Horde foot soldiers became frantic in their attempts to detect their enemy before being shot. The terrain was horrible. A Horde troop could sink into to a bog with his feet on top of an Oglaks and just think the Oglak was another large vine.

The Horde troops hadn't been fitted with night vision glasses in conditions where ordinary eyesight was almost useless. The invading Horde troops couldn't understand the battle strategy of their Oglak enemy and none of the Horde foot soldiers wanted to be there anymore.

The Oglaks, in their foxholes, had them surrounded and the only time the Horde soldiers saw an Oglak was while the Oglak's machine-gun was bup, bup, bupping at them or one of their magnetic Gatling guns was slicing them to pieces.

The Horde air cover could have been good for their troops if the troops had been in an ordinary situation. The Horde fighters remained with the troops but the Oglak ground batteries shot them down with metal projectiles from rapid firing cannons that went completely through their fighters, or hit something inside and exploded. Once the

Horde fighters were hit the Horde crews died or couldn't return to space.

The fighter pilots called in vain for the destroyers and cruisers to spot the ground batteries for them, but the spacecraft above the atmosphere couldn't detect ground batteries through the thick atmosphere and ground clutter any better than the fighters could. The loss of air power was beginning to be serious. The Horde fighters' scanner screens blossomed from ground clutter, and they could only identify very large objects. Everything on the planet seemed wet and their scan pictures were almost useless because of the strong scanner return from the multitude of small collections of water and water soaked vegetation everywhere on the planet's surface.

The Horde ground Commanders realized they were in a lose-lose situation. This planet they assumed to be empty was filled with Oglaks and all of them fired weapons. None of the Oglaks fought in the open like an army should. The Horde Commanders ordered their troops to use grenades on the suspected foxholes. The troops couldn't see well enough to identify a foxhole-bog or an Oglak. The grenades usually blew up a lot of mud to no particular military advantage. The Oglaks still popped up unexpectedly from everywhere else and killed a few people each time one of them popped up.

The Horde Commander in charge of the ground operation ordered the retreat of his troop. But, the retreating Horde troops were in a broad circle that had been encircled by the Oglaks. The Horde lost so many troops in the attempted retreat that they had to reversed the direction of the retreat. The retreating Horde Army had to form itself into battle quadrants and keep moving toward the open center of the broad Oglak encirclement.

While Horde ground Commanders called for transports to return and lift the retreating troops off of the planet, they continued to retreat toward the center of the Oglak encirclement.

The retreating Horde troops set up a field of fire aimed at the ground, directly in front of their retreat where they hoped the Oglak foxholes would be. Every puddle and bog was thoroughly cleansed with lasers and grenades as they approached it. The heavy Horde fire during the retreat kept the Oglaks inside the encirclement in their burrows. That reduced the Horde casualties, but few of the Oglaks were killed.

The Horde Operations Commander, Skursk, was in a frantic quandary. The Emperor, himself, had ordered him to take the planet Iklug. He could not, with the future of his career in jeopardy, disobey his Emperor. The battlefield appeared to stabilize after the Horde retreat and that gave him some time to plan. He didn't want to risk his fleet near the surface and he didn't want to abandon the assault by sending in his transports to evacuate his troops. He needed an attack method that would insure the success he so desperately wanted.

Commander Skursk decided to call his leading commanders to a meeting on his flagship. The meeting took place in Commander Skursk's briefing compartment. Skursk sat tall in his command chair, appearing to be the epitome of an efficient and forceful commander. His second in command opened the meeting, "We have lost one hundred fifty thousand ground troops. We have lost four hundred ground support fighters and many others are damaged. It is very possible that the Iklug military Commanders have led us into a trap. Commander Skursk has a plan to overcome these losses but wants your ideas on how to restore the invasion effort before he offers his plan."

The first to speak was the commander of the Horde Fighter Group. "We expected to see many Iklug spacecraft but we have seen none. We know they have fighter spacecraft and perhaps a few spacecraft larger than fighters, but all of our fighter losses have been to ground fire. We have found no spacecraft bases. At some time we will have to deal with their space war machinery. I think we need to be cautious about grouping too many of our spacecraft too close together. They may be waiting for us to end the wide disbursement of our space-based resources to simplify their attack on us. They are obviously reserving their resources for some reason."

Skursk replied, "The Argans kept the entire Iklug planet under control with sixteen Argan cruisers under the command of an Admiral Brak. Chief Commander Grol's attack on Arga destroyed more than half of the Argan fleet and those he didn't destroy ran from the battle in terror for their lives. I don't think an Iklug space fleet will be a problem for this fleet. They are keeping their fleet out of the battle for the same reason the Argans are keeping theirs out of the battle; they know they will lose their fleets if they fight. The sooner the Iklug fleet fights, and we will have to force them to fight, the sooner we will destroy them and be done with it."

The second to speak was a ground Commander who had not been on the planets surface but was familiar with the problems, "This planet is far different from what we were told to expect. We were told the battle conditions, although not totally known, would be within the weather and terrain models our troops are familiar with. This planet does not fall within any model boundaries I have ever seen. This planet's surface is very different from what we were told to expect. I suggest we check our coordinates to determine if we are on the right planet."

Skursk stormed at the Commander, "These coordinates came directly from the Emperor. I have, of course, checked and rechecked the Emperor's coordinates for accuracy. We are, precisely, where the Emperor, himself, told us to be. Are you suggesting that the Emperor doesn't know one planet from another?"

The ground Commander's comments were quickly withdrawn and his apology was duly recorded. The next to speak was one of the Honor Guard commanders, "The Iklug's weapons are archaic contraptions using some kind of explosive firing mechanism. They have used no lasers, pulse cannons or particle beam weapons. I think we should consider the possibility that their primitive weapons are the only weapons they have and gear our assault to the parameters of their weaponry."

One of the Imperial Fortress commanders added, "We are unable to support our ground troops from space. Cloud layers and the inordinate thickness of the atmosphere quickly dissipate our weapon's discharges fired through the Iklug atmosphere. We can't expect to overcome the Iklug ground army unless we take our spacecraft low enough to make our armament systems effective. I suggest we send several of the Honor Guard ships across the planets surface as a test of the Iklug firing power. We should not concentrate entirely on the area we are in. We must know the Iklug's capabilities across the entire planet."

Skursk's Communication Officer gave the Imperial Fortress Commander his information, "We have no translations of their language but we have detected many of their communications from different areas of the planet. We have identified what we believe to be their major population centers. Those population centers should receive the bulk of the fire power from the Honor Guard ships and I can give you the planetary coordinates of those centers."

One brave ground Commanders, who had been on the surface of Oglak, stated, "All of this activity is useless unless we can invade and subdue the Iklug Army. We have no hope of subduing them with the troops we have here and the two million we are expecting from the planet Nordic aren't enough for an operation of this size. We must have more of the troops from the Argan invasion to be successful. I don't believe our spacecraft can get low enough in the atmosphere to destroy their cities without being shot down by their antiquated metal projectiles."

Skursk felt his opinion was necessary after hearing the obvious logic of his ground Commander, "We expect our ground troops to secure a perimeter around each of their cities. That perimeter will be broad enough to keep our spacecraft out of the range of the Iklug weapons, and allow us to destroy the Iklug cities by bombarding their entrances. That bombardment should secure the cities to our control.

"Your ground troops must secure an area large enough for our ships to descend and put our firepower where it will do the most good--into those entrances. Two million additional troops should be effective enough to accomplish our goal. We can quickly and efficiently destroy these three cities and all of their cities, one or several at a time if we do it on a planned basis. The heat of our weapons will destroy the Iklug cities' populations and their defending ground troops."

Skursk felt the meeting had progressed far enough for him to offer his formulation of an offensive posture for the invasion. He offered his master plan to the assembled military ignoramuses attacking the wrong planet; "We will send twenty of our Honor Guard class ships on a course to fly over the cities from which we have received the greatest concentration of Iklug communications. Those ships will fire on targets of opportunity; but, if they can identify them as they pass, they are to fire on troop concentrations, and into the entrances to the Iklug cities. They will scan the surface of the planet for Iklug troop movements advancing in the direction of our ground forces.

"Our ground troops will hold their positions until further orders. Our reinforcements from Nordic should arrive in five days. The ground troops must hold out until then. They are not to engage the enemy unless the enemy attacks; and, in that event, our troops will defend themselves. When our two million reinforcements land from Nordic, we will put a decisive end to Iklug.

"We will have determined the Iklug space defense capability before the troops from Nordic arrive. After their arrival, our troops, with support from our spacecraft, will bring victory to our efforts. This meeting is finished."

The communications the Horde were abundantly receiving, without understanding them, were the Oglak instructions transmitted to their different nations and defense forces. The Oglaks were conducting their own planning meeting at the same time the Horde had theirs. The Oglak meeting was being held by remote communication from various secure transmission facilities. The Oglaks didn't know the Horde were on the wrong planet and couldn't understand the Oglak radio transmissions even if the Oglaks had been transmitting in the clear.

The Oglak Commander of the international Oglak Army, General Shsiska, was the man who had kept the planet Oglak from being conquered by the now deceased tyrannical Veolsh Council. When the planet Veolsh conquered the other planets in the area, the Veolsh Council considered the planet Oglak to be one of the members of its mighty Empire. The Veolsh Council tried many times to bring the Oglaks under their control, but the Veolsh Empire received no taxes from the Oglaks. The Veolsh Council's claim of conquering the Oglaks was a lie they used to frighten people of nearby planets.

General Shsiska was bombarded with questions about the battle capabilities of the Horde. He replied, "Their ground troops are poorly equipped for our planets ecology. They have no night vision glasses, and they are dressed for the climate of some other planet, like Iklug. The Horde weapons do not function very well on this planet and they are confused about how to properly use them to their best advantage. They have kept their larger spacecraft above the atmosphere where they can keep them safe. That altitude keeps the Horde from using them for ground support. They are using Dragon Spit Corsairs as low level ground support fighters. Our fighters can destroy their corsairs at low level using the same methods we used on the planet Tuplej. They have no hope of conquering this planet with the force they have brought, if they continue using their present methods. Without a much larger space fleet, and fifty times the number of ground troops, I don't think they can conquer us using any method."

One of the Oglak generals stated, "They will try to locate our cities with a low level mission of some kind. How are we to respond to that attempt?"

Shsiska answered, "You are to fire on them with our standard cannons. You are not to fire at them with your lasers, pulse cannons or particle beam weapons. All city entrances will remain open for their identification. We want them to bring their larger spacecraft low enough in our atmosphere to use their weapons on our cities before we use our big guns on them."

The General didn't understand that strategy. He asked, "Won't they leave when they understand our weapons are more powerful and longer ranged than their spacecraft weapons? If we use our heavier weapons on them now, they will leave and our people will be safe."

Shsiska replied, "They probably would, that is why we can't use our heavy weapons until we can kill them all. If they leave here, they will join the battle over Arga. We must, at all cost, keep them here fighting us. Every moment they are here gives Arga a better chance for survival. The only reason the Horde can have for their delay in attacking us is because they are waiting for more ground troops. We will allow the ground troops to land without opposition. Once their troops land, they will never leave this planet.

Another asked, "Are we going to lead their ground troops into our inter-city tunnels?

Shsiska answered, "Our tunnels are difficult to build and keep dry, and they are lighted. From that standpoint it would be better if we fight them on the surface. The Horde troops may fight better in dry, lighted tunnels if we choose to fight them there. On the surface, Horde troops aren't very good. If they find and enter our tunnels we will not fight them there. We will use the standard method to take care of that problem."

His Space Commander broke into the conversation, "My pilots can take out everything the Horde have except the Horde destroyers and we are eager to prove it. We have half of our spacecraft here. The other half is with the Galactic Forum fleet under Admiral Chosteel. Half is enough for what we have to do. We are going to lose many more people because we are keeping our spacecraft hidden underground."

Shsiska retorted testily, "The Argans have lost half their fleets and millions of Horde ground troops are now landing on Arga. We have some nut here, that thinks he can conquer this planet with a small fleet and a few troops. If anyone, for any reason, makes that nut think he can't win, I will, personally, shoot him. We will take whatever losses we must to keep that nut here until we can destroy him and our part of the Horde invasion force."

The last question was about the armored city gates, "Are we going to close the city gates after the Horde ships identify our cities?"

Shsiska replied, "We will keep all city gates open until our big guns begin firing on the Horde Destroyers and cruisers. At that point, I suggest we close them quickly. Until then our cities must appear to be vulnerable to their weapons. We will use the same tactics we used against the Veolsh Council. Everyone understands those tactics and they need no discussion."

The Horde passed the five days on Oglak with only enough light skirmishes for the Oglaks to keep their troops awake. The Horde believed the Iklug army's weak opposition to their invasion was an indication of the Iklug fear of the power of their large invasion force. The two million Horde troops landed with the loss of only two of their transports from the Oglaks, antiquated, artillery. Skursk and his Commanders were becoming very pleased with the military progress of their conquest of Iklug.

The Horde troops moved to surround the three cities they had failed to surround with one fifth of their present force. Resistance to the increased Horde invasion was light and they believed their additional troops made the difference.

The Horde discovered the vents to the Oglak's underground tunnels that were used for inter-city travel. They stationed troops around them to prevent the escape of civilians trying to flee before being fried by their Destroyers' weapons, or the use of the tunnels by the Iklug troops running from the coming battle. The tunnels were heavily guarded by the Horde but none entered them. They didn't want their troops to be inside the tunnels when their high-flying destroyers and cruisers lowered to toast the Oglak city dwellers.

Commander Skursk declared to his Commanders, "We can use this identical plan on every city on the planet." He immediately sent his most optimistic communiqué, which prematurely informed the Emperor, "Your plan for the invasion of Iklug is a success. The Iklug Army has retreated from the battle. We are in control of the Iklug's air space and its surface. It will take an undetermined amount of time to destroy their cities and the remnants of their military defenses. Our success is a certainty. You are to be congratulated on your grasp of battle tactics. I am now in the process of positioning my fleet to destroy their cities."

The Emperor was very pleased with the news from Commander Skursk. The main battle on Arga hadn't begun yet but it would begin as soon as he informed Grol of his triumph. The Emperor felt the pleasure of being able to tell Chief Commander Grol that the last of the Nordic troops Grol was waiting for to begin the battle against Arga had been diverted to Iklug.

The Emperor enjoyed his personal triumph for a few hours before he gleefully informed Grol, "I, alone, have commanded the defeat of the first of the enemy planets. Chief Commander Grol, you may begin your battle for Arga whenever it pleases you. You have all of the troops that are available for this battle. I, personally, ordered half of the home fleet to attack the planet Iklug and I ordered the use of the last two million troops from Nordic in the ground invasion of that planet. Commander Skursk has already informed me of his success. He is, at this moment, lowering his spacecraft through the murky atmosphere of Iklug to destroy their cities."

Grol was stunned by the Emperor's announcement of the loss of two million troops, but something about the Emperor's last sentence caught his attention. Grol asked, "What murky atmosphere? Iklug doesn't have a murky atmosphere, it's almost like Arga."

The Emperor exclaimed, "You are mistaken! My Commanders on the planet say the planet is dark and it never receives the full light of the sun because of its thick atmosphere. Commander Skursk tells me the Iklugs have abandoned their defenses and he is assured of success."

Grol went Ashen faced before he yelled into his transmitter, "Give me the coordinates of that planet!"

The Emperor refused to give Grol an answer but one of his aides relayed the coordinates to Grol, who again yelled into his transmitter, "Get Skursk off of that planet! He's in a trap! That isn't Iklug! It's Oglak! We only wanted to keep the Oglaks from using their fleets in space to keep them from helping the other planets. Our people can't live on Oglak. Its damned atmosphere will kill us in months."

The Emperor was adamant. Whatever planet it was, Skursk had informed him that victory was immanent. The Emperor absolutely refused to take the first victory from himself, and let that first victory go to Commander Grol and the Argan offensive.

Skursk patiently and carefully lowered his fleet closer to the Oglak surface. His Honor Guards lowered with his Imperial Fortresses. The Honor Guards were below the

Fortresses; but keeping the same rate of descent, and the Honor guards were dispersed over a wider area. Skursk kept his Fortress flagship above his other spacecraft to monitor the battle formation and, perhaps, to be in a better position to leave quickly if his prediction to the Emperor wasn't precisely correct. The Horde scanners filled the gloomy atmosphere, still carefully on guard for an attack from the Iklug spacecraft they thought were too cowardly to attack.

The Oglak scanners filled the same gloomy space. The Oglak Commanders tensely waited for the right moment to strike. The Horde fleet descended to one hundred thousand feet. General Shsiska ordered, "All weapons on line." The Horde fleet slowed its rate of descent. General Shsiska ordered, "Hold your targets and follow them down. Wait! Wait--until we can get them all." The fleet stopped its descent with Commander Skursk's flagship at fifty thousand feet. The Horde fleet wheeled to bring each ship in the fleet to its best firing position over the cities. General Shsiska gave his order to the ground batteries, "commence firing!" He turned to the Commander of the Oglak Ground Army and said one word, "Attack!"

The Oglak ground Commander instantly ordered his waiting fighters to attack the Horde air support protecting the Horde ground troops.

In the moments they had before they were attacked, the Horde invaders on the ground peered upward through the murky clouds expecting to see a massive barrage of fire penetrating the Oglak cities. They watched, with sinking hearts, as hundreds of lasers, pulse cannons and particle beam weapons spewed hissing arrows of fire and death from the Oglak surface batteries, splitting the dense fog around them to terminate in explosions the Horde could barely see from the ground.

Too late, Skursk realized his error in miscalculating the power his invasion faced. He couldn't save his fleet or the invasion. He barely saved himself by shifting his Imperial Fortress above one and then to the next of his falling ships, using them as shields to keep from sharing their fate. If he hadn't been higher then they were and kept his dying fleet between his Imperial Fortress and the planet's surface, he could not have escaped.

In terror of what was happening below him and in terror of facing the wrath of a disappointed Emperor, he plunged upward through the Oglak atmosphere and put his ship on a heading for the Emperor's safe haven near Arga.

The poorly equipped Horde Army was stranded without its fleet. Their Horde support fighters had no overhead armada to retreat to. The Army could do nothing but defend its positions. Oglak fighter formations were crowding the horizon before the destroyed Horde fleet had finished falling to the ground.

The Oglaks had quietly brought their ground troops to the battle in the five days it had taken the Horde to bring theirs. Oglak machine-guns and magnetic Gatling guns began spreading death through the ranks of the Horde ground troops.

The quick turn of events stunned the Horde commanders. The hunters were suddenly the hunted. Every second of the battle became a dance with death. The Horde commanders, frantically, attempted to reposition from offensive to defensive warfare.

The Horde Army was surrounded, outnumbered, out gunned, out maneuvered, and no one was asking them to surrender. The Horde commanders didn't know a word of the Oglak language. They didn't know how to petition for surrender.

The Oglak fighter spacecraft came from every direction in waves of death. Every Oglak pilot pushed his ship to the max, but all of them couldn't be first. It took some of them longer to get there than it did others because they had farther to fly. They had waited patiently in their underground hangers for the order to fight, and they were impatient to enter the battle.

The air battle began low over the wet, steamy Oglak surface. The Horde fighters couldn't maneuver near the surface as well as they could in space. The Horde fighters kept steady dogfight climbs to higher altitudes in an attempt to avoid the increasing number of Oglak fighters near the surface. The number of Horde fighters diminished during each minute of battle.

The Horde fighters were faster than the Oglak fighters in space. When their battle for survival reached the upper limit of the Oglak atmosphere; the surviving Horde fighters retreated to deep space, leaving the Oglak fighters behind. They also left behind the help they might have been for the Horde ground army.

The Oglaks had taken control of the air over the battleground, but air cover for an Oglak army is sketchy business. The Oglaks are close in guerrilla fighters and it's difficult to give ground troops air cover when they are up close with the enemy. The Oglak fighter pilots had to focus on large Horde troop concentrations to prevent Oglak losses from friendly fire.

The Horde helped the Oglak fighters in that effort by collecting in many defensive formations across the battlefield. They protected themselves with blazing fields of lazer fire around their defensive formations' perimeters. The Oglak pilots targeted the laser lighted Horde ground formations, spreading their own lasers and pulse cannons against the brilliance of the Horde defense.

The Horde Army had no place to retreat. Oglak Army troops slashed the retreating Horde Army on all sides, forcing them into ever-smaller zones of death. The retreating Horde remembered the air vents to the Oglak inter-city tunnel system. They didn't know what they were for but they knew they were big and warm air came out of them.

The Horde Commanders, who could not open the vents, ordered their troops to blow them open. Horde troops began pouring into the tunnels that might give them some hope of avoiding certain death at the hands of the charging Oglaks on the surface. The Horde troops could see better in the lighted tunnels than they could on the surface, but Oglak lighting leaves a lot to be desired for people with normal daylight vision. The tunnels were still dark; they were just, not as dark as it was outside.

The surface battle went from worse to the worst for the Horde. If they stayed in large groups, Oglak fighter pilots eager to defend their homeland pounced on them. If they fought in small groups, they were cut down by the Oglak foot soldiers they couldn't see until it was too late. In the next two days the Oglaks killed the Horde Army by the hundreds of thousands.

The Horde survivors were forced ever closer to the entrances of the three cities. Oglak Army troops arrived in droves through the inter-city tunnels to defend their beleaguered cities. The new Oglak arrivals poured through the city gates and fired into the flanks of the retreating Horde Army as it was forced into their range. Oglak soldiers pouring out of the cities, sandwiched the Horde between the cities and the encircling Oglak army, and cut the Horde down in withering crossfires.

One of the Horde Commanders managed to regroup enough of his troops for one more desperate try. He hoped to assault one of the city entrances, get his troops inside, take the city and defend that position. The Commander and his troops fought their way to the entrance and gained a foothold inside the cities huge storm gates. The Oglak defenders met the attack with tenacious ferocity. Barrages of small artillery, mortars, machine-guns, lasers and magnetic wire Gatling guns spewed into the attacking Horde and stopped their advance.

The effort of the Horde Commander and his troops was too little, too late. He had Oglak foot soldiers at his rear and the cities defenders in his face. The Commander and his troops were the only Horde soldiers to see the inside of an Oglak underground city; the view was brief. They all died at the entrance.

The planet conquering war on the surface dwindled to an Oglak mop up of the conquerors but there were still tens of thousands of the Horde Army in the Oglak tunnels. The Oglaks tunnels gave a short, false ray of hope to the last of the ill equipped planet conquering Horde troops who were fighting a losing battle on the wrong planet. The Oglaks didn't fight them. They identified the tunnels they were in, closed off the Horde infected tunnels and flooded them. The Oglak soldiers guarding the vents the Horde had blown to get into the tunnels, reported no Horde escapees from the flooded tunnels. The Horde war to conquer the planet Iklug was ended with an Oglak victory.

14
CHIEF COMMANDER GROL'S NEMESIS

Grol was weary from the long hours he had forced himself to remain on the command deck. He had many misgivings about the coming battle to destroy the Argans. He recognized the Argans as superlative warriors, tougher than his own men, and obviously more experienced. His troops had yet to capture their first major city. The Argan ground batteries were still in operation, and waiting for his fleet to come close enough for the Argans to use them.

The Horde had captured a few outlying ground batteries but the Argans used explosives to blow them to pieces before they fell into Horde hands. Grol had no hope of getting them repaired to use against the Argan spacecraft he feared would reappear. Every weary bone in his old warrior's battle wise body told him the space battle wasn't over.

Grol's ground commanders wanted to use the three hundred miles of mountain rim area as a staging area for all of the troops brought in from the planet Nordic. Grol refused to permit them to concentrate the entire force in one area. He demanded they use forest bivouacs in nearby areas of the mountains for the greater number of troops. He also insisted they use the beachheads they had already established to bivouac others.

He allowed them to bivouac fifteen million Horde troops along a front at the bottom of the three hundred mile rim. His ground Commanders were taking days after the last troops had landed to prepare their troops for the advance on specific targets. Grol felt every minute of that time brought them closer to disaster.

Grol couldn't get the nagging questions, 'where are the two fleets and what are they doing?' out of his mind. Among his other distractions, the Emperor insisted on sending Commander Skursk to him to explain Skursk's losses on the planet Iklug. The fool of an Emperor, who refused to recall Skursk's fleet and troops when he could, hadn't bothered to explain to Skursk that the coordinates the Emperor had given him were for the wrong planet.

Skursk was still unaware that he fought and lost his battle against the planet Iklug on the planet Oglak. Skursk wanted to discuss his plans for a new assault on Iklug with Grol, but someone would have to explain to Skursk where Iklug is. Grol's worries about the battle against Arga had put him in the wrong mood to be the one forced to brighten one more dull imperial wit.

Skursk entered Grol's command deck with some apprehension. Losers are always apprehensive on their Chief Commander's command deck. The Emperor had told Skursk about Commander Varst's, terminal, misfortune in the same situation. He looked to where Grol was studying scan maps of Arga. Skursk's apprehension level elevated when he looked into Grol's face. Grol's face looked mean. His usually chalk white face had turned a mean gray color. His black eyes looked mean. Grol's jaws looked mean and tight. Grol looked silently back, toward the latest imperial dull wit, and his silence appeared mean to Skursk.

Skursk said nervously, "Iklug was nothing like our information led us to expect. The atmosphere was so thick we couldn't use our fleet weapons until we were within fifty thousand feet of its surface. Our troops didn't have the proper gear for the climate, and the Iklugs were much better armed than we expected. We lost the battle because we were misinformed about the planetary conditions and the Iklug's ability to defend their planet."

Grol asked in, what sounded to Skursk like a mean tone of voice, "If the planet was so different from what you expected, why didn't you retreat and reconsider your options, instead of landing, losing two and one half million troops, and causing the destruction of your entire fleet?"

Skursk tried to float his, Emperor, hole card, "We were under the direct orders of the Emperor to take the planet, retreating was unthinkable. The Emperor, himself, gave Iklug's coordinates to me. He ordered me to take the planet. Performing our duties in any other manner would have been an insult to our Emperor."

Grol gave Skursk a moment of mean, silent, steely-eyed disgust. He then said, "The coordinates the Emperor gave you are the coordinates for the planet Oglak, not Iklug. Oglak is one of the planets I hoped to do battle with, one at a time. The Oglaks are too well armed, too dangerous, and too experienced, to fight with, two at a time."

"I was directly under the Emperor's orders," Skursk insisted, near to panic from fading nerves. "He would have destroyed my career for disobeying."

Grol noted with contempt, but bypassed Skursk's career fears, and asked with pointed disgust, "How is it that you and your, Personal, Imperial Fortress are the only escapees from the Oglak disaster, you personally arranged?"

Skursk tried to bluff out a reasonable answer, but bluffing isn't easy for a man who is afraid he has one foot in a casket and his other on a death warrant, "It was my incredible good fortune to be directing the Emperor's fleet form a slightly higher altitude than the other ships. The enemy opened up on the Emperor's fleet with an incredible barrage of weapons, weapons we thought they did not possess. There was nothing I could do; the fleet below me was dying. I saved my Imperial Fortress and myself from destruction to be able to regroup, and lead an entirely new attack--as--as the Emperor--himself, said he wants me to do."

Grol looked at the foremost of the Emperor's favorite cowardly incompetents for several minutes without answering. His anger abated during those minutes but his disgust remained as solid as his own flagship. He finally addressed the quaking blob of military pus before him, "You are a military imbecile. You are undeserving of a command, or even service, in any military unit in any galaxy, friend or foe. I am not going to kill you. You are relieved of command. Your flagship will remain with me to be used in this battle.

I am giving a fleet wide order to have you shot if you so much as step on any command deck in the Imperial fleet, except the Emperor's. A fighter is waiting to take you back to safety with the Emperor. Now--get out of my sight--before I change my mind about not shooting you."

Grol didn't like this war. He fought hard in the wars to establish the empire. He considered those wars to have been for good purpose. Many of the nations he helped to conquer were glad to be rid of their leaders.

Grol knew the people in those wars, understood the weapons and the end result was good, until the Emperor he fought for died, and his idiot of a son became Emperor. Since that time of great mourning for an old comrade in arms, he and many of the older warriors began wondering about the wisdom of forming large empires.

This war with the Argans wasn't about anything but survival and both sides knew it. He admired the people he was fighting. They were the best-damned fighters he had ever encountered. Faced with a war of annihilation they would fight to the last man, woman and child. With stark bitterness in his guts, Chief Commander Grol ordered the ground attack on Arga to begin.

General Sokeasel's main battle focus was on the fifteen million Horde troops at the bottom of his three hundred mile rim. He kept hoping they would shift more of their troops to the rim country but he was to the point of admitting defeat on that hope. Still, they had their largest encampment right where he hoped it would be. When the first of the Horde troops began their preparations to move out, he would give up his last hope for more Horde troops and push the button.

The days were long until Sokeasel's command post received the information that the Horde troops were about to make their move. He looked to the men waiting at the rows of remote detonators and nodded his head. They quickly began pressing the rows of switches. Sokeasel had set his explosives on the rim to begin exploding from both ends. The detonations of high explosives would end at the center of the rim country. It would take only a few seconds to press the correct sequence of switches for the entire rim to explode.

Most of the Horde troops were still waiting near the cliffs along the rim when massive explosions began rocking the countryside. The exploding rocks sent the terror of hurtling death through their ranks. Only those nearest the rim had a brief glimpse of the tons of shattered rock flying toward them. Those farther away were confused about the method used for the explosions, and they couldn't immediately grasp what was happening to them. Some thought the Argans were counter attacking with bombs.

Deadly rock poured from the walls of the rim, careening for miles past their bivouacs, and flowing down the slope of the land. Large and small flying rocks killed the Horde troops as they tried to run for cover. The hoped for cover from their own battle equipment was ripped apart as tons of exploding rock sliced it to bits. Their armored personnel carriers, mechanized weapons and supporting fighters were turned into broken pieces of useless junk torn apart by the blast hurtled avalanches of rock and dirt.

Surviving Commanders along the three hundred miles tried to rally their troops to lead them away from the exploding rock walls. Delayed explosions began taking the lives of troops who survived the initial blasts. The terrific explosions caused landslides to rip through the Horde encampments. Troops half buried in debris screamed for rescue. Troops with arms and legs blown off by flying rock yelled for medical help.

Ground Commanders called helplessly for the fleet to rescue them from the terror of the disastrous explosions. Grol knew his fleet couldn't help. He knew the Argans had laid the trap and the trap would include well-hidden, very powerful, ground batteries to destroy his spacecraft.

The ground war had to be won on the ground. He had landed the ground troops to make it safe for him to bring his fleet close to the surface and destroy Arga. His fleet was still too vulnerable. The Oglak victory over Skursk, the imperial dim wit, was fresh in is mind. Grol had to accept the trap his army was caught in to keep out of the second trap he knew the Argans had prepared for his fleet if he ignored the first trap.

The explosions ended with swirling dust packed air. Horde Commanders had to wait for the dust to clear to see if they could regroup their few survivors and move them from the killing field. The air was just beginning to clear when the survivors along the rim heard a deep rumble and felt the ground shake under there feet. The fault line that originally raised the rim from the depths of the earth was becoming active from the explosive power of Sokeasel's three hundred mile trap.

Within minutes of the first rumble, an earthquake shook the entire rim. Huge landslides flowed down the mountains, sweeping down the sloping hills below the rim to slide across the valleys and climb the upsweep of the mountains on the other side. A few of the Horde survived but for battle purposes, Sokeasel's personally arranged trap that became a natural disaster was a complete success.

Horde Commanders in the safer areas of Arga felt they still had enough troops to take the nation. They assumed there would be many survivors from the rim disaster and wanted the survivors of Sokeasel's trap in the battle.

To rescue the survivors, they began moving their large space transports into the mountains along the same safe route, they had previously used with success. A few of the hidden ground batteries, Grol feared the Argans had waiting to trap his fleet, destroyed the Horde space transports over the forests the Horde thought were safe.

When his last transports were shot down, Grol came to his first military understanding of the Argan battle strategy. He knew the Argans had decided to allow as many of the Horde troops on their planet as the horde were willing to put there. The Argan strategy was to kill enough Horde troops to prevent their attack on the neighboring planets, even if it cost all of the Argans their lives, homes and planet.

For the first time, Grol's old warrior's worries became deep fears. Grol stored his fears in the silence of his own heart. He quieted his fears with the thought, "If the Argans lose and I can hold this one planet, we will still have enough time and power left to rebuild out armies and conquer all of the other planets."

Grol ordered his Horde ground Commanders to continue their strategy of assaulting large population centers and destroying ground batteries. He felt there was no other choice. After the Argans shot down the last of the Horde troop transports, the Horde no longer had a means of being evacuated from the planet. The Horde ground Commanders knew their only hope for success was to make Arga safe for the Horde fleet to join in the attack.

There were some other strategies the Horde hadn't considered that were coming into the battle for Arga. General Sokeasel, in his minds eye, had fought this battle many times in his rise to the top of the command structure. He knew Arga better than any living man. He had walked it, scanned it, and studied its surface like a mother studies the face of her first born child. He knew where the Horde Army would find bottlenecks for their troop movements, where the natural barriers were, knew every pitfall for a foreign army. More than that, he knew where every element of the Horde Army was and every step it would have to take to kill the nation he loved.

The Argan Army was still seriously outnumbered, even with the destruction of fifteen million Horde troops, but they weren't beaten. Sokeasel knew the Horde troops would no longer be trying to take the easy routes to their objectives. They had fallen into too many traps not to know the easiest ways were the deadliest ways. The Horde would be moving across the most difficult terrain to avoid the traps.

Sokeasel knew his biggest problem wasn't saving cities; it was saving the powerful ground batteries that kept the Horde fleet away from the surface. If he lost too many ground batteries, Arga was finished. The Horde fleet would be able to descend and destroy the Argan army and the cities.

The nation of Arga covered two continents and a large part of a third. The largest continent had the capital city of Poshalla on it. The Horde Army was concentrated on that main continent. The Horde believed, accurately, if they could conquer the main continent by destroying the ground batteries surrounding Poshalla, they could win the war. They could conquer everything on the other two continents and win nothing. The main continent would still be an implacable fortress waiting to destroy them.

With the help of the Horde fleet, the Horde Army could conquer the entire planet; but the fleet had to be able to avoid the massive ground based protection spread across the main continent. The only way for the fleet to avoid that massive protection was for the Horde Army to capture or destroy it. Destroying Poshalla had to be the beginning of the destruction of Arga.

Grol believed he could lose his entire ground force on Arga, and still win if they could destroy the protection on this one continent while they died. The Horde could eventually transport as many as one hundred fifty million men to the war but the preservation of the space fleet was critical to the transportation of more troops. He had already lost too many of the Empire's thirty thousand man space transports to bring in reinforcements quickly.

It was apparent to Grol that his space fleet must be rebuilt to full power to conquer the other planets and that would take time. He needed to save every ship he could save, finish the defeat of the Argan fleets, and be successful in conquering Argan. If he could defeat Arga in this first battle, all of the other problems would become solvable.

The Horde marched sixteen million troops through the Argan forests to attack Poshalla from two sides. With that many troops they thought Poshalla would be an easy victory. The Horde felt their losses so far, although massive, had not changed the basic fact of for the Horde's overpowering numbers favoring a battlefield victory.

The Horde planed to use the fifteen million Horde reserves troops that would not be in the Poshalla battle, to keep the widespread elements of the Argan Army away from Poshalla. With a major part of the Argan Army kept out of the Poshalla battle, the Horde could quickly bring the capital city under their control. They thought the Argans had, at the most, four million troops dug in to protect Poshalla. The Horde planners were right about the number of dug in Argan troops surrounding Poshalla.

Eight million Horde troops traveled through the Lersta Mountains to attack Poshalla from the South. Eight million Horde troops traveled through the Kerst Mountains to attack on the north side. Both armies had good cover for most of their seven-day march, but the last few miles would be on open ground. Poshalla was built on a plain. Crossing the open plain to Poshalla was the most dangerous area for the Horde.

The Horde ground troops used a variety of attack vehicles, all armed with lasers, pulse cannons, missiles or all three. There were three man Hoplats, armored and used as airborne assault vehicles to quickly support troops in trouble spots along their offensive line. They used lightly armored one man Seldeks to fly large numbers of Special Forces Troops behind the enemy lines to attack from the rear. The heavily armored Malstuf was used to move as many as one thousand troops, per Malstuf, from well-established areas of the front to wherever they needed more troops. The Horde depended heavily on hovering unmanned remote platforms called Bastus mounted with a variety of weapons that could be positioned and fired from a Command Post, or by ground controllers.

The Horde battle Commanders used heavily armored moving Command Posts they called Stycols. The Stycol was a quick mobile unit that could hover for long periods of time. It could hover above the battle lines or rapidly change position to view the entire battle area and it could operate from positions on the ground. The Stycol had an excellent armament system with all of the firing options of their assault vehicles.

The heavier assault equipment the Horde used for ground attack was just as impressive. Their major weapon was a large vehicle that ran on metal tracks. They called it a Kurstuf. It had a crew of ten and could fire all of the weapons in their attack arsenal including the short-range anti-personnel missile installed on some of the Bastus. The Kurstuf was heavily armored and had a long sloping nose designed to deflect laser and pulse cannon hits into the air to keep the ground troops from being hit by their scatter.

Following the Kurstuf into a conventional Horde battle was a line of self propelled vehicles called a Brust. The Brust stood eight feet tall and twelve feet wide. The Brusts had no weapons. They were used in a long line to form a protective wall for advancing troops receiving heavy fire. The Brust gave the troops a shield to protect them from whatever small arms were being fired at them.

The Horde had many high tech weapons but they couldn't use any of them until they marched their sixteen million men to the battle. Getting there would be half the fun and a little less of the danger.

Sokeasel's troops gave the Horde little time to contemplate the beauty of the countryside on their march to the plain. The Horde dared not move in large open areas. They kept their army moving, laboriously, through the thick cover of trees across the slopes of the mountains. Mechanized Earthmovers cut trails for the armored equipment and foot soldiers, but earthmovers aren't very good at clearing large trees.

Sokeasel's penchant for booby traps made itself known almost immediately. The Horde Commanders first used their Kurstufs to topple the trees in their path but too many of the trees were booby trapped with enough explosives to destroy the Kurstufs.

Their next move was to send teams of experts to check the trees for explosives. The explosives were buried beneath the trees and the only way the experts could defuse a booby-trapped tree was to dig beneath it. When they dug beneath the trees the explosives' proximity fuses set them off and killed the experts.

The Horde commanders decided to use explosive charges on the trees, which worked, but also began starting forest fires as they moved farther into the deep forests. General Sokeasel had thoughtfully used incendiary explosives on a large number of his booby-trapped trees. The Horde was in the deep forests of Arga with millions of troops. They couldn't afford forest fires. They continued to use explosives on the trees, but they had to put enough troops nearby to put out the forest fires.

The Horde feared meadows, or any other large open areas, but they didn't like trees anymore either. Sokeasel and his Argans booby-trapped everything the Horde troops could walk on or by. The Horde were watched every step of their march by Sokeasel's troops, who knew the best time to press a remote switch and blow them up. The horde entered the open areas they couldn't avoid by first filling the ground in front of them with massive amounts of laser and pulse cannon fire.

The Horde began using their three man Hoplats to fly over the area and check for traps. When the Hoplats reported nothing, they ran Kurstufs or earth graders across the area to see if the heavy vehicles would set off land mines. If nothing happened, they moved troops across the open area. When their troops filled the area, the Argans triggered remote controlled land mines and killed many of the troops.

The Horde lost fewer men to exploding trees than they did in the open areas. The Horde skirted the open areas, sometimes with great difficulty, and dealt with the exploding trees, after they had a few tries at the shorter routes.

Each of the Horde armies lost approximately one hundred thousand men killed or wounded on their march to the open plain of Poshalla. With millions on the march, two hundred thousand didn't seem to be a large loss to the Horde.

They knew the plain of Poshalla they were finally facing was the most lethal of the mined areas they had encountered. They hadn't yet figured out how to detonate the many varieties of mines. It would be suicidal to take sixteen million troops across the plain to attack the capital of Arga before they found a way to detonate the mines.

The Horde ground Commanders asked the help of Chief Commander Grol to find a way to explode the mines before the attack. Grol knew more about mines than the ground commanders. He knew a remotely fired device had to have an electronic trigger of some kind. He knew, having experienced the Argan genius for explosive devices, all of them wouldn't have the same trigger. He had learned the Argans were very professional about war. They wouldn't use mines that were easily detonated.

Grol worked the problem while the Horde army kept steady firing patterns going into Poshalla from their positions on the edge of the forests. Horde Kurstufs on the ground and Hoplats in the air pounded the Argans across the flatlands. The Horde Bastus weren't in range and couldn't be used. The Argans returned fire on the Horde with lasers and pulse cannons from their dug in positions. The distance between the two armies filled with unceasing barrages of pulse cannon and laser fire.

The Horde tried to bridge the gap between themselves and Poshalla's defenders with hundreds of low flying Hoplats. The three man Hoplats worked well with a large troop movements, or used with other weapons, but getting them, unsupported across an open plain to attack dug in troops wasn't their strong point.

The Argan troops raised their sights and burned the Hoplats out of the air with heavy lasers. The Hoplats glowed like jack-o-lanterns for seconds before they crashed to the ground to be blown apart by the land mines. The Horde withdrew the Hoplats to save the survivors for use in the closing attack maneuvers. The Horde had to shift the battle to something less vulnerable than the Hoplats.

The Kurstufs weathered the long distance fire with ease and the Horde were able to keep the battle going with the Kurstuf as their main weapon. Both armies suffered many casualties but the Horde was in a more exposed position and received the brunt of the losses.

The frustrated Horde commanders decided to increase their kill rate with aerial attacks by their fighters. The Horde fighters swarmed the Argans with low level strafing runs around the circumference of the Poshalla defensive lines. At first, the Argans had little luck against the fast moving Horde fighters. The Horde fighters stayed too low to the ground to be hit by heavy space batteries and hand held lasers or pulse cannons were useless against them.

The Horde fighters were forced to remain near the ground to keep from being shot down by the Argan defenders space batteries. The fighters' ground skimming strafing runs worked on the dug in troops until the Argans began using their Oglak machine-guns and magnetic Gatling guns in a desperate bid to stop the Horde slaughter of their troops.

After facing the more effective weapons, the Horde fighters became burning piles of debris around the Argan front lines. After many losses, the fighters had to withdraw. If they stayed low, the Oglak weapons brought them down. If they went higher, the Argan ground batteries brought them down. Their losses forced them to stop the aerial attack. The long-range ground battle seemed a permanent fixture for both armies until Grol came up with a solution to the buried mines.

Grol used his fleet computers to determine various analog and digital combinations of signals to detonate the mines. He then flooded the Arga plain with those electronic signals. It took his computers an entire day to find the right combination of signals to begin detonating the mines. Large patches of mines blew up as each trigger was found. Finally, there were no more mine explosions and the Horde considered the minefield cleared.

The Horde plan for their attack on Poshalla included crossing the plain at night to take advantage of the Argans decreased visibility of the Horde troops. When it was full dark, the armored Kurstufs were ordered to take the forward position with the three-man Bastus overhead. The troops would follow the Kurstufs on foot, preceded by the self propelled Brusts to protect them from the Argan lasers and machine guns.

The front moved easily until the Horde closed half the distance from the forest to Poshalla. Heavy land mines began exploding under them, destroying Kurstufs and killing foot soldiers. Someone, or something, pressing down on the trigger sets off contact mine. Anything from the size of a foot to a heavy vehicle will do it. Clever electronic triggers don't work.

The Argan defenders had waited for the contact mines to begin going off before they fired flares to light the Horde positions. As soon as the flares lighted the targets, the Argans began firing short-range missiles at everything they could identify. Many of the Kurstufs were destroyed and many Bastus and Hoplats were hit and downed.

The Horde was in an exposed position. The amount of frustrated radio traffic between their command Stycols was terrific. The Horde had the lethal remnant of a tremendous mine field to cross while Argan lasers and pulse cannons fired continuous deadly volleys into their ranks. Buried mines blew up the Horde's Brusts that protected the attack. Horde foot soldiers became directly exposed to the Argan heavy fire. The flares exposed their positions and the Horde were now close enough to hear and be hit by the damned bup, bup, bup machine-guns, and their commanders wouldn't let them retreat.

To add to the problem, Horde Commanders were receiving reports of machine-gun fire along the advance of their reinforcements coming from the forest behind them. The Horde had developed a healthy respect for machine-guns and the short thin wire coming from silent magnetic Gatling guns at eight thousand rounds per minute.

They knew the Argan Army was trying to move in behind them under the cover of night, and they would be receiving casualties from the rear of their battle formation. The Horde had left a rear guard to take care of a rear attack problem, but the rear guard wasn't reporting any activity. Perhaps the rear guards weren't as familiar with the Argan's deep forests as the Argans were. The Horde Commanders were beginning to fear that their rear guard might have gotten lost--or maybe killed!

The Horde Commanders recognized that they couldn't retreat. They had to take Poshalla and hold out until enough of the fifteen million Horde troops who were supposed to be keeping the rest of the Argan army busy, could reinforce them and complete the Poshalla operation.

The Horde didn't know how many Argans were in the attack on their rear. They hoped they were too few, and the Horde Army could take Poshalla while keeping the Argans attacking their rear between them and the 15 million incoming Horde reinforcements.

Horde Commanders ordered their troops to go forward through the minefields and take Poshalla. The troops would have to concentrate their fire directly on the ground ahead of them to detonate the mines as they advanced, and keep the Argan defenders under constant pressure with the same weapons.

The Horde Commanders ordered thousands of their Special Forces Troops to man the one man Seldeks for a rear guard attack. The Special Forces troops in the Seldeks would land well behind the Argan defensive perimeter; assemble in the city as quickly as they could form into groups. they would attack the dug in defenders from the rear. That was the simplest maneuver the Horde could use to break the Argan defensive line.

Grol studied the Horde battle reports with great interest. He approved the battle Commander's plan to go through the minefields to take Poshalla. Grol ordered the fifteen million troops spread out over Arga's main continent to form into five units and converge on Poshalla. Grol felt the Argans had committed the bulk of their ground forces to save Poshalla, their most important city. Grol believed the battle had become so focused by both sides that the entire planet would be won or lost at Poshalla.

The two Argan fleets on Nordic were finally ready. Their pellets of black hole metal were in the firing mechanisms of the thirty-two cruisers. Jeonk ordered the two hundred eighty-eight Argan cruisers, waiting for instructions near the Galactic Forum fleets, to attack the Horde fleet in its stationary orbit over Arga. They would attack at their maximum speed, hit hard and sucker the Horde fleet into following them into deep space. Jeonk hoped the Argan attack would lead the Horde fleet high into the roof of the galaxy on a course that would take it out of the galaxy.

The Argan cruisers increased their speed to maximum and came in at flank speed to attack the Horde fleet. Grol put his fleet underway quickly when he realized his fleet was targeted. He had no choice but to run ahead of the Argan fleets and try to increase the speed of his fleet to match the speed of the Argans. If the Argans struck while his fleet was moving too slowly, it would be a disaster for the Horde fleet.

Grol dispersed his destroyers and cruisers to give them maneuvering room for the battle. He ordered flank speed to better match the spread of the Argan cruisers. Grol's fleet's battle stations were manned and all of its weapons systems were on line before the attack.

Grol felt a strange surge of enthusiasm for the war as the attacking Argan fleets closed on his. The new enthusiasm sat easily on his shoulders. He had been counting on the Argan Fleet Commanders to realize Arga was about to fall. He had felt certain they would enter the only remaining major battle that held some possibility of saving their planet. Grol was content that this final space battle his fleet would fight with the Argan fleets was beginning. He savored their impending destruction. This final battle in space would insure the victory for the Horde.

Grol didn't have enough time to gain his fleet's maximum speed before the Argans came into their firing range. The Argans fired the last of their missiles and every gun they had as their cruisers swept over the top of the Horde fleet.

Both fleets were hit hard in the attack. The Argans lost sixty-two cruisers. The Horde lost eleven Imperial Fortresses and seventy-three Honor Guards. Grol believed the Argans had lost too much in their initial assault, while his much larger fleet could survive the losses. The Argans passed his fleet and began to climb higher.

Grol knew the Argan cruisers could outrun his fleet in open space, but he thought they would gain the distance they needed and then wheel their fleet for another attack. He maneuvered his fleet to meet the attack he expected head on, spread so its maximum fire was dead ahead.

Grol followed in pursuit for many long hours that spread into days. He thought he could pick the time when they would turn for the attack. Grol's timing was wrong, they continued on the same course. He decided they were trying to lead him away from Arga to prevent him from supporting his ground army.

The Argan cruisers kept climbing, always higher, away form the planets below. Grol's Deck Officer announced. "Two Argan cruiser fleets are coming in fast. One is approaching from behind our fleet's left flank; the other is approaching from behind our fleet's right flank." The speed of the two fleets was a shock to Grol and his command deck personnel. Grol knew the two fleets must have been traveling for a long distance to gain that much speed. They two fleets had to know where their targets would be and to have planed the ambush for a high-speed attack.

Grol's nagging questions about the two missing fleets and what they were doing was about to be answered. Grol quickly understood that Arga's two fleets had put his in a trap. He instantly ordered his fleet to reposition to repel the new threat. Grol's crews weren't good at repositioning and firing at the same time. The Horde repositioning was made difficult by the Argan's unexpected attack vectors and fleets' speed. One Argan fleet went over Grol's fleet; the other went under it.

Only two of the Argan cruisers were hit as they swept across the enemy fleet. Both damaged Argan cruisers rammed Horde destroyers in the last moments of their navigational control. The Argan crews knew when they were hit, that they had lost their ability to fire the black hole pellets. They knew they wouldn't be able to escape from their cruisers. They would die as soon as their anti-gravity screens lost power.

The two fleets fired their black hole pellets into the Horde fleet as they went over and under it. The Argan crews would have a short wait to see the results.

The two Argan fleets finished their attack runs, and then programmed their flight patterns to join the Argan cruisers that had set the ambush for the Horde fleet.

Grol was confused. He expected to be hit hard. The two fleets fired on his fleet and did some damage but considerably less than he expected. They flew a crazy X formation across his fleet and then ran for their lives. Grol's scanners showed his Horde fleet to be moving to catch the Argan fleet. He ordered his Communications Officer to get a fleet damage report.

In the Argan fleet, Shok reported, "All weapons have fired successfully. We're in the clear. We only lost two cruisers. I thought we would lose most of us."

Jeonk looked toward Shok and said, "Order our two fleets to swing wide, away from the Horde fleets trajectory and the trajectory of the pellets. Even one of those pellets is a death warrant. I'll order the fleets that led the Horde here to fly far enough away from the Horde course to avoid any possible contact with the pellets. The Horde ships that escaped being hit by one of the pellets may have some of the pellets following them."

Grol's scanners showed the Argan cruisers arcing away from his fleet and leaving the battle area. Grol's Communications Officer reported, "I've just identified King Jeonk and Admiral Shok's voices on the same cruiser. I'll keep them on scan until we destroy them and their cruiser."

Grol felt a surge of triumph at the report. He would finally be able to battle the two most dangerous Argans. Grol felt the final victory in his grasp if he could kill these two leaders. With a blast of relief from his lungs, he ordered his fleet to pursue and engage the enemy.

Grol's flagship was in the front and center of the fleet. He brought his destroyer to the new heading to track the Argan cruisers. He couldn't outrun them, but he could follow until he caught them, and deliver the final deathblow. Only three of his destroyers and twenty-eight cruisers followed him. The remainder of his fleet kept its original course, still moving through the darkness of space toward the position the Argans had just left.

Grol's feelings about the battle changed from being mystified about an attack that seemingly caused little damage, to the cold, hard, quiet of an old warrior's terror. He once again ordered damage reports form his silent Commanders. He received no replies. In total frustration, he ordered his operational spacecraft to return and circle his silent fleet. Grol could see nothing out of the ordinary in the outward appearance of his fleet on its journey to nowhere.

Grol ordered one of his flagship's fighters to fly through the silent fleet for a closer visual inspection of the dead fleet. He kept the fighter on scan as it weaved its way through the fleet. The fighter's crew radioed that they could see no visible damage. After that one report, the fighter's radio emitted a final growl and died. Grol tried repeatedly but could no longer raise the fighter crew on his radio. He watched his scanner as the fighter stopped weaving between the ships in the fleet and slammed into one of the Honor Guards, killing the fighter, but leaving the Honor Guard cruiser--no less dead.

Grol, once again, ordered damage reports from his fleet. There were many ways to use the fleet's radio equipment to respond to the order, and he expected a response.

A thick, dark silence hung over Grol's command deck, formed by the deadly quiet from the silent fleet. The only Commanders who made their damage reports were in the ships that had changed course with his. To increase the mystery and terror Grol felt; twelve of the twenty-eight Honor Guards circling the dead fleet with him had gone silent.

Grol briefly considered returning the remnants of his fleet to the main fleet for a closer inspection. He reconsidered that option when he thought of the fate his fighter had met while passing through the silent fleet, and that he could no longer contact twelve more of his Honor guards. Grol was unable to alter the course of his, apparently dead, main fleet on its galaxy-exiting course.

Grol bitterly accepted the defeat of his fleet as an Argan victory, and set his course for the Emperor's safe haven. The final twelve cruisers he lost contact with didn't change course with him; they were on a silent course that would return them to their own galaxy. Grol, without knowing why, knew they were dead or dying.

MARVIN E. FOX

The black hole pellets that hadn't attached themselves to a Horde spacecraft would be moving through space with the Horde's dead fleet. Most of the loose pellets would eventually attach themselves to ships in the fleet they had just killed, but some could have changed course to be pulled along behind the Horde ships that escaped the initial bombardment. Eventually, all of the loose pellets would be pulled to the nearest material that was subject to gravity.

The Argans knew their cruisers weren't immune to the danger. They would also attract the deadly pellets if they came anywhere near them. The Argans were being very careful to keep their spacecraft far from the infected space the survivors of the Horde fleet were traveling in.

The battle between the Argan and Horde fleets took both fleets days from the planet Okron. It would take the same amount of time for them to return. Grol and the remainder of his fleet were returning to the Emperor, who was unaware of the defeat. The Argan fleets were returning to support the Argan Army in the life or death battle for survival.

The battle for Poshalla's ground batteries was finally going well for the Horde. The Horde Bastus' were taking a heavy toll of the Argan soldiers. Horde Kurstufs were surviving against the constant barrages from the Argan defenders. Horde troop spearheads made the first beginnings of a break through past Poshalla's defensive perimeters.

The Horde Army attacking Poshalla was losing tens of thousands from Argan troops' flank attacks. The Horde losses were from Sokeasel's Argans fighting their way through the forests and advancing on the rear of the Horde army assaulting Poshalla. The Argan march across the plain destroyed the Horde's rear units. The first Horde army was now sandwiched between Poshalla's defenders and Sokeasel's Argan reinforcements. Being surrounded by Argans was a major horde worry but the Horde expected to stop those losses when the reinforcing Horde troops came into the battle from the same forests the Argan Army had marched across to make its attack.

The Argan Army marching to help Poshalla knew Horde reinforcements were coming up behind them in the forests. The pressure to save the Poshalla's space batteries kept them on the move to help defend against the most active assault on Poshalla. The Argans were forced to fight a forward and rear action at the same time, no matter what the cost.

The Horde reinforcements, Grol had ordered to join the battle, were just beginning to come out of the forests behind the Argan reinforcements. The Argan reinforcements had just exited the forest and were beginning to cross the plain to help defend Poshalla.

The layout of the Poshalla battle looked like a target. Poshalla was the bull's eye. A thinning line of Argan Army defenders ringed the outskirts of Poshalla. A thicker ring of Horde attackers surrounded the Argan defenders. The third ring was the Argan reinforcements fighting its way cross the plain. A final rag-tag ring was made up of the Horde Army just emerging from the forest, and spreading out behind the Argan reinforcements.

General Sokeasel's Argan troops were handicapped by a lack of heavy armored vehicles and Arga had nothing to match the Horde's Bastus. The flying weapons platform was difficult to bring down and it had a devastating array of weapons.

The Horde fighter spacecraft were able to give the Horde Army a sharp fighting edge until the Horde fleet left to attack the Argan fleets. When the horde fleet fighters were ordered to return to the fleet, the Argans were free from attack from the Horde fleet fighters supporting the Horde ground attack fighters. The Argan ground support fighter craft, now being less outnumbered, began a concentrated attack on the Horde air cover.

The dogfights with the Horde fighters brought the destruction of many of them, and reduced the massive Horde air cover. Fewer of the Horde airborne fighters gave Sokeasel's foot soldiers a chance to spread their advance behind the attacking line of the Horde army that was sandwiched between Sokeasel's first arriving reinforcements and the Poshalla defenders.

Earlier Horde advances had broken the Argan defense of Poshalla in two places, one on each side of the city. Poshalla's armed citizens joined in the defense of their homes and were successfully keeping the Horde from making a rear attack on the Argan defenders. The Horde soldiers in the breakthroughs were forced to fight a house-to-house battle in the areas they had penetrated. The Argan citizens had an array of assault weapons and used them like professionals.

The frustrated Horde invaders destroyed many Argan homes with explosives in an attempt to set up an offensive perimeter for themselves. Before the Horde army could blow up one area of homes, The Argan citizens retreated and attacked the Horde from the homes facing the destroyed ones. The Horde lost too many of the troops that had penetrated into Poshalla. There weren't enough Horde troops to make a flank attack on the defending Argan army. The Horde killed a large number of Argan citizens, but there were always more to take the places of the fallen ones.

The one-man seldeks, the Horde launched into Poshalla in the early part of the battle, to form a rear attack on the defensive line, ran into the same problem. The Horde Special Forces Units flying the Seldeks were unprepared to face citizen warriors. They expected to find people so frightened they would run away in fear when they came face to face with a Horde professional soldier. Instead, the Horde Special Forces were fired on, from whatever cover was available, by people who knew how to use the cover and their weapons. The Horde Special Forces Units had spread themselves too thin over too wide an area to group up and make a counterattack on the armed citizens. The angry citizens shot down most of the seldek pilots one at a time as soon as they landed. The remainder was killed trying to find a safe way back to the Horde battle lines.

The Horde Commanders were beginning to worry. They had broken through the Argan military lines. They discovered their breakthroughs were in danger of failure from armed citizens, well armed, and in military lines of defense. Their air cover was melting before the Argan fighter's air attacks. Argan fighters had attacked the Horde Command Stycols with such vehemence the commanders were forced to leave them and remain on the ground.

They were beginning to realize they would have to take Poshalla one house at a time unless they could get fleet support to destroy Poshalla from space. They requested fleet support, but the fleet was silent; it made no reply to their many requests for help.

General Sokeasel knew the value of Poshalla in the war. He knew the Horde had bet everything on taking it. He knew that whatever remained of the fifteen million Horde troops would be coming at him from the forests in a very short time.

Sokeasel had troop units positioned in the mountains to fight the approaching Horde millions. He ordered them to concentrate on taking out the Horde Kurstufs and Bastus while they were still in the mountains, and at their most vulnerable. They were also ordered to smash as much of the Horde advance as they could with hit and run tactics. Sokeasel felt that, if his units along the Horde advance could destroy most of the Horde Kurstufs and Bastus, the Argans might still have a chance.

Sokeasel's reinforcements were fragmented. They were widely dispersed, and coming from the many places the Horde might have attacked. With the Horde concentrating on Poshalla, Sokeasel relieved his widely spread troops of their defensive duties in the other cities. The fresh Argan troops finally began to advance behind the Horde reinforcements attacking Poshalla. The Horde was about to get the feel for being the center of someone else's sandwich.

The Horde began the battle with a large fleet of support fighters but the Argans fighters were making a big dent in their ability to provide air cover for the Horde troops on the ground. The Argan fighters knocked out most of the Horde Kurstufs and Bastus near Poshalla. The Horde foot soldiers were reduced to fighting primarily with their standard weapons, one man lasers and small pulse cannons carried by three men teams.

The battle between the two armies raged furiously for three days. The air around Poshalla was constantly filled with the brilliance of laser and pulse cannon fire. The Horde were unable to take advantage of their breakthroughs because the citizens of Poshalla fought them from every window, roof top, basement and tree along the broad streets of their homes. Many Argans died in the streets but there were always more to take their place. It seemed all of Poshalla's fourteen million were eager to defend their nation.

The battle began to favor the Argans on the fourth day. The Argans needed little sleep. They could remain awake for several days with no ill affects. The Horde weren't so fortunate. They were a very tired army and the intense pressures of battle kept them constantly awake. Exhaustion itself was making them careless and unable to respond quickly to the Argan battle tactics.

The Horde Army had already lost half of its sixteen million attackers in the battle, but the battle was far from over. The Horde dead lay where they fell. The exhausted Horde surrounding Poshalla were one day from defeat. Sokeasel's sandwich had the Poshalla defenders in the face of the horde, and the Argan army attacking the rear of the Horde from the forests. Squeezing the horde from the front and rear at the same time was breaking the backs of the Horde troop concentration that had originally surrounded Poshalla. The Horde in other areas of the same battle was not close to defeat.

Horde Commanders at Poshalla began frantically calling for the fifteen million Horde reinforcements to attack the rear of the Argan Army surrounding them. The fifteen million had been reduced to less than thirteen million during the hit and run tactics of the weaker Argan force, but the Horde Army wasn't stopped. The Horde continued its march to complete the destruction of Poshalla. Their Kurstufs and Bastus had been little help to them in the forests. They Horde lost most of the troops to Argan attackers. Still, millions of Horde reinforcement had finally advanced to the battle.

The fresh Horde reinforcements hit the Poshalla plain at the run. Sokeasel's rear units began to crumble before the power of the Horde attack. The Horde poured from the forest by the hundreds of thousands. Horde Commanders felt the Argans were finally doomed by the overwhelming power of their Army.

The raging battle at the rear made little difference to the Horde troops fighting the Argans near Poshalla. Those Horde soldiers were too far away, and making too much noise themselves, to hear the change of the battle raging in their rear.

Ten million Argan troops had finally come together after traveling across the nation. The Argans were just beginning to leave the forest to begin the attack on the rear units of the huge Horde Army moving across the plain and attacking Sokeasel's army on the Poshalla plain.

The Horde troops between Sokeasel's dug in troops around Poshalla, and sokeasel's reinforcements surrounding them, realized the advancing Horde Army had Sokeasel's reinforcements trapped between them and the advancing Horde reinforcements coming from the forests. The thought of millions of fresh troops entering the battle at the rear of the Argan reinforcements gave the Horde new courage.

The Horde Commander at Poshalla ordered his troops to split into two fronts. One front would hold its position facing Poshalla. The troops in the center would do an about face and reinforce those who were fighting a holding battle against Sokeasel's troops on their rear. The Horde Commander hoped the Argans wouldn't be able to hold out with an attack force pounding the Argan front lines and a massive attack from the Horde forest reinforcements on the Argan rear.

The Argans on the Poshalla plain were now in the Horde sandwich. They had to fight the Horde on their front and on their rear. Battle losses had depleted the Argan air cover that had been protecting the Argan ground war. The Argan pilots were giving them as much cover as they could but the Horde fighters still outnumbered the Argans. It appeared Sokeasel's reinforcements would be massacred between the two Horde armies.

Grol was silent on his return to the Emperor. His thoughts turned again and again to the conditions that caused the war and his rise to power as the Chief Commander of the Empire. Grol thought the old Emperor, Dak Lu Skaj, had appointed him Chief Commander for Life to reward him for the many battles he had won to establish the Empire, and to insure that an old friend had a secure place in the Empire. Grol knew that Dak Lu Skaj had little confidence in his son, Sinleek, who had never risen to military importance in those battles. Grol thought he might have to agree with his wife and replace Sinleek. This meeting with Sinleek, and the Horde defeat, would tell him.

Grol's wife Aklee, who had known Sinleek from childhood, had told Grol many times to depose Sinleek and take over the Empire himself. Aklee had said, "Yit, you have to get rid of Sinleek. He was a self-consumed egotist even as a child. Sinleek has no feeling for the people of this Empire. He uses it and the people as his personal possession. The Empire is nothing more to him than a cheering section, and a way to force more people to cheer him. He has nothing to give. He will kill the Empire and all of our chances to escape these two galaxy grinders."

Grol always had the same answer, "I know he is weak, and I know he is a poor Emperor, but I can not kill the son of a man I admired so much for his courage, intelligence, strength, and most of all, his love for the people of this Empire."

Grol's thoughts moved to the bitter day Emperor Sinleek had changed the war plan from a plan of conquest to a war of annihilation of the people in the brother galaxy. He would have killed the Emperor on that day, but by that time Sinleek had installed his own sycophants in government. It was too late. Grol knew Sinleek would have replaced him too if his father, Dak Lu Skaj, hadn't made Grol the Chief Commander for Life, and announced that to empire before he died.

In the battle for Arga, more was happening to affect the war than the Argan Army or the Horde Army knew. Grol had arrived with the remnant of his fleet at the Emperor's safe haven. He had chosen not to inform the Emperor of the defeat until he was in the Emperor's presence. Grol knew the Emperor was a quick tempered, foolish man who might kill him when Grol told him the bad news. Grol decided to take his bodyguards with him when they met. Grol's bodyguards were on the Imperial payroll, but they had been carefully chosen for their fighting ability and loyalty to Grol.

Grol docked his ship to the Emperor's. His bodyguards accompanied him from the docking station to the meeting inside the Emperor's Imperial compartment. The Emperor had his bodyguards, more than Grol had, waiting when they met. The Emperor asked, "Why are old friends meeting surrounded by our personal bodyguards? Is there a problem we must resolve with weapons?"

Grol replied, "Certainly not your Majesty, but I do have bad news. I feared some of your crew might respond to it with violence."

The Emperor was still confused by Grol's actions. He asked, "You have brought only a small portion of the fleet with you. What have you done with my Imperial Fleet?"

Grol answered, "The Imperial fleet was beaten in battle by the Argans. I don't know what weapon they used. I have never experienced anything like it. Most of the fleet is dead and locked in a trajectory that will take it out of the galaxy. Twelve of our Honor Guard class ships are on a heading my navigator said would return them to our own galaxy. The twelve ships went dark after I completed my inspection of the main fleet. Their crews are dead. The small fragments of the fleet I brought with me are the only survivors."

The Emperor stood stunned with disbelief during Grol's confession of the loss of the Imperial fleet. He blurted, "We must have the fleet! The ground war is in jeopardy! Our Commanders have been asking for fleet support for days."

Grol responded, "Tell the ground Commanders to surrender. We no longer have the means to conquer the Argans or any other planet in this galaxy. They have won!"

The Emperor reached for the personal radio he used to talk with the ground Commanders and said, "This is Emperor Sinleek speaking, keep fighting! We are coming to give you victory. You must fight on, do not surrender. Victory is within our grasp!"

He then turned to Chief Commander Grol and said, "You are relieved of duty. You have forgotten your place and your mission. We have a fleet of twenty Imperial Fortresses and six hundred Honor Guard spacecraft at home. The Argans have, at the most, two hundred of their cruisers left to fight with. Our superior numbers will be more than enough to win this war. I am appointing Commander Skursk to replace you."

Grol aimed his sardonic laugh at the Emperor and said, "Do you remember why the Gamacs and the Prsskians refused to join us in this war against Arga? They said, 'If the Argan's tactics, or guts don't kill you, their blind luck will.' They have not fought us with luck and they are not blind. Their tactics and guts are superb. I suggest you tell our army to surrender or they will die.

Commander Skursk is a military idiot and he suits you well. I am taking what's left of my-fleet home. If you wish to stop me, start shooting." Grol left the Emperor without the necessity of shooting his way off the ship.

If the Emperor had been listening as Grol and his small fleet made its final turn for home, he would have heard a few very loud pings on the top of his Imperial Destroyer. Seconds later, his ship's systems began shutting down. The Emperor was getting his first and last experience with some of Arga's blind luck. A few of the black hole pellets had been pulled along behind Grol's flagship and had just ended the journey on the top of the Emperor's personal Imperial Fortress. The Emperor had no time to call for the home fleet before his ship became a silent death trap.

General Sokeasel stood with his beleaguered troops, calculating how long they could last while being attacked from the front and rear. The first arriving Argan reinforcements weren't enough to fight their way through the Horde troops, enter Poshalla, and join its defenders. The fresh Horde troops pressuring them from the rear were too many. Sokeasel couldn't hope for his men to fight the horde off for much longer. His army couldn't hold out long enough for his Argan Army attacking the Horde in the forest to change the battle in his favor.

Sokeasel was weary from the days of fighting. He watched helplessly as the last of the Argan fighters fruitlessly tried to clear the air of the Horde support fighters. Then, a breath of relief blasted from his lungs. Hundreds of fresh Argan fighters came from space, blasting the Horde fighters with the devastating fury of their pulse cannons and lasers. The Horde fighters fought back with an intense fury of their own before the desperation of their impending destruction forced them to gain altitude to find a safer place to fight.

As they made it to higher altitude, the Argan cruisers opened up on them. Lasers and pulse cannons pierced their hulls. The Horde pilots knew a Horde fighter was no match for Argan cruisers. They dived low to avoid the cruisers only to be attacked by the

Argan fighters climbing to meet them. The Horde fighters again climbed to get away from the Argan fighters and were, once more, pounded by the cruisers. It took very little time for the Argans to take the air over the battlefield from the Horde.

Two hundred and fifty Argan cruisers descended to near ground level around the perimeter of Sokeasel's nearly defeated Argan Army. They positioned themselves to surround the beleaguered Argan army. The Horde soldiers tried to destroy the cruisers with their ground assault weapons but they were too puny to harm the cruisers. The cruisers' gunners swept the plain with deadly fire, destroying the Horde Army by the hundreds of thousands. The Horde army advance became an insane rout, each man fleeing to return to the forest he came from.

Argan fighters began strafing runs against the Horde army sandwiched between Sokeasel's troops and the dug in Argan Army surrounding Poshalla. When the Horde tried to advance toward Poshalla to escape the airborne lasers, the dug in Argans cut them down. When they tried to retreat toward Sokeasel's encirclement, Sokeasel's men cut them down. The Horde was faced with destruction in front of them, destruction behind them, and destruction above them. More kinds of death than they had ever seen poured into their positions. Whether they would have surrendered, or not, is unknown. In the final analysis, they had no time to surrender.

The millions of survivors in the Horde Army were now retreating in two directions. The Horde from the battle on the plain retreated into the forest they had come from. The Horde in the forest, attempting to reinforce the Horde troops on the plain, retreated through the forest toward the plain. They were being attacked by the ten million man Argan Army behind them in the forest. The two retreating Horde armies connected each to the other in the forest. Argan troops attacked them from both sides. The Horde air support was gone, they had no camouflage, and weren't particular good against the Argans, who were very good at fighting in their own forests.

The fact that there were still millions of the Horde Army foot soldiers in the forest gave their commanders a false sense of security. To add to their misconception, they believed the dead Emperor had a plan to rescue them and win the battle if they held out a little longer.

The Argans, no longer in any particular hurry, and having no desire to slaughter a surrounded, controlled, and in the Argan minds, a defeated enemy, drew back and waited for their surrender. The optimistic Horde Commanders mistook the Argan withdrawal for a retreat from a regrouped superior enemy. The Horde commanders ordered an attack.

The Horde attack really pissed off the Argans. They hit the Horde with every weapon they had brought to the Horde infested forest. The cruiser based Argan fighters were ordered to get out of the way so the Argan cruisers could strafe the forest. Millions of balls of super heated pulse cannon rounds, and thick shafts of laser fire penetrated the dense forest. The Argan ground troops, surrounding the Horde, heated the battle with their fire, leveling the Horde and woodlands in front of them with machine-gun and magnetic Gatling guns.

The forest turned into an inferno of burning trees and underbrush. Crown fires swept above the Horde and heated the ground below to horrendous temperatures burning everything in their paths. The Argan Army made a quick retreat from the burning forests. The Horde Army became sole owners of the wrath of the forest fire.

The weapons fire coming into the forest from the Argan assault, and the fire raging among them from the burning forest completed the destruction of the Horde invasion of Arga. Only a few of the Horde survived both infernos. Those who did found it was time to surrender, no matter who said they were about to become victorious.

15
THE AFTERMATH OF WAR

The Argans found an amazingly small amount of damage done to their nation in the war they feared might cost them everything. Most of the damage was on one continent and the most devastating loss was to their people and the capital city. They lost twenty-two million people, counting both military and civilian deaths. They would mourn their dead for many years. They felt very fortunate that Poshalla was the only one of their major cities to be badly damaged.

Large areas of Poshalla would have to be rebuilt, two thirds was burned in the war. Fires caused by missiles, lasers, and pulse cannons had taken their destructive toll on the city. Most of the citizens would need to be moved to other cities while the rebuilding was going on but that problem was considered to be minor.

The Argan space fleets were severely damaged. More than two thirds of their cruisers were destroyed in battles with the Horde. A crash program to restore the fleets was quickly begun. The Argan Army was badly depleted but General Sokeasel was already busy rebuilding it. There were many new recruits, and they were volunteering from every part of the nation.

The Galactic Forum nations had been spared most of the losses of war because the Argans had taken the pressures of war on themselves. They sent the Argans many teams of people to help with the restoration of Poshalla. The Galactic Forum fleets under the command of Admiral Chosteel of Paraca were patrolling Argan space until the Argan fleets were rebuilt.

The nearly eight hundred Forum nations sent tons of Gold and Silver to restore the Argan treasury. King Jeonk told them it wasn't necessary because Arga wasn't a poor nation and could afford the restoration. He was told, in return, that the money was not a loan and was not returnable. The Forum nations insisted it was the least any could do. They would accept no rejection of their efforts to do something to show their gratitude for the sacrifices made by the Argan people.

Chief Commander Grol wasn't going home to the applause of the crowd. He was in a foul mood. His first concern was to determine if his removal was known in the capital. Grol walked with an air of confidence into his office. Everyone in his outer office respectfully rose to his feet. That didn't tell him much; that would have been done, even if they had know the Emperor fired him.

Grol's Staff Commander approached and said, "Chief Commander, we have heard nothing about the war for days. We have no word from the Emperor and no word from you. Will you be holding a briefing session for the Command staff?"

Grol smiled for the first time after his meeting with the Emperor. He gave the Commander a long list of trusted civilian and military associates who were once high in the command structure of the Empire. He ordered, "I want all of these people in my briefing room as soon as they can get here. If any of them are off planet or can't be here in twelve hours, I'll start the briefing without them, and speak privately with them soon after they arrive."

The large briefing room was nearly full of Grol's trusted associates. He began, "We lost the war. The Argans kicked our butts hard. They introduced a new weapon none of us here have ever been exposed to. The weapon killed nearly the entire fleet within a few minutes. The fleet was traveling at flank speed when the Argans struck. It took thirty-two of their cruisers to kill the entire fleet. As soon as I could, after I lost the fleet, I suggested to the Emperor that he order our ground troops to surrender to the Argans. He refused my suggestion. The Emperor considered himself to be in charge of the war. He could not believe he could lose a war with he, himself, the Emperor, in charge.

"My guess is, since the Argans could bring what remained of their fleets to support their ground troops, our ground troops are dead or captured. Most of them will be dead. The Emperor ordered them to fight on in the vain hope he gave them for a rescue he was about to mount. The Emperor wouldn't believe the Argans had won even though he knew they destroyed the Imperial fleet. He fired me and replaced me with that stupid bastard, Skursk, at the final hour.

"No one has heard from the Emperor or Skursk since that moment. They were alive when I left them but I believe they are both dead by now. Skursk was stupid enough to attack the Argans, and the Argans are smart enough to attack him first. Because of their silence, I think the Emperor and Skursk are dead. If they are not, we still need to get rid of Skursk and the idiot we have for an Emperor. We will also have to remove the ass kissers the Emperor promoted to screw up the Empire. I think we may still be able to save the Empire, but not by war. I'm going to try to save it. Are you with me or against me?"

The old custom of drawing swords was observed. If they plunged their swords into Grol instead of the conference table, they were against him. They plunged their sword points into the conference tables instead of Grol. Grol's old comrades were with him.

Grol shook his old warrior's head in relief and in recognition of their confidence in him. Grol continued, "The first order of business is to promote all of you to the positions you lost to the Emperor's pet military nitwits. You are now in command of your military units. We now have military control of the Empire.

"If any of you think you will have trouble with the Emperor's men you have just been promoted above, you may tell them they are responsible for the loss of the war and have been demoted by Imperial order. Those you are replacing are the ones who convinced the Emperor he was right in waiting for the Argans to attack the Empire.

"If being fired doesn't convince them of the finality of their replacements, a few well-aimed lasers will settle those problems. I am assuming the duties and the authority of the Emperor until he returns. If he returns, a well aimed laser will settle that problem."

The meeting was interrupted by Grol's Staff Commander who announced, "There are forty-two Honor Guard ships from the Emperor's personal guard preparing to land at the Imperial base outside of the city. The Emperor's Imperial spacecraft is not with them. They have refused to give us any information about the Emperor until they report to the Chief Commander. What do you want done with them?"

Grol replied, "Order the Honor Guard's Commanders to report to this meeting room. Have them escorted by armed guards. Make sure they speak with no one until after they leave my office."

The Staff Commander left to carry out Grol's instructions, while Grol returned his attention to the newly appointed military Commanders, "I think I know what the Commanders have to say about the Emperor and the eight missing Honor Guard ships that should have landed with them, but I want you, and me, to hear it from them. I would like their confirmation of my belief by hearing it with everyone here."

Room was made in the front of the meeting for the Commanders of the Emperor's personal Honor Guard ships. They entered and Grol asked them to report. The ranking Commander among them stated, "I am sorry I must be the one to report bad news. We think the Emperor is dead. His ship went dark shortly after the Chief Commander's ship left his royal presence. I don't know what happened to the Emperor or his ship. His Imperial Fortress returned no response from our transmissions and we received no requests for help from his command crew. His Imperial Fortresses' systems appeared to suddenly power down, even their life support systems.

"Two of our Honor Guard's docked to determine the cause. They, also, went dark. We landed several fighters on the Emperor's ship but we heard nothing from them after they entered the fighter bays. Six of our Honor Guard spacecraft, which were near the Emperor's ship, went dark after that.

"We had no ides what was happening to our fleet. We spent hours scanning for damage. There seemed to be a very minor amount amount of structural distortion to the ships exterior. We could not make a determination for the distortion being a cause or just natural. We circled the Emperors ships many times over the hours and tried to communicate with it from many different angles and distances to see if that might be of some help. Nothing helped! We finally left the area to keep the ships that were still functioning from suffering the same fate. Do you have any information to give us Chief Commander? We are at a total loss for an explanation."

Grol's reply was blunt, "You were attacked by the Argans. They have a secret weapon that silently kills spacecraft and crews. No outer damage to the spacecraft is apparent. Any spacecraft that docks with, or lands on those dead ships suffer the same death. We don't know what the nature of the weapon is, and without further information it's too dangerous to fight against. Why they didn't use it earlier in the war is unknown. The weapon may be so dangerous, even to the crews who use it, that they can only use it under special circumstances.

"Did the Emperor give any last orders or issue any statements before his ship went dark?"

The Honor Guard Commander replied, "The Emperor said nothing after you left."

Grol asked, "Did you check the progress of the ground war before you left?"

The commander answered, "No, our radios weren't functioning well enough to monitor transmissions from Arga. We assumed the Argans were losing. We thought it best to return here and report the Emperor's loss to the Empire."

Grol responded, "You were correct to bring your ships back to Pik. You were incorrect about who won the ground war. The Argans won the ground war. There was nothing you could have done to stop them. There will be a full inquiry concerning your actions and his Imperial Majesty's death, but you are not being blamed. The inquiry is only a formality. You are dismissed.

The Honor Guard Commanders left the room and Grol returned to his coup partners, saying, "The death of the Emperor makes it easier for us. I am now required by law to assume the duties of the Emperor while the Empire is at war. We will not declare this war; we have lost, at an end until further notice. There is a possibility the Argans might attack us in the future, but I think it is a slim possibility. They will probably be rebuilding their fleets and their army to repel our next attack. We will stay in our galaxy. If they stay in theirs, as I think they will, there will be no continuation of this war.

"We have major problems at home. The first is how to escape from this galaxy to another that isn't in the process of destroying itself. I think, without knowing it, the Argans solved the problem of inter-galactic travel. Their spacecraft are faster than ours. They solved the problem that has puzzled us for years. They know how to increase the speed of our spacecraft to inter-galactic speed. We must discover what the Argans already know. We will have our best scientists working on this problem. The Emperor's favorite scientific ass kissers have been consistent failures."

An old friend of Grol's interrupted him, "I have a friend, a space propulsion engineer, who tells me the reason we are not inter-galactic is because we don't use the total spectrum of light in our propulsion systems. Perhaps we should give him a chance to prove he's right."

Grol replied, "Tell your friend to pick his team and start moving on the project. He will have the money and support he needs from now on. I also want to make sure any other likely theories are fully developed."

An interplanetary manager brought up a different problem, "There is resistance to the Imperial rule on most of our planets. The Emperor allowed very little self-determination for planetary decisions. We need to allow local problems to be solved locally without Imperial interference. With the Imperial fleet destroyed, we can't continue as the Emperor did, we'll have revolutions. We can't move troops around like we once did. I understand most of our troop transports were destroyed in the war. How are you going to handle the problem?"

Grol answered, "The Empire was originally formed to help all of us escape from the collision between this galaxy and the neighboring galaxy. We're back to that point. The Empire is no longer an ego journey for a good Emperor's no-good son. If any of the original nations wish to separate from the Empire, we should allow them to depart with our blessing, but they need the Empire's help to escape the coming destruction. If they want that help, they must remain with the Empire and help us solve the problems.

"I, as Emperor, am not going to involve myself in local matters. I will be working full time on the Empire's major problems. When we find a new home and the Empire has served its purpose, the Empire will cease to exist and we will have some new way to maintain our security and friendships. Perhaps we should do as the Argans did and establish a Galactic Forum. Their Galactic Forum is designed to help the nations of neighboring planets to support and protect each other. Having just fought a war with them, I know that works for them and it could work for us.

"We will not rebuild the Imperial fleet to force our planets to stay in the Empire. We need to build an escape fleet for passengers, not a war fleet. Any of the Imperial nations that want to walk away from the Empire can do so freely. For those who stay; we are leaving, and we are taking all of our people with us."

An old friend from Space Command asked, "What will we do if we can't solve our inter-galactic speed problem?"

Grol's answer showed some of his frustration, "The Argans, in their war with us, used the technology our idiot of an Emperor gave to the planets Tuplej and Kashtool. Our technology was given to the two planets so they could conquer their galaxy for 'us'. The Argans beat hell out of both of them and then improved--our--technology. They fitted every ship in their fleets with it in less than ten years. I don't believe our scientists can't take our technology--and improve it like they did!

"Sooner or later, the Argans will contact us, or we will have to contact them for the return of our prisoners of war. I think I learned something about the Argans while they were kicking our butts. They are a decent people we should never have gone to war with. They will not kill our prisoners of war. They will want to be rid of them as humanely and as quickly as possible.

"When contact with the Argans is made, I intend to be one of those who bring back our prisoners. I will meet with the Argans and try my best to convince them we are now their friends. If we can't solve our propulsion problem, they may be decent enough to share their advances in propulsion technology with us. It won't be easy but I may be able to convince them we will use it properly to save our people."

Grol seemed to be leading the Horde back in the direction of a national recovery of their main goals.

The Argans and the Galactic Forum nations, who might eventually have the same problem, were not addressing it yet, but they had more time to consider the solution. The Argans considered their most immediate problem to be making certain the black hole metal pellets they used against the Horde fleet were going out of the galaxy. They decided to scan the routes the black hole pellets should have been taking to make sure they were still on course. They made scan searches for pellets that might have bypassed the Emperor's small fleet. The Emperor had dutifully collected all extra pellets.

Admiral Chosteel took it upon himself and his Galactic Forum fleet to patrol the area around the Emperor's destroyer. He was the first to notify King Jeonk that the Emperor's dead ship, the two cruisers docked to it and the six cruisers floating dead nearby, were drifting toward the planet Okron. They began following the planet when Okron's orbit brought it closest to the dead spacecraft. The gravity pull of the black hole pellets had begun to interact with the gravity of the planet Okron. The pellets were bringing the entire mess of spacecraft toward the planet's surface with them.

Jeonk, Shok and a dozen of their best space engineers were the first Argans to inspect the dead Horde destroyer and cruisers from a safe distance. The cruisers that hadn't docked with the destroyer were drifting closer to the destroyer with each passing day. It was obvious that the destroyer and the eight cruisers would not only hit Okron, but land somewhere on Arga as one large mass of metal.

The crash of the spacecraft on the planet's surface would be far worse than a large asteroid hit. Each of the black hole pellets, no bigger than a grain of sand, was heavier than a large asteroid and no one knew how many of the pellets were attached to the dead spacecraft.

The space engineers calculated the speed of the planet Okron and the closing speed of the dead spacecraft. Their calculations, if correct, gave the planet, and Arga, three months of peace and quiet before the crash with the dead spacecraft. No one wanted to test the accuracy of their time frame by letting them crash. The decision was to get rid of the mess as soon as possible.

The first try would be the quickest and easiest. The plan was to position a fleet of cruisers near the dead spacecraft. The Cruiser Commanders would put the cruiser's tractor beams on full power and pull the entire group of dead spacecraft to a course that would trap it in the sun's gravity, and crash it into sun. The heat of the sun would melt the spacecraft and cause the pellets to expand to their pre-black-hole size. The fleet and the pellets would become nothing more than additional fuel for the sun.

The Argans stacked their fleet of cruisers on the sun side of the dead spacecraft, each separated by only a few yards. Another few yards separated the nearest Argan cruisers and the dead Horde fleet. All of the cruisers' tractor beams were trained on the dead spacecraft. The cruisers began accelerating, slowly, to pull the massive dead weight toward the sun.

The collection of tractor beams moved the mass but not toward the sun. The Weight of the dead fleet, plus the immense gravity power of the black hole pellets, and the black hole pellet's gravity pulling toward Okron, was too much for the Argan fleet's tractor beams. The best the Argan effort could do was shift the dead fleet so it would impact at a different place on Okron. They couldn't tractor beam the dead fleet out of Okron's gravitational pull.

The six Horde cruisers were forced into contact with the destroyer during the first attempt at pulling them.. The space mess was now, effectively, one piece. That changed nothing of problem the dead space ships were causing.

They made one more try with additional cruisers. They stacked the Argan cruisers as close as they dared to pull the dead fleet backward and slow its approach to the planet Okron. They did, indeed, manage to slow its approach. According to the new calculations, they added almost three days to the estimated time of the crash. Their dead fleet pulling effort took three days, so they didn't win any prize for that effort.

The Argans learned three things from their effort. They could move the wrecked fleet around their planet and they could change its speed. The third was that they could pick the place for it to land because of the other two things.

They weren't satisfied with the results of their efforts. A bunch of black hole pellets hitting their planet any place at any speed wasn't what they had in mind. They wanted the mess on a peaceful journey to its new home in the sun.

Jeonk looked to his old friend Shok sitting at the command pedestal of the cruiser and said, "You have any ideas Shok? This black hole pellet idea was yours and up to now I thought it was a pretty good idea. It got rid of the Horde and won the war for us, but it has gained a certain backfire quality we could do without."

Shok was never short of a solution. He replied, "If it was just two or three average sized ships separated by a respectable distance we could put gravity screens around them, remove the pellets and recover the spacecraft. The real problem is: this fleet is too big, it's locked together and we don't know how many pellets are in it. If we could slow it down enough, and find a nice empty piece of land for it to crash on, we could still take care of the problem on the ground but that solution has a few uncertainties about it.

"I think our best shot is to get Jarl Gast working on it. If anyone has the ability and equipment to put that mess into the sun, its Jarl."

Jarl Gast was an old Argan space engineer who, many years ago, had gone into the space salvage business. He knew more ways to move dead weight in space than any man living on any planet. Jeonk and Shok worked with him on several occasions and both had a great respect for his abilities. Jeonk responded, "I guess your right but Jarl's talents are only exceeded by his bad manners. We'll have to listen to his guff about having to hire him to get the job done because we military experts couldn't do it."

Jarl looked up from the large table spread with his own pictures of the Horde's dead fleet. Jarl remarked, "I knew the two of you couldn't get it done. I sent one of my crews to take these pictures, and I've been planning the operation since Chosteel told you about it. You want it pushed into the sun, right?"

Shok answered, "That's the general idea Jarl. Do you think you can get it done?"

Jarl remarked, "Do campers crap in the woods? Of course I can get it done. I was just waiting for you military heroes to screw it up and get the hell out of the way so I can begin the job."

Jeonk wasn't quite satisfied with Jarl's bragging. He asked, "How do you intend to do it? Are you going to blow it into the sun with some of your hot air?"

Jarl laughed and replied, "That's plan one. If that fails, I can give it one more try before I come up with something else."

Shok asked, "Do you mind expanding on your method of operation for us dumb military heroes? We'd like to know the details."

Jarl's bad manners were in full flower. He remarked, "The process is too complicated for the military mind. You are welcome to come along and watch. You'll only be gone a few days. I and my crews have been ready to leave for the last two days."

"We wouldn't miss it for a new war," Jeonk remarked. "We're right behind you."

They entered jarl's favorite home away from home, a massive weird looking recovery spacecraft that Jarl called his junk flagship. Jarl's junk flagship had six tongs extending from its underside that looked like huge warped landing pods. The tongs were long enough to grab an Argan cruiser and bring it under his junk flagship's upper structure.

There were many other spacecraft as strange as his flagship but they were smaller by comparison and more specialized. One of the strangest things about all of them was the monumental size of their thrusters and the huge metal beams used to attach the thrusters to the spacecraft. Jarl called his larger space junk recovering spacecraft, Space Tugs.

As the salvage fleet approached the Horde fleet from the Okron side, Jarl remarked, "You military heroes managed to put the whole mess in one pile. That was nice of you. I won't have to rearrange the hardware to work with it."

Jarl ordered three of his ships to take up positions twenty miles from the dead fleet. They were ordered to erect a huge metal cone. He then ordered the crews of what remained of his weird collection of space going deformities to train their cutting laser beams on the dead spacecraft and begin their work.

Shok asked, "If you are going to cut it apart, why were you glad we put it in one connected pile?"

Jarl replied, "There is no way to separate the different spacecraft in that fleet. We are going to cut it up so its parts will be pulled closer together by the gravity of the black hole pellets you guys destroyed it with. We aren't just cutting it; we're melting it down to the smallest size we can make it. We won't lose one ounce of it in the process.

Jeonk asked, "What will you do with it when you get it as small as you can make it?"

Jarl resurrected his bad manners, "That's why I brought you along, to see how a genius like me performs. Stop giving me a lot of guff and watch, this may take a while."

It took Jarl's crew two days of cutting and melting to work the dead fleet into a small round mass of metal about two hundred yards in diameter. His crew, twenty miles away, signaled their need for one more day to finish their work. One more day would be well worth the time for Jeonk and Shok if it helped get rid of the mess

From Jarl's command deck they could see the huge metal cone Jarl's crew had built and locked onto the rear of one of his Space Tugs. Jarl said they needed the extra day to work on the opposite side of it. The cone's support structure needed to be strengthened. Jarl's salvage fleet spread out over a wide area of space while waiting for the cone crew to finish.

The grunt work was finished and it was time for Jarl to put his genius where his mouth was. The giant Space Tug that was locked onto the cone began feeding a very large cable through its center. The cable was made of very strong, lightweight, flexible metallic coils and it stretched the twenty miles from the cone to the melted fleet. Jarl's crew had no trouble feeding the cable to the melted metal, and attaching it to the metal. The gravity pull of the black hole pellets would let the cable go nowhere else and once a plate on the end of the cable was attached to the metal of the melted fleet, its hold couldn't be broken. Just to make sure its hold couldn't be broken, Jarl hit the large metal plate with lasers to melt it into the main mass.

The towing Space Tug's thrusters were turned up to maximum power. The cable stretched as far as it would go and that measured twenty-two miles. Jarl radioed the Space Tug pilot to be ready on his mark. Jarl launched a nuclear missile and exploded it behind the melted down fleet. The missile explosion boosted the mass of metal a short distance. The Space Tug's thrusters may have helped to pull it along but it was difficult to tell. Jarl launched missile after missile, always moving the melted fleet a little farther toward the sun.

Jeonk remarked, "Jarl, I don't think we have enough missiles on Arga to get that chunk of metal from here to the sun."

Jarl countered, "It's closer than it was and it's going all the way. I'm trying to do this the cheap way first. If I can start it moving so my tug can keep it going away from the planet, even an inch at a time, it will be moving faster every minute after that. The problem isn't how to get it there, it's how cheap it is to get it there and it's time for phase two."

Jarl ordered the Space Tug to disconnect from the huge cone the cable was attached to and let the cone and the cable go free. The Space Tug disconnected and made a fast run forward. Jarl aimed a missile near the back of the cone as it was being pulled toward the melted fleet by the recoiling cable. The missile exploded and shot the cone forward, stretching the cable to its full length. The explosion moved the metal mass but not far enough. Jarl kept his missiles spaced to keep the cone moving forward with the melted mass following it on the stretched cable.

While Jarl was expending the remainder of his one hundred or so missiles on the project, Shok said, "That takes care of the first hundred miles. If we can figure out how to get it the rest of the way we're all set."

Jarl ordered his Space Tug to reconnect and see if it could pull the mass. The Space Tug reconnected and could hold the mass of metal well enough to keep it from drifting toward the planet surface but it couldn't tow it.

Jarl stretched back on his command pedestal and said, "Cheap is out! Now you space jockeys are going to see some real flying." He reached for his radio and ordered, "You guys on Tug number two bail out. We're going for the big money."

The crew on Space Tug two flew their utility shuttle to Space Tug number three. They were on board before Jarl picked up his remote control. Jeonk said, "Jarl, if you're going to try to push that pile of junk into the sun and your Tug touches that melted fleet it will become a part of it. Its systems will shut down and you'll have that much more weight to move."

Jarl retorted, "Just sit there and watch. It's my Tug and I have it on good authority that the King of Arga will buy me another one when I'm finished. Cheap is out!"

Space Tug two had been fitted with a large thick metal plate on its nose. Jarl brought his big ugly flagship in behind Tug two before he sent two forward. Jarl made his final check of all system before the final operation was allowed to begin. Tug two moved slowly forward on its way to make a permanent connection in the center of the melted mass of metal.

Jarl explained, "Do you see the long slender rod behind the Tug? That's the antenna for my remote control unit. I've put anti-gravity screens inside the Tug, all around its working systems. The intense gravity of your pellets caused the electronics in the Horde spacecraft to shut down. When their electronics shut down, everything stopped working. My Tug will work. I'm going to lose one high priced Tug, with a few really expensive anti-gravity screens because I can't back the tug away from that mass of metal. But, all of my Tug's systems will still work. Now, watch this!"

Jarl moved the controls on his remote control. Tug two continued its move gently toward the clump of spacecraft and nudged it softly. When Tug two's contact was certain, Jarl put its thrusters to full thrust. Within seconds the mass of metal began to slide slowly forward. With Tug One pulling it and Tug Two pushing it, the metal mass gained speed rapidly. Within two hours the melted down fleet was far enough away from Okron's gravitational pull to make the job easy.

Jarl's Space Tugs stayed on the job. His pulling tug disconnected when the mass was close enough to the sun to unalterably doom the entire collection of dead spacecraft to a fiery end. Tug two completed the job of pushing the mass into the fire of the sun.

Jarl, for all of his bad mouth and manners, saved Arga billions of gold skirbs in cost, and who knows how many more deaths would have been caused by the planet-crashing remnant from the Horde war. The new Tug, paid for by the King of Arga, and built to replace Tug number two, was being built to Jarl's very expensive specifications. Jarl's new Space Tug was to become the masterpiece of his Space Salvage business. It was so massive Jarl intended making it his flagship, and he swore it would be the most beautiful thing anyone would ever see in space.

The Horde weren't so lucky. They had no Jarl Gast and never heard of black hole metal. They had no knowledge of how to handle it. Twelve space ships contaminated with the dangerous metal were on a collision course that would crash them on the planet Turt. The Horde's first notice of the incoming spacecraft was from their deep space probes positioned to warn them of a possible Argan attack.

Emperor Grol was notified immediately when the probes detected the incoming spacecraft. He didn't know what or whose they were but he knew they weren't an attack force. He launched an inspection team while the small fleet of spacecraft was still approaching far from his home planet. His inspecting Commander informed him that the spacecraft type was Honor Guard class spacecraft. All twelve of the ships were connected together in an odd, jumbled pattern as though they had drifted together. They were obviously dead and they were on a collision course with Turt. The Commander asked for Grol's orders to take care of the problem.

Grol didn't know what he wanted done with them but he knew where they came from, and he knew they were bad news. He called a meeting of scientists and military Commanders to determine the options. The military people didn't like the product of a secret weapon coming at them and they wanted to blast them to pieces and be rid of them. The scientists, being more curious, wanted to tractor beam the dead spacecraft to a desolate part of the planet and study them.

Grol didn't agree with his military leaders. He had different ideas about what he wanted done with the dead spacecraft. Grol had lost a war because of what had happened to the spacecraft. He wanted more knowledge about the secret weapon that caused his defeat, so he agreed with the scientists. Grol knew the ships represented a threat none of them understood, and could become very dangerous. He, also, knew the Argans had aimed the deadly weapon away from their own planet. He thought, "If we have to face this weapon again, we must find out what it actually is. The cost of that knowledge may be great, but what is the cost of not knowing?"

The committee decided to allow the dead spacecraft to drift on their present course until they came closer to the surface of Turt. They planned to change the dead spacecraft's path of collision with the planet, and tractor beam the connected craft to a soft landing in a pre-selected remote area on the planet. The final plan seemed simple enough and the committee agreed on that choice of action.

The big day arrived with the dead spacecraft gaining speed in its planet-crashing trajectory. Three Imperial class spacecraft using The Horde Space Command's largest tractor beam were launched to guide the twelve dead spacecraft to the selected surface area. The three Imperials' tractor beams locked on but they had very little effect on the incoming trajectory of the dead cruisers. The destroyer commanders attempted to move the mass of spacecraft out of the gravity attraction of Turt. They found they could move the dead spacecraft around in space, but the mutual gravity attraction remained solid.

Grol sent six more of his Imperial ships as the dead spacecraft aimed at the planet. More Imperial ships allowed the Horde to slow the dead spacecraft and move them across the planet's surface but their incoming speed wasn't slowed enough for any kind of a soft landing. The tractor beams were too weak to force the dead spacecraft to land in the designated area, or to tractor beam them to a deserted landing area. The twelve ships slammed into the surface of Turt at fifteen thousand miles per hour near the shore of a ten square mile lake forty miles from the center of Turt's capital of Pik.

The twelve ships made a deep crater as they slammed into the planets surface. A huge plum of dirt exploded from the crater and spread through the atmosphere to a diameter of twenty miles. Some of the heavier debris in the dust cloud was driven to the ground by the power of the explosion. The cloud of dust and smaller debris reached the limit of its slowing journey; and then, remaining airborne, the gritty substances reversed its first path to slam back into the crash impact area. The air over Pik was quickly, if mysteriously, cleared. The water in the lake flowed through the cracks made in the lakes basin by the crash and covered the remains of the twelve spacecraft.

The people of Pik were terrified by the explosive sound of the crash and the strange sight of the dust cloud spreading into the city and then rapidly pouring back to where it started. The survivors closer to the impact were having difficulty walking away from the direction of the crash and some of them were pulled to their death. Those able to flee the disaster could see a large uneven looking bubble of water sticking up in the air where no water should be possible. Flocks of birds flapping their wings as fast as they could were pulled backwards into the bubble of water.

In the first moments after the impact, everything in the air was pulled toward the bubble. The surviving suburbanites, farther than fifteen miles from the site, had difficulty walking away from the ugly looking chunk of water but everyone else in the city began leaving as fast as he could.

Panic is a small word for the feelings of people trying with great difficulty to go one way while their personal belongings insist on going in the opposite direction. Small airborne vehicles, attempting to get a closer look at the strange sight, were pulled into the ball of water. Nothing was alive for very long within fifteen miles of the crash center and everything loose within thirty miles of the crash was being pulled toward it.

The increased gravity in metropolitan Pik affected everything in the city. Walls of large buildings on the outer fringe of Pik began to bulge in the direction of the crash site and the some of the smaller ones crumbled and slide toward the strange ball of water.

Grol and his Imperial offices were on the opposite side of Pik. At sixty miles from the center of the Impact area they could feel the strength of the increased gravity. Evacuating the city was no problem. Everyone who wasn't trapped in the pull of gravity was already leaving. The ability to leave was far exceeded by the desire to leave. Grol ordered the military and civil agencies to aid in the evacuation. He moved his Imperial offices three hundred miles away to the city of Tipa.

Grol's bureaucrats were terrified. The papers they were pushing and all of the small items in their offices were stuck to their office walls nearest the crash. Grol had to evacuate with his bureaucrats but he didn't leave with their panic driven urgency to the new imperial offices. Grol went directly to his Imperial flagship and put it in the air over the impact area. He was more astounded by what he saw at the crash site than he was by his Imperial fleet after the Argan bombardment destroyed it.

A huge ball of clear water sat from ground level to two miles in the air. The ball wasn't round. Its surface was irregular and in some places the water protruded for hundreds of yards. The largest protrusion was nearly half a mile of water hanging in the air partially over dry land with its sides sloping evenly to the main surface of the weird bubble of water. The water was as clear as any untouched beach on Turt. Everything in the water, or going into the water, was instantly drawn to the bottom of the strange contortion of water. No one could believe it without seeing it.

Grol thought, "Only idiots would fight a people who can build a weapon to do this. How did they control, whatever it is, and shoot it from their cruisers? No wonder they wanted my fleet on a heading to leave the galaxy when they destroyed it. They--sure as hell--didn't want an uncontrolled residue of the weapon to land on their planet."

Grol remembered the Emperor's Imperial Fortress and the eight Honor Guard ships that had died with it. He wasn't sure if they were close enough to the planet Okron to be drawn toward it but judging from the gravitational pull of the twelve that crashed on Turt, he believed they might be. He thought, "The Argans know how to control this stuff. They'll be watching for the Emperor's spacecraft to begin drifting toward their surface and they'll know how to take care of the problem. If anyone knows how to clear up this mess, it's the Argans."

Grol went to his new office in Tipa and ordered the imperial scientists to start working on the problem. They knew the problem was gravity and all of the spacecraft in the Empire used gravity and anti-gravity equipment. The technology wasn't new, but the severity of the problem was far beyond the abilities of their available knowledge and equipment to solve it.

Grol began a crash program to increase the Empires anti-gravity technology. Meanwhile, the scientists were ordered to measure and monitor the strength of the gravity field at various distances and times around the circumference of the impact area. None of them knew if the disaster had peaked with the crash or if they were just beginning to see its effects.

Grol decided that, under the disastrous circumstances, it was time for him to stop waiting for the Argans to come to him. He would fly to Arga, meet with them and check on the return of his prisoners of war. He would take all of the available information about the crash of the dozen spacecraft with him. He feared it might be too much to ask a recent enemy to offer his Empire help with a problem the empire caused with its own belligerence, especially since Grol, as the new Emperor, would have to make the request himself. The Argans were still recovering from the problems he had caused them as the Chief Commander.

Grol's scientists fed his Imperial office constant updates on the situation including the increasing number of problems the large change in the gravity spectrum of the planet might produce. Among the problems they predicted. might happen, were earthquakes, volcanic eruptions, a possible shift in the planets orbit around its sun. The water in nearby rivers and lakes was already tilted toward the impact area. The scientists gave him all of the problems they could think of, but nothing they said sounded like it might become a solution. Grol hoped the Argans would give him an undeserved break to help solve this one problem.

16
EMPORER GROL MEETS HIS ENEMIES

Grol's flagship entered Argan space alone. He dared not antagonize the Argans, whose help he needed and hoped for, by bringing a fleet. Grol flew his Imperial Fortress directly to the coordinates where he had left the late Emperor. The dead Emperor's Fortress, and the eight Honor Guard ships, were gone.

Grol made long range scans of the area in an attempt to locate them but found nothing. He assumed the Argans had successfully recovered or destroyed the Emperor's spacecraft, and he didn't particularly care which. In either case, they knew how to handle the gravity problem. He was certain the Argans were monitoring his arrival. Grol was afraid they would give him very little time before the shooting started. He didn't think another dead Emperor would solve Turt's gravity problem.

Grol ordered his Communications Officer to contact the Argans on a wide band of frequencies to make sure they listened before they began shooting. He identified himself as Emperor Grol, and requested to speak with His Majesty, King Jeonk, about the disposition of the prisoners of war, and other important matters, leaving the other important matters unexplained.

An Argan military official returned his greeting and informed him they had set a beacon for him to follow. The beacon would bring his spacecraft to Shok's Perlta cruiser base close to Poshalla, the city he had tried his best to destroy.

As his ship descended, Grol had his closest look at Poshalla. He noticed there were building projects throughout the city to repair the damage commander Varst's attack and the Horde army caused. The forests areas nearest the city were blackened for hundreds of square miles.

King Jeonk and Admiral Kelly met Grol as he exited his spaceship. Without discussion, he was taken to the Admiralty building in Poshalla. Grol's first sight of his principal enemies in the war was also his first face-to-face meeting with an Argan. The Horde hadn't captured one Argan in the entire war. Grol asked, "Admiral Kelly, I understand you are usually called Admiral Shok, Is that correct?"

"I'm better known as Shok than Kelly," replied Shok. "Even my close friends call me Shok."

Grol continued, "His majesty and you were reported to the former Emperor as the most dangerous of all the Argans. The informants we spoke with, from the planets Prssk and Gamac, told the late Emperor that King Jeonk and you would hunt him down and kill him the minute you discovered he was your enemy. The Emperor believed them. That's why you had more than a year to prepare for war. The Emperor thought we could win by waiting for you to attack us. I advised him against that course of action but he wouldn't listen. We lost because of it. Our late Emperor was as stupid as the rest of your enemies."

As they entered the Space Command briefing room, Grol noticed more than half the chairs were empty. That reminded him of how much he was gong to ask of the

Argans. The war had killed more than half of their military leaders, and he knew the dead were also the friends of the survivors. He and his side lost more in the war, but the dead on his side were the ones who started the war.

Jeonk opened the meeting, "Emperor Grol is here to inquire about the disposition of our prisoners of war. I will make that determination now. We have no reason to keep any of them. They are free to be transferred from our control to yours at any time you have transportation for them.

"There are approximately one million three hundred thousand survivors. We will allow your military transports to come to this planet for that purpose. The military transports must be unescorted by any other spacecraft. The transports will use the cruiser base at Tischel to load the prisoners. You will be given the directions necessary for your transports to descend on that base. Do you have any objections to that plan?"

Grol was struck by the fact that they asked nothing in war reparations for the return of the prisoners. He had expected to pay dearly for them. Grol responded, "I have no objection, and I wish to thank you for your direct means of handling the problem. I will have transports here within thirty days after I leave. We no longer have enough transports to move them all at one time but they will all be removed from your control as quickly as possible."

Admiral Rakoup asked Grol, "There is one very deep mystery that I would like to have explained. Why did you attack the planet Oglak? Each time I think of it, I become more curious about that absurd part of the war."

Grol shrugged his shoulders, and then stated, "The late Emperor wanted to plan a first victory to his own credit. He commissioned one of his close friends, a Commander named Skursk. I had left Skursk guarding the home planets to keep him out of the war. Skursk was ordered to attack the planet Iklug, but the Emperor gave Skursk the coordinates for the planet Oglak by mistake.

The room erupted in laughter. King Plask, who loved a good joke, slapped Rakoup on the back and said, "The Iklugs would have been terrified by the Horde attack. The Oglaks were glad to see them. The Emperor might as well have sent his men into a meat grinder. That attack was the only fun old General Shsiska has had for years. I

After a few minutes of the Admirals discussing how stupid anyone would be to attack the planet Oglak, Jeonk brought the meeting back in line. He said, "Emperor Grol you said you have, other, important matters you wish to discuss. Now would be a good time for the discussion."

Grol didn't like to be the butt of a joke but he was grateful for the change in the somber mood of the meeting. He needed cooperation from people who had no need to cooperate. He hoped their good mood would help. He explained, "At the time you destroyed the Imperial fleet, twelve of our Honor Guard class spacecraft were inadvertently on a course for the Imperial planet of Turt. While they were on that course, they were drawn into one mass by your gravity-based weapon. They impacted forty miles from the center of Pik, Turt's capital city. Our scientists have no knowledge of how to handle it. The problems surrounding the crash are growing.

"I realize you have no reason to offer your assistance in this matter and, in fact, have many reasons to refuse. Our attack on your society was a useless and stupid act of desperation that brought nothing but disaster and pain to both sides.

"Our scientists have been monitoring the crash sight of the twelve ships, but monitoring the site hasn't helped. I have brought photographs of the site and the accompanying scientific data with me. You may be interested in seeing some of the after effects of your weapon, even though you may decide to refuse my request for your help in cleaning it up."

Grol took his photographs from his briefcase and showed them to the amazed Admirals. Shok was the most interested since he was in charge of the project that produced the weapon system for the black hole pellets. He asked, "Has the column of water changed in shape since the crash?"

"It seems to be stable in that shape," Grol answered. "The water remains clear because the dirt, debris and everything else coming in contact with the water is pulled through the water to the bottom of the crater. The crater is more than six hundred feet deep. The twelve spacecraft stopped going deeper when they hit bedrock."

Admiral Doskel said, "Our scientist can determine the number of pellets in the water by its shape." Doskel looked toward Jeonk and Shok standing together at the table and said, "It's a good thing you two figured out how to get rid of the destroyer and the eight ships with it. We might have had a real problem if they had crashed into one of our oceans."

Pellets and, get rid of, were the words Grol keyed on, "You killed a whole Imperial fleet with a pellet gun! How did you get rid of the Imperial Fleet after you pellet gunned it to death?"

Shok explained the black hole pellets to Grol, leaving out the security information about the pellet firing mechanism and how they were produced. He then told him, "We melted the Emperor's destroyer and the eight cruisers into a ball of metal and towed the ball of metal into the sun. It took many days, the loss of a very expensive space tug, and expertise we had to learn on the job to get the job completed. That was the cheapest way we could get rid of them.

"I think we can put a team together to take care of your problem if his Majesty and the Admiralty want that done. It will be an extremely expensive operation to complete. I see no reason why we should help a people who were obviously trying to annihilate our entire population and the population of every other planet on this side of our galaxy."

"You are correct," Grol responded. "We have given you no reason to help and you have every reason to refuse. I fought a desperate war with you without ever having met one of you. I came here against the advice of everyone on my staff to meet the people I have come to admire more than any other strangers. That war is over and the Emperor who made it a war of annihilation is dead. I want my people and your people to be friends and no help from you is required for that friendship.

"As a parting gesture I would like to give you one piece of information about your technology that I don't believe you have. Your spacecraft, the cruisers you used so brilliantly, have inter-galactic speed. You took our technology and improved it to a point we have been trying to reach for decades. If we had been able to develop our technology as well as you have, there would have been no war. I'm sure you understand the war was our effort to buy time to develop our space technology for inter-galactic speed.

"Perhaps our scientists will find a way to remove these--black hole metal pellets, perhaps not. We will do what we must to cure a problem we caused. I think, gentlemen, it's time for me to leave."

"Just a moment your Majesty," Jeonk advised. "We Argans love to work on tough problems. Shok always has a plan. He was responsible for the black hole pellet idea that killed your fleet. If Shok didn't already have a plan for those pellets, he wouldn't have said we could take care of your problem. If you leave, he will tell us what it is. We'll be arguing for years about whether his plan would have worked or not. If you don't like his plan; you will, at least, have heard what the most feared and respected tactical genius in this galaxy thinks of the situation."

Grol allowed himself a small ironic smile. He had finally met the man who engineered his defeat and the same man was about to tell him how to save his planet. Grol remarked, "I wouldn't miss it for the propulsion specifications for your cruisers."

Shok began, "To begin with, my plan isn't how to finish the job. The plan is how to organize the people and equipment we need to finish the job. We need the team who helped us get the black hole metal out of the mine on the Mog 5 planet. They will be able to figure out exactly where each pellet is. When we know where each pellet is, we will know where the easiest to lift will be.

"Next, we have to get rid of the two-mile high bubble of water. The only people I know of who have pumps strong enough to handle the job are the Oglaks. We could build the pumps we need, but building them will take time and I'm sure the Oglaks have them on hand. They'll help if we ask them. The Oglaks can build the water pipes they'll need from the metals available on Turt.

"Once we get rid of that two mile high mass of water, the Mog 5 mining team can get close enough to the pellets to set up anti-gravity screens around the sight. The team can probably remove the pellets alone but it would take them years to do it. I think we need to do this more quickly, if the data Emperor Grol showed us is accurate.

"Finally, we need the help of Jarl Gast. He has the only equipment strong enough to pull those pellets, one or two at a time, out of the crater and sling them into the nearest sun. Our anti-gravity screens will make them light enough for Jarl to start them moving. Once they are moving; he can keep them moving.

"Jarl Gast is the real problem. One, he may tell us to go to hell because he don't like the Horde. If Jeonk and I talk to him together, we may be able to convince him to take on the job, but if he says no, he means no. Second, he has very large spacecraft and they are reasonably fast but it will take him more than a year to get to the other galaxy. We need a way to transport his equipment to the crater. The only spacecraft big enough and fast enough is a Horde destroyer, but the inside of two of them would have to be changed to handle the load. I don't know if that can be done."

"Shok," Admiral Doskel asked, "what makes you think the Oglaks can pump a two mile high bubble of water dry? The water they pump to keep their tunnels dry is below ground."

Shok replied, "The bottom of that bubble is at least six hundred feet underground and the Oglaks are the only ones with the expertise to get near it even with the help of our anti-gravity screens. We'll need to take some of their earth borers with us but I think we can squeeze them in with Jarl's stuff."

"What do you think of Shok's plan?" Jeonk asked Grol. "Do you have anything comparable for your people to use?"

Grol replied, "The plan sounds all right to me. We have nothing comparable ourselves. Our best anti-gravity equipment allows us within five miles of the crater, and that's going as close as we dare."

Jeonk turned to Shok and asked, "Do you want to do this job or not?"

Shok replied, "Not my call. You and the Admiralty make it a go or it's a no-go."

Jeonk looked to his father and said, "Father would you show Emperor Grol into another room for a few minutes. We need to discuss this problem privately."

Plask left the room with the Emperor. As Plask shut the door, he turned and said, I'm going with Shok if he goes."

Jeonk gave Shok, his best friend, a long look before he said, "All of us know you want to take on that bubble. Why don't you just say, yes?"

"I like the problem, and I think it can be solved," Shok answered. "On the other hand, I don't care if those pellets eat the whole damn planet. That's a dangerous job. Why should we risk ourselves, and our friends to get the worst enemy we have ever fought out of fix he brought on himself? Even so, it's an interesting situation and I sure would like to see how the pellets made that weird column of water. You and the Admiralty call it; doing it may be my plan, but whether to do it or not is outside of my area of expertise."

Admiral Rakoup burst out, "What's this area of expertise crap? I've never heard you mention anything that is outside of your area of expertise. Shok if you don't do this we'll all be wondering, forever, if whatever crazy plan you have works. I say we do it and any one who says no can kiss my ass."

Admiral Brak voted his conviction, "I wouldn't vote against Shok's bubble for a fleet of cruisers. I say Shok has to do it, and I'm with Rakoup on the ass kissing. This is the first time I have ever heard Shok admit anything was outside of his area of expertise, whatever that means."

The curious Admirals voted their curiosity, and all of them were curious about the project. Shok had to accept the weird project because of the unanimous vote of the Admiralty; added, of course, to his own unbridled curiosity.

King Jeonk's true feelings were revealed when he voiced his permission for the project, "I think we need to assess a price for Shok's expertise in this matter. We didn't capture even one of the Horde's destroyers. Our price is the plans and specifications for the destroyer. If Grol doesn't want to pay the price, let him get rid of his vertical bubble of water all by himself, or start evacuating his planet. The Horde will also have to pay the enormous cost of Jarl Gast's bad manners plus everyone else's cost for the project."

The Admirals agreed quickly with Jeonk's price analysis for the job. All of them wanted to see the destroyer plans, especially the destroyer's outer protection they had so much difficulty penetrating with everything they could throw at it.

Emperor Grol returned with King Plask to hear the good news. His chalk white face turned ashen, and he squirmed in his chair when he heard the price, but he finally agreed. He also agreed to modify the necessary two destroyers to transport Jarl Gast's equipment.

There was one hang-up that hadn't, as yet, been dealt with. Jeonk and Shok still had the dubious task of convincing Jarl Gast to take the job. Without Jarl, the job might take years of dangerous work to complete. No one wanted to spend that much time on it.

Jeonk and Shok entered Jarl's office with Grol's photographs and scientific data. Shok said, "Jarl, we have an interesting job to do and we want you to take a look at it. We hope you'll help us with it." He spread Grol's photographs for Jarl to see.

Jarl Gast was blunt, to an ever-living fault, and his first question was, "Does this have anything to do with that Horde destroyer at Perlta? That pile of water--sure as hell--isn't from around here, and it was obviously made by some of Shok's pellets."

Jeonk stepped in quickly to keep Jarl from saying no immediately, "Your right Jarl, the mess you see in the photographs is on the Horde Imperial planet of Turt. We have a national interest in helping them get rid of it and you have the only equipment that can lift those pellets off of their surface."

Jarl didn't say no but he retorted, "I do my work in space. Nobody piles water in space. The Horde wanted a fight; let them fight that pile of water."

Shok decided to pique Jarl's mercenary side, "You can name your own price for this one. I don't think they are in a position to argue. The Horde Emperor has already promised Jeonk the plans of a Horde destroyer for the job and we need those plans." Shok continued with his explanation of how they wanted Jarl to help lift the pellets off of the surface of Turt.

Jarl's patriotism finally kicked his blunt bad manners, and his dislike of the Horde, over to his mercenary side. He said, "Well, for the sake of the national interest, if they meet my price, I'll do it but I want my money first. If Shok's plan don't work, I still get paid."

The plan was set. Jarl was willing to take on his part. The Oglaks insisted on bringing enough troops to protect the operation and to make sure the Horde didn't get a chance to kill Jeonk and Shok. They promised to bring their strongest pumps and earth borers to the job. The Oglaks insisted on flying their own spacecraft to Turt. They thought that, by the time the Emperor returned and transported Jarl to the planet, their slower spacecraft would be waiting.

General Shsiska insisted on being in command of the Oglak detachment. He wanted to see where the people came from who had fought so stupidly on his planet. Shsiska said, "If we arrive early we'll be able to use the only lake sticking out of the planet to find the right place to land."

It took both of Grol's modified Destroyers to hold Jarl Gast's Space Tugs and they had to be loaded in space. Jarl's two largest tugs looked like behemoths crawling into leviathans as they entered the huge destroyers. Jarl's collection of space Tugs were too heavy to be loaded on the ground, even a Horde destroyer wouldn't be able to lift them.

The Argans flew two fleets of cruisers to Turt, the same two fleets they used to destroy the Horde Imperial fleet. The Horde were not informed and never learned that the pellet firing mechanisms had been removed from the cruisers after the war. The cruisers were to keep Horde Commanders; there might be a few rogues, from making a spurious and vengeful attack on the operation. Jeonk and Shok, the most celebrated of the Horde butt kickers, would be on Turt to supervise the operation.

Their first look at the giant bubble of water was staggering, absolutely unbelievable. Jeonk looked at Shok and said, "What have you gotten us into this time?"

"The bigger they come, the wetter they fall!" Shok exclaimed. "Let's get to it." He started his Argan crews moving their anti-gravity screens and had the Oglaks land their earth borers at a safe distance. The earth borers would have to be protected by the large anti-gravity screens just to get to the positions where they could begin boring underground to lay the drainage pipes.

The Argan scientists decided there were only eleven pellets in the crater. Somehow, a Horde cruiser that hadn't been pellet infected must have come in contact with one that was. That was a break for Shok's plan. The big fear was that there were more than twelve pellets, not less. By the general appearance of the column of water, they guessed the pellets were resting on bedrock in separate places except for three that were locked together or very close to one another. Those three and the uneven disbursement of the others caused the half-mile of water to protrude from one side of the bubble.

Two miles of water could be seen above ground but no one knew how much there was below ground. The cruiser's scanners couldn't give accurate information about the bottom of the crater because the dense field of gravity holding the bubble in place distorted their scans. Since the bubble was spread over a large area of ground as well as above the crater, the decision was made to run above ground pipes to the water and pump the water above the surface of the crater to a new location.

A scientific analysis of the pellets gravity field said it would take a pipeline ninety-seven miles long and downhill from the crater to pump the water to someplace where it couldn't be drawn back to the crater. A dry canyon found to be a little farther than the ninety-seven miles and nine hundred feet lower in elevation would be used as a basin for the draining process.

The disaster team found they could work as close as ten miles from the crash site without anti-gravity screens if they were strong enough and used tethers to keep them from being drawn any closer. The only people strong enough were the Argans and the Oglaks, but getting closer wasn't enough. They needed a method to get equipment close enough to drain the water.

Shok ordered his flagship's crew to use their lasers to burn a solid roadbed to the bubble of water. While that was happening, the Oglak and Argan teams began putting together a rail system with wheels under the rails. After completing the ten miles of rails with heavy metal crossbeam supports, they welded thirty pipes down the full length of the rails. Protruding from the front of their rail system was one hundred feet of free floating pipe that would be pushed into the vertical bubble of water.

A suspension system was used to support the free-floating pipe to keep the pipe from being bent downward by the gravity of the pellets. When the first pipes on the rail system were inside the bubble, the pipes at the rear would connect to a larger pipe ten miles from the bubble. The water would be pumped through the thirty smaller pipes to the large pipe. The large pipe and the Oglak pumps would force the water to the dry canyon nearly one hundred miles away.

It was complicated to build but they got it done. Jarl Gast used his largest Space Tug, and one of his long cables, to pull the ten miles of pipe down the laser burned road to the bubble. He left his cable tethered to the front of the pipe system and landed twenty miles from the bubble with the other end still attached to his Space Tug, in case some recovery work might be needed.

The Argans and the Oglaks connected the thirty smaller pipes at the rear of the large pipe. The Oglak pumps came on line and water began to flow in the canyon. They reduced the water level by one hundred feet but that wasn't much of a dent in the two-mile high bubble.

After being repositioned, the rail system began sinking into the crater. The pellets were drawing everything loose near the edge of the crater into the crater. The ground under the bubble became saturated with water and the weight of the rail system began a collapse at the crater's edge. The collapse allowed the leading edge of the rail system to be pulled into the crater.

Outside of the bubble, dry ground was still dry because the water being held by the pellet's gravity couldn't seep into it. There was no solid footing for the wheels of the heavy rail system inside the bubble of water. The first try was a failure. The bubble was still standing high and Jarl Gast had to use his tethered space tug to pull the rail system out of danger and keep it from becoming part of the problem at the bottom of the crater.

The Oglaks had gotten into the mood of the job and they wanted to bring their own expertise to the problem. They decided to build a ten-mile pipe the same size as the pipe they were fitting the smaller pipes into. They would have flex joints in various positions along its length so it wouldn't break when it was towed.

At the bubble end of the pipe, they put a three hundred feet long snout pointing down into the bubble. The entire length of pipe would be towed to the center of the bubble by a space tug. Jarl Gast would do the towing. He would have to remain above it with his Space Tug tethered to the pipe to keep the long snout from being pulled into the bubble of water.

Jarl wanted wheels on the ten miles of pipe. Even a Space Tug can only drag so much weight. He also wanted more money because he would have to stay above the bubble with his thrusters going pretty hard to hold the weight of the three hundred feet of pipe extension in the intense gravity field caused by the pellets.

Jarl's deal had been to lift the pellets out of the hole if, and after, someone removed the water. Jarl said, "This new job isn't part of my contract. I'm not spending my profit money to buy fuel for a pipe hanging job." A deal was struck with Emperor Grol, to Jarl's benefit, and the project went forward.

A Horde tunneling organization constructed the pipes the Oglaks designed. The pipes were sent to the work site in sections. The pipes were fitted together by the Oglak and the Argan team, and installed on the wheels demanded by Jarl Gast. Jarl towed the miles of pipe to the center of the mass of water. The other end of the pipe was connected to the outgoing water pipe they had previously used. The Oglak pumps began pumping once again and water began flowing to the, now not so dry, canyon.

It took nine days to pump the bubble of water down to the minus three hundred foot level of the crater. Below the pumping level, the crater was filled with water soaked silt and debris from the collision. They could remove no more by pumping unless they constructed a longer snout to hang in the crater and they weren't sure that would work.

Shok was able to photograph the crater's surface area from a cruiser brought close above the crater. He found the crater's surface looked much like the bubble of water. The lowest places in the crater were above the buried pellets.

Based on the new photographs, Shok and his engineering team formed a new and supposedly simple plan. If Jarl Gast dropped a heavy, pointed probe into the water soaked silt, the point would be drawn to one of the pellets. When the probe connected with one of the pellets, the connection couldn't be broken because of the extreme gravity force holding it. Jarl could then bring the pellet, and whatever was connected to it in the crater, out of the crater. The high-density debris would begin its journey to the sun. Jarl would do his best to guide his probe to the separated pellets before he tackled the three that were connected, or very close together.

The pellets were spread over a half-mile area at the bottom of the large crater and the big money was on that being far enough apart for the plan to work. Everyone ignored the fact that nothing, so far, had gone according to the original plan. The water was gone, by whatever means, and that was according to the original plan.

Jarl decided to use a twenty-mile long cable for his probe. He figured he needed twenty miles of cable to allow him enough distance above the crater for his big thrusters to exceed the gravity in the crater. The three pellets they were trying to avoid were on the city side of the crater.

Jarl would drag his metal probe across the ground from the lakeside, and let the pellet he was after drag his probe down through the silt mess to make his connection. Doing that from twenty miles above the surface was no easy task, but that's why they paid Jarl so much money. Shok would guide Jarl's efforts from his flagship. Shok's flagship would be low enough to the surface for Shok to track the operation, and give instructions to Jarl on his space tug command deck.

Jarl was alone with his crew twenty miles above the surface. Shok's cruiser's command deck had never had so many people on it. Everyone with enough clout to watch was there. Grol was on the command deck with some of his military friends. They were more interested in the cruiser than the pellets. Jeonk was there and his father Plask, Admiral Rakoup, Admiral Brak, Admiral Doskel, the Oglak General Shsiska and some of his Oglak Generals were there. If Jarl Gast had known how many important people would be on Shok's command deck, he would have asked for more money.

Jarl slowly lowered his probe on the lakeside far from the crater. Shok told him when it was on the ground, and to begin dragging it to the crater. Dragging a probe on the end of a twenty-mile flexible cable to a specific place is tedious. It took hours to get the probe to just the right point on the lip of the crater. The probe went over the lip and immediately plummeted to the bottom, pulled by the powerful gravity of the pellets. The probe made its connection quickly. Shok notified Jarl and told him to begin the lifting operation.

Jarl put tension on the cable to check the connection and satisfied his professional side that a connection had been made. He turned his thrusters up to one hundred percent. The cable was under great stress but it was obviously moving skyward. A dignified but obvious cheer went up from the important assembly on the cruiser's command deck as a large ball of muddy looking junk came out of the crater. The ugly ball had an irregular shape.

Photographs of the exiting ball of wet debris were made and new photographs of the crater were made. The photographs of the crater showed Jarl had pulled out two of the pellets he wasn't after, but had left the pellet he was after in the crater. No one was sorry about freeing an extra pellet. Freeing the two pellets created a nearly twenty percent decrease in the gravity field. The problem was, they couldn't guide Jarl's probes to any specific pellet and his probe had angled toward the three pellets they considered the most dangerous to handle.

The Argan scientists cautioned the disaster team that there should to be no other pellets in the crater when they went after the three worst-case pellets. Lifting the three pellets might also lift the others at the same time. The Scientists didn't think Jarl's Space Tugs had enough power to pull more than three pellets from the planets surface at one time.

The situation called for some new planning on the part of the disaster team. Everyone on Shok's command deck had gotten up close and personal with the pellet removal and they had just been treated to some success. All of them wanted to be present for the new planning and their presence amounted to one more complication in a hazardous project.

None of the Horde dignitaries were familiar with black hole gravity. One of Grol's Generals asked, "If the pellets can't be disconnected from the probe dropped into the crater, how can the Space Tug pilot disconnect it when he drops it into the gravity of the sun?"

Shok answered, "You noticed that very strong men can walk within ten miles of the crater. Gravity is weaker as the distance is increased from its source. The pilot of the Space Tug is twenty miles from the pellet's source of gravity. He uses an explosive charge to disconnect his twenty-mile long cable from his Space Tug and he has no problem disconnecting. Once he is disconnected, he lets the pellets, the probe, and the cable, continue their flight into the sun. The Space Tug makes a wide turn to avoid the pellets and the cable. When Jarl is free of his load and the pellets are on their way to the sun, he returns ready for the next part of the job. Jarl brought plenty of extra cables and probes."

Grol's aide asked how something smaller than the size of a grain of sand could have so much gravitational pull. Shok explained, "No one understands the dynamic forces in a black hole. Our understanding of what little we do know is from the rare materials we find in space that we believe came from a black hole. We think the material is very old and has lost much of its strength over a long period of time.

"The gravity in a black hole compresses everything going into it to the same gravitational level as the original black hole. A black hole can be overloaded with too much material. When that happens its center becomes super heated beyond its ability to contain its energy content, and it explodes. The energy loss due to the passage of time after the explosion makes the material weaker and prevents the many exploded parts from becoming new black holes.

"A very small piece of the material from a black hole, which appears to be a very dense metal, may weigh as much as a planet and have the same gravitational force as a planet. We used black hole metal that had been wandering in space for, perhaps, billions of years in our weapon system.

"The old black hole metal we use is very heavy and it can cause many problems. Even though it is small, it still retains the gravity complement of the size it was before it was compressed to its present size by a black hole. That's why the dense gravity field of the pellet is pulling everything in the area to it. The city of Pik and a large piece of the surrounding countryside would be covered by the pellet if any one of those pellets suddenly expanded to its original size."

Grol asked, "How did you increase your gravity protection to the point where you can work with such a dangerous material?"

Jeonk explained, "If you have noticed, our anti-gravity screens are very large. Each of them has a small piece of black hole metal inside under constant control. We use electromagnetic modulators inside the screen housing to affect the metal and redirect the gravity field of that small piece. We control its gravity to produce a counter gravity field that nullifies the gravity field of the black hole metal we are working on. We increased our screen sizes in small steps over a long period of time. For each increase, we used a denser material to bring ourselves to the present level of control."

General Shsiska revised the learning period, "How are we going to get rid of the pellets we have in the crater? Do we try to pull them out with Jarl Gast's Space Tugs or dig tunnels to them and use your anti-gravity screens to remove them? We can do it anyway you want, but the quickest way is probably the best way."

Shok remarked, "We've taken the stuff out of space; we've worked it on the ground and we have mined for it, but we have never before removed it from beneath three or four hundred feet of muddy slush. The photographs indicate that we may be able to remove two or three more pellets with the Space Tugs before we tackle the slush.

There are three pellets close to the bottom rim of the crater on the city side. If we say the three are at twelve o'clock, there is another at four o'clock and two more on a line between the four o'clock pellet and the twelve o'clock pellets. If Jarl drops his probe over the edge of the crater at four o'clock and the same thing happens that happened on his first drop, he will snag one or both of the pellets between the four and twelve o'clock pellets. I think it's worth a try. We'll see what we have after that operation before we decide what to do later."

Jarl Gast was told what they needed him to do. He put his Space Tug in the sky and followed the same procedure he used before. His fifteen-ton probe dragged over the rim of the crater and plummeted to the slushy depths at the four o'clock position. It appeared he had a connection. He cranked his thrusters up to one hundred percent. His cable stretched to its maximum but he couldn't pull the probe out of the depths of the crater. Jarl ordered his second space tug connected to the front of his pulling Tug, with a shorter cable, and the removal effort was renewed with the thrusters of both Tugs cranked to one hundred percent.

The people in Shok's cruiser watched Jarl's expert maneuvering and held their breaths. It was certain that Jarl was going to pull the pellets out of the crater or break the twenty-mile long cable. Something had to give and it wasn't going to be Jarl Gast.

Slowly, the cable began to lift out of the slushy mixture. As the crazy looking ball of slush and debris broke the surface, the watchers could see parts of Horde cruisers sticking out of its surface. From the looks of the mess, Jarl had pulled three pellets and some of the destroyed cruisers out of the crater.

As Jarl's load passed within view of Shok's flagship, two of Grol's Generals saluted their fallen comrades in the departing Horde cruisers. Grol looked at them as though they were crazy. Grol didn't think a passing ball of weird looking mush deserved a salute no matter who was in it. Grol barked, "Why didn't you salute the whole damned crater? They were all in the damned crater."

New photographs were made of the slush pit and a new planning session was called. Jarl Gast insisted on being among the planners for the remaining removals involving his Space Tugs. The photographs showed Jarl had removed the pellet at four o'clock and the two pellets they thought he would get later in the line between the four and twelve o'clock pellets. The experts guessed that the pellets were raised in the same lift because they had remained attached to the cruisers lifted at the same time.

When Jarl snagged the pellet he was after with his probe, the other two pellets and the attached cruisers were pulled into the one he snagged. The dead Horde cruisers still attached to the pellets, and responding to the same demand of gravity, came with the pellets they had been hit with.

There remained the three troublesome pellets on the city side of the crater, and the three separated pellets to be dealt with. The one they thought was at three o'clock was really at two thirty but they weren't concerned about a small error in calculation. There was another pellet at six o'clock and one at nine o'clock. The removal of five pellets had reduced the gravity around the crater by forty five percent.

The Grol faction among the group was filled with admiration for the disaster crew. The Horde Generals wondered why the Argans hadn't made one of their expected brash attacks on them first to destroy all of their planets. They certainly had a weapon that would do the job. They didn't know the Argans had never used a weapon like it before, and it wasn't a part of their usual arsenal. None of the Grol faction wanted to stir up their recent differences by asking why the Argans had suffered so much damage to their military instead of making a preemptive strike on the Horde planets.

The planning session began with more onlookers than planners. Jarl Gast wanted to go for the gold. He had lifted three pellets and he thought he could lift the three on the city side of the crater. After that, only individual pellets would remain and it would be easy to cleanse the crater of all of the pellets one at a time.

The more cautious scientific planners were afraid the three grouped pellets might be sitting on bedrock instead of being anchored to cruiser frames. If they were on bedrock, there was no way Jarl could lift them by breaking enough bedrock to tear them loose. The experts were afraid Jarl would break his cable after his connection was made and they would have some portion of the twenty mile cable in the crater connecting the six pellets together. That would be a worse disaster than they now had.

The problem was whether to dig, remove the slush from the pit and use anti-gravity screens to go after the pellets, or find a way to remove the three separated pellets by lifting them.

Shok always had an idea handy and he came up with a scheme from the Earth planet's whaling days. They would rig a harpoon with a long cable on it, shoot the harpoon into the dirty depths of the crater and connect it with one of the pellets. The scheme would require using anti-gravity screens aimed at the edge of the crater nearest the pellet they decided to remove, and the decreased gravity from the other removals made that much easier.

High power compressed air would be used to shoot the harpoon down the side of the crater. Once they made the connection, they would use the preset harpoon and its cable to guide Jarl Gast's probe to the proper pellet.

The Argan miners and the Oglaks worked together to produce a firing system strong enough to get near the edge of the crater and fire the harpoon to the bottom. The Oglaks decided to reposition a six-mile length of the water pipe they had previously used to remove the water from the crater. They would bring the large water pipe to the location at the crater's edge above the targeted pellet. The pipe was large enough for the Argans and the Oglaks to walk in.

The Horde workers transported the sections of pipe to the other side of the crater. Jarl Gast, obligingly, and without any serious insults, snaked the reconstructed sections from where the Horde workers left them to the position the Oglaks wanted them. Jarl used one of his smaller Tugs to line them up where they could be put together.

The anti-gravity screens were turned to full power. The Argans rolled the large screens to the edge of the crater, using the Oglak earth borers as mules to push the anti-gravity screens. The Oglaks and the Argans walked down the pipe, protected by the prepositioned anti-gravity screens, to the edge of the crater. They loaded their short, heavy harpoon into the newly constructed harpoon gun, aimed it at the pellet in the six o'clock position, and fired it into the slush pit.

The harpoon made its connection with the pellet. Jarl Gast allowed the Oglak and Argan harpoon experts to guide his larger probe along the harpoon's cable guideline to make his connection. He pulled the pellet and its share of silt and Horde cruiser remains to the surface, and made one more journey to the sun. There were no salutes from Horde Generals as Jarl dispatched another chunk of unwanted gravity from the surface of the planet Turt. With the repositioning of the equipment, the pellets at the two thirty and nine o'clock positions were gotten rid of with the same tedious and dangerous ease.

There remained the three pellets nearest the capital city of Pik. The unwanted gravity in the area had been reduced by seventy- three percent. An Argan or an Oglak, with the use of a tether and without anti-gravity screen protection, could now move to within approximately two and one half miles of the crater without being drawn into the pit.

Shok didn't want to begin a digging operation for the last three pellets. The mining crew would have to dig down to the six hundred foot level and begin their earth boring operation at two and one half miles from the pellets to get them out by digging. It might take months to tunnel to the pellets using anti-gravity screens throughout their digging effort. It could be done but it was a nasty, dangerous and, worse, a time consuming job.

The disaster planning team decided to let Jarl Gast snag the pellets with his fifteen-ton probe. He would have no trouble doing that because wherever he dropped his probe into the slushy pit, it would be drawn to the three pellets. Jarl agreed with that solution. It was what he had wanted to do in the first place.

There was no need for anyone to be near the crater. All personnel were ordered to leave the area and wait a safe distance away in case something unforeseen went wrong. The command deck of Shok's cruiser was crowded with high-level onlookers anxiously waiting to see the last vestiges of the horrible problem begin its journey to the sun.

Jarl Gast dropped his probe into the slimy depths of the disaster pit. The probe cable could be seen angling toward the city side of the slush pit. As it stopped abruptly, the onlookers knew Jarl had his connection with the three pellets.

Jarl cranked his thrusters up to one hundred percent. The cable held but nothing moved in the pit. Jarl's number two tug hooked to Jarl's number one tug. They both cranked to one hundred percent. The cable held but nothing moved in the pit. The three pellets remained firmly anchored. Jarl aborted the removal, separated his Space Tugs, and landed his number one tug with the cable stretched to its full twenty-mile length.

The planning session was in motion even before Jarl landed his Tug. They still didn't want to dig tunnels for the pellets. They needed a new plan. Shok had already formed a plan--just in case this happened. The Argan scientists had mentioned that the position of the three pellets suggested the clutch of three might be buried in the bedrock at the bottom of the pit, and Jarl wouldn't be able to move enough bedrock to pull them out.

Shok's plan was to use the Oglak pumps and water pipes from the top of the pit. Using anti-gravity screens, they could now get close enough to pump most of the silt and debris out of the pit. If they could get the pit cleared of most of the silt, water and debris, he knew how to free the pellets.

The problem of emptying a six hundred feet deep pit filled with ultra heavy garbage didn't seem to be too much for people who had been through as much as they had. They had already enjoyed the success of seeing most of their efforts bear fruit. Besides that, they trusted Shok. If he said those pellets were coming out of there, they were coming out. They would all wait and enjoy seeing what kind of plan he had for getting it done.

With the help of Horde pipe fabricators, the Argans and the Oglaks constructed the pipes they would need to suck the pit partially dry. Most of the pipe was already on site because of the extensive use of pipe in the removal of the bubble of water.

The stronger Argans and Oglaks moved their ant-gravity screens to the nine o'clock edge of the pit so they could use their metal tunnel to get to the work area. They added two more anti-gravity screens aimed at the bottom of the pit so their six hundred foot siphon wouldn't be pulled to the opposite side by the gravity of the three pellets. The anti-gravity screens would also allow them to remove more of the contents of the pit. They would empty the contents of the pit into a hastily constructed depression a safe ten miles away.

With the help of Jarl Gast's second pipe hanging operation, the job was completed within a few days and everyone on the cruiser could see the still large ball of goop around the area of the three pellets. Jeonk asked Shok, "What's this magic method you have of freeing the pellets?"

Shok confidently replied, "Jarl had two possible problems in lifting the last three pellets. One was that the pellets are actually anchored to the bedrock, but I don't believe they can be. The pellets went into the pit attached to Horde cruisers. It's almost impossible for them to have been dislodged from those cruisers even in the crash.

The other problem is this, Jarl was trying to lift the entire contents of the pit with his Tugs and his tugs weren't strong enough to lift that much weight against the gravity of the planet interacting with the gravity of the pellets. I think that was the real problem.

We've solved the weight problem by reducing the contents of the pit. We are going to solve the possible interaction problem with explosive charges."

Grol listened from his vantage point just behind Shok. He asked, "Now that the weight problem has been reduced, why don't you have Jarl Gast try one more lifting effort and see if that works."

Jarl turned to Grol and said, "The cable I have to use is already attached to the mess in the crater and we used it for the last failed attempt. I think the cable is still good but I can't check the part of it that is still in the pit. If it breaks when I lift, part of it will go into the crater. One more lifting failure might be more stress than the cable can take. The next lift try had better be the last for that cable. I want to know how Shok is going to set explosives under that whole mess of debris."

One of the Argan mining engineers suggested, "We have one big ball of goop left in the pit. I can take a crew into the dry part of the pit, rig up a suction unit and clear the remainder of the slush. After that is finished, we can move the anti-gravity units in close and remove the three pellets. Why don't we just do that?"

Shok asked the engineer, "How long will it take you to do the necessary work after you discover the pellets are attached to three or four crumpled up cruisers and you find you have to disassemble the cruisers to get to the pellets?"

The engineer replied, "I don't know how long that will take. It could take two or three months to cut them up under these conditions. The work would have to be done very carefully."

Shok said, "To answer Jarl's question, "I intend to lower two anti-gravity units into the crater. We will place shaped charges as near to the base of the ball of goop as we can get them. The shaped charges will be aimed below the surface of the three pellets. The shaped charges must be anchored to the bedrock, so they won't be pulled to the pellets when we lift the anti-gravity units out of the pit. The charges must be strong enough to shatter the bedrock under the three pellets. When everything is set, we'll move the anti-gravity units out of the pit.

Jarl will put his two connected Tugs in the air and have their thrusters pulling at one hundred percent. As soon as he tells us he's at one hundred percent, we blast the bedrock with the shaped charges. The shaped charges should break up the bedrock under the pellets and give them a push to start them moving. If Jarl's Tugs can keep them going, we are home free on the pellet problem. That's the plan. We can use my plan or dig for a few months to get rid of them. I think Emperor Grol should make the decision. He's the one who wants to be rid of the pellets."

"I agree with Shok," Jeonk added. "Emperor Grol's interests should be served in this matter. What's your pleasure your Majesty, quick or slow?"

Emperor Grol needed some consultation to make his decision. He asked, "Do you have somewhere private for a quick meeting? I'd like to discuss this with my aides."

They were taken to the private conference compartment on the cruiser and their discussion began with one of his old friends, "Our Imperial ship's thrusters are stronger than the two Tugs. Why don't we offer to use them and lift the pellets out of the crater ourselves?"

Grol replied, "Our ships may also be strong enough to break the cable if the pellets don't come out of the pit. We don't want twenty miles of cable loose in the bottom of it. Besides that, I want to see how they finish this job. So far they haven't done anything the way they originally planned, but the job is getting done. I have been amazed by the individual inventiveness of these people in totally new circumstances.

"King Jeonk watches every move of the operation but he doesn't say anything unless it's important to the operation. Shok goes for the guts of the problem, but he lets everyone have his say. He always admits to a good point but brings his own logic to the problem. After hearing his logic, the experts have agreed with Shok every time and, so far, he has been right every time."

Another of Grol's aides said, "I've noticed you looking for something when we move around this cruiser. What are you looking for?"

Grol answered, "This is Shok's flagship. This cruiser and the others they brought with them are the cruisers they used to destroy the Imperial fleet. The pellets in that hole in the ground came from one of these ships. I've been looking for the armament system they fired the pellets from. I haven't seen the slightest sign of such a complicated armament system. I think these two fleets are armed with the pellets just in case we were drawing them into a trap. I believe they would have already used the pellets on us if they wanted revenge. We have no defense against their black hole pellets and they know it."

Another of Grol's aides remarked, "I guess we are going to tell them to use Shok's quick disconnect on the crater?"

Grol responded, "That's right but I thought making it appear as a thoughtful decision might be better. There is one more consideration. I want each of you to pay special attention to this ship for the remainder of your time on it. This cruiser can beat the hell out of ours. If we hadn't been able to use our Imperials Fortresses in the war, the Argans would have won without their black hole pellets. I hope we never need to fight another enemy as tough as the Argans but if we do, I want our cruisers to be as tough as this one."

The meeting ended and the disaster crew was told of Grol's choice to use Shok's plan. The anti-gravity screens were lowered into the crater and the crew began sinking the shaped charges around the ball of debris, moving the screens for each new position. Photographs were made from every angle. If the lift failed they would have photographs to compare the differences in the debris structure. Any shift in the position of the three pellets could be determined by comparing the before and after photographs.

Before the lift began, Shok's cruiser was brought to its lowest level for a last visual of the strange looking mess at the bottom of the crater. There were three distinct lobes sticking up from the craters bottom. Half of the power of the pellets was underground. The visible lobes appeared as three interlocked bubbles of debris whose bottom half couldn't be seen. None of the material remaining in the lobes touched the wall of the crater. The mangled parts of Horde cruisers could be seen protruding from the three bubbles at bedrock level.

Jarl insisted on sinking one more cable into the pellet hole before he would begin his exit thrusts. He was worried about the stress on the first cable. Shok didn't like that idea because of the weight of the additional cable. Jeonk tried to convince Jarl that Shok was right but Jarl insisted he was the expert on pellet lifting.

Jarl would listen to none of their attempted revisions of his decision and became adamant about his own plan. He wouldn't budge his tugs until they let him sink the second cable. Jarl proclaimed, "I do it my way or no way. Kings and Admirals hire me to get it done. They don't tell me how to do it. If you want that pile of crap moved, it will be with two cables."

Grol and his crew of advisors were astounded when Jeonk and Shok finally agreed to let Jarl drop his second cable over their own objections.

Jarl, his two tugs and two cables began their stretching climb to altitude. Shok said, "I would have put a lot more explosives in that hole if I had known he was going to do that."

"Jarl knows his business better than we do," Jeonk remarked to Grol. "I hope he's right on this one."

"What are you going to do with him when he's finished?" Grol asked. "You can't allow him to get away with insulting you, and he did insult you. He insulted Admiral Shok at the same time."

"Jarl has done many jobs for Shok and me," Jeonk replied. "When he's being nice, he is only a little less insulting. Jarl is undeniably the best there is in his business. If he needs to insult someone to do it his way, he is insulting. He has been that way ever since I've known him. What we are going to do with him when he's finished is pay him and congratulate him on doing a fine job. Problem solving experts are a welcome, and a necessary, resource. Shok, most Argans, and I don't give a damn if those experts are insulting or not.

Grol laughed and said, "That's a point worth remembering. If it brings the results to us as it has your people, I will make the change for the better in this Empire."

Jarl Gast's two tugs connected and signaled they were at one hundred percent thrust. Shok gave the order to set off the shaped charges. The simultaneous explosions caused the bubbles of debris to shift and become more like one bubble. Nothing else seemed to happen for a few seconds. Then, the bubble began to slowly lift from the bottom of the pit. Jarl squeezed the last ounce of thrust from his Tugs. The top of the ball of debris began lifting above the upper lip of the crater as the ball of slush moved slowly upward. Finally the crater was cleared and the debris ball began to gain speed. Jeonk said, "If Jarl's cables hold all the way to the sun, I think his insults paid off."

"If he gets that ball of trash off of this planet," Grol remarked, "I'll let him insult me a few times."

Shok's command deck was filled with cheers as the last of the pellets disappeared from sight. Jarl was on the way to the sun with his last load but the job wasn't quit done. Shok noted a trembling in the miles of pipes that had been laid from the crater to the lake. He ordered the immediate evacuation of all workers and equipment. Because the anti-gravity screens could become as dangerous as the pellets, he ordered the screens moved first and everything else second.

The workers on the ground felt the tremors Shok had seen from the air and they were very quick about getting themselves and the equipment loaded. Argan cruisers quickly descended to pick up the gravity screens. The Oglaks were just as fast to get their earth borers off of the surface and in the sky. The less important equipment was considered expendable and left behind.

Grol, seeing the beginning of the frantic activity but not what caused it, wanted to know, "What's your hurry? You've removed the danger. Relax and enjoy yourselves. The entire Empire is waiting to meet the heroes who accomplished what we all thought was an impossible job.

I hope you'll stay long enough to get to know us better. Allow us to show you we can be something better than mindless makers of war. Bring your mining crew and your friends the Oglaks. Bring Jarl Gast with you. He has my permission to insult anyone in the Empire. If he runs out of insults, I'm an experienced hand with insults, I'll teach him some of my insults."

Jeonk replied, "We aren't hurrying to get away from you or your people. Shok noticed earth tremors in the area. That may be the beginning of an earthquake or perhaps volcanic activity. We're getting our men and equipment off the surface to keep them safe from whatever is about to happen.

The eleven pellets may have put stress on a fault line and Shok put some very deep dents in the bedrock. The explosion may have cracked the bedrock over some magma working its way to the surface. This is also your closest planet to the galactic collision. Maybe the gravity of the planet is being affected, and the planet's crust is responding to gravity fluctuations from that source. We don't know what's causing the tremors. You may be lucky your capital was evacuated earlier."

"The city below us is an empty shell." Grol responded. "What happens to it isn't important. The new Capital is three hundred and fifty miles away. Whatever happens here won't affect it. Our scientists tell me Turt won't feel the pressure from the collision for nearly a hundred years. Come to the new capital with me and allow me to show you our hospitality."

Jeonk didn't like the idea of an extended stay on the planet but he thought it would be all right to make a short visit. He agreed to a two-day visit to Grol's new capital of Tipa.

17
GRAVITY"S ATTACK ON THE HORDE

Shok was silent as they repositioned the two fleets over Tipa. His silence was the average sign of an unresolved problem and Jeonk recognized it. Even with the unusually large crowd on Shok's command deck. Jeonk asked, "What's on your mind Shok. You're usually one of the first to recognize something wrong and it looks to me as though you have."

Shok replied, "When were not doing something necessary on the surface, I think we should all be on our cruisers. The Oglaks refused to stay with us on the planet. Before he left, General Shsiska told me the Oglaks working on the surface said there is something wrong on Turt. They think the whole planet is going to have something bad happen to it.

I've ordered one of my cruisers to the Hika space station. I want Admiral Nonazk to give us an update on what's happening with the gravity around the collision. We are as close to the collision here, as the Hika are in our galaxy. Whatever is happening to them is probably happening here. Grol's scientists might have missed something Nonazk has detected. I think we should ask Grol to check the seismic activity on the entire planet of Turt. If there is unusual seismic activity occurring across the entire planet, that's a problem."

Jeonk walked to where Emperor Grol was speaking with his aides and informed him, "Shok is worried about Turt. He believes your planet may be in danger from the gravity pull of the collision. He just told me he sent one of his cruisers to the Hika space station to get an update on the collision from Admiral Nonazk. Nonazk is the Admiral in charge of the Hika space station. Shok suggested you check for unusual seismic activity everywhere on your planet."

Grol replied, "Shok didn't ask you before he dispatched one of his cruisers? I find it unbelievable that an Admiral would do that when his King is within asking distance."

Jeonk became testy at Grol's comment. He said, "If Shok had been on your side before you began your war, you would have won it. We had him on our side and we won it. He has the authority of the King, my authority, in all matters. He has that authority because he cares for nothing, more than he cares for the solution to our problems. He sees them first. He plans a solution first and he attacks the problems first. He needs, and uses my authority to do that. I respect him and his decisions more than any other living man. If he says you need to check the seismic activity on your planet, I suggest you do it."

Grol realized he had crossed the wrong boundary when he challenged Shok's actions. He replied, "Of course we'll check whatever Shok thinks we need to check. I apologize for not understanding Shok's importance, and for questioning your judgment in allowing him so much freedom of action. The seismic checks will begin as soon as I get to the surface."

Grol was as good as his word. He ordered data on the planets seismic activity as soon as he entered Tipa. His wait for its return was very short. The planet surface had already been covered with sensors because of their closeness to, and worries with, the collision.

The Imperial central office for seismic data collection had been trying to contact Grol. Its scientists had detected unusual seismic activity across the planet. Grol ordered four of his Imperial Fortresses to the collision area to gather new information from the collision but it would be several days before they reported back.

Grol asked Jeonk and Shok to look at the data with him. He didn't know how an Admiral and a King would be able to help but Jeonk had shown a great deal of faith in what Shok said, maybe one or both would have a suggestion.

Grol said, "Shok was right about the seismic activity. It's occurring damn near everywhere and it seems to be strong. Earthquakes are occurring in many different places on all of our continents. Volcanoes are appearing where none have ever been. The activities in Pik have grown to earthquake proportions. I'm told we have a volcano growing there, and it's getting bigger by the hour. Jeonk, you were right, we were lucky Pik was evacuated. Look at the data and give me your opinion. Maybe Shok will see something you or I are missing."

Both studied the seismic data for a few minutes. Jeonk turned to Shok and asked, "What do you think Shok? Do you think there is anything we can do?"

Shok answered, "Not much, except help with the evacuation of the planet."

Grol jumped up and exclaimed, "You think we have to evacuate the planet! Why should we do that?"

Shok replied, "If what I think is going to happen actually happens, everyone on this planet that isn't evacuated will die."

Jeonk looked sharply at Shok and said, "Shok, if you told me we had to evacuate a planet and I could do it, I would. But, I want to know why. Do you mind explaining your reasons?"

Shok explained, "This planet is obviously going through some kind of a global trauma. The unusual earthquakes and new volcanoes appearing globally are an indication there is a planetary shift of some kind about to happen. The only planetary shift I can think of, that seems similar, is one that has occurred on Earth. In the distant past, the magnetic field of the planet Earth has shifted, some say as many as fifty times in the history of the planet. The magnetic field nulls at the weakest point in the shift. During that null, the crust of the Earth can shift with it. The crust can slide around the magma in the Earth's center, like a loose skin.

"There is nearly total destruction of the population when the shift occurs. Oceans sweep over continents, the cold Polar Regions may become deserts; tropical areas and the warm areas on the planet may become frozen polar regions. Everything on the surface of the planet is displaced. How far the surface slides is unpredictable, but it doesn't really matter. Even a small shift can cause global floods, earthquakes, climate changes, and contamination of the atmosphere kills almost everyone."

Grol asked, "How fast does it happen and how can you be sure it is going to happen?"

Shok replied, "No one has ever witnessed one. No one has enough data to predict its beginning. The Earth's scientific theorists say it happens very fast. Once the shift begins it takes only hours to be completed.

"The theorists don't say how long it takes a planet to recover from the shift. As far as knowing it will happen, no one can be sure it will happen, but I've got a feeling in my gut that says this one isn't very far from its beginning. The feeling in my gut says days."

Grol angrily remarked, "I can't evacuate this planet in days. It would take several months of intensive effort just to evacuate most of the population. If I could, I wouldn't evacuate it because you know a planet such a shift may have occurred on, and you have a feeling in your gut about this one.

"I have already called for the most expert people in the Empire to make an assessment of the global problem. I will mention your magnetic shift theory to them. They may have more information on the subject than you do. If they think it's a possibility, I'll evacuate as many as I can while we wait to see if it actually happens."

Grol left to see how his experts were coming along, leaving Jeonk and Shok to themselves. Jeonk turned to Shok and said, "If the shift you're expecting begins while we are here, you and I will leave immediately."

"That will be too late," replied Shok. "Few will be able to leave this planet once it begins. Our cruisers won't be able to land and we'll be lucky if we can get a ship that is on the ground off of the surface."

"Let's get on board your flagship," Jeonk suggested. "Maybe the information you asked for from Admiral Nonazk will be waiting. I'll leave word so Grol can reach us if he needs anything.

"I think Grol will be glad we're gone. You gave him the worse news he's ever heard in his life. I told him you're always right. I might think you were wrong on this one if the Oglaks hadn't left because they think something bad is going to happen to this planet. They live on the inside of their planet and they develop a special sense for what is about to happen. I trust the Oglak's instincts."

"I hope I'm wrong about the shift," Shok remarked. "I've tried to come up with a less damaging solution to what's happening but my guts keep telling me I'm wrong when I find one."

Two days later the ship Shok sent to Admiral Nonazk began transmitting from a position where it could transmit and receive data to Shok's flagship and Admiral Nonazk's space station at the same time. The report received by Shok was shattering. Admiral Nonazk reported, "Two rogue suns have entered the collision area. The smaller sun has been traveling from the Milky Way galaxy toward the Magellanic Cloud. The largest sun is traveling from the Magellanic Cloud toward the Milky Way. The large sun could be causing the problems with the planet Turt.

"The two suns have been lining up on their opposite courses as they approached each other. Each sun has begun to accelerate due to their mutual attraction. The two rogues are now on a collision course that would cause magnetic and gravity changes on two of the Hika planets."

Nonazk was asking for permission to use the planet Nordic as an evacuation destination for the two planets. The evacuation to Nordic was already in progress. Jeonk gave his permission and requested instructions from Nonazk for whatever help they needed.

Jeonk suggested they take the Hika information to Grol. If the small sun was causing problems on the Hika planets, Grol certainly should be told about the large sun's possibility for the trouble on Turt. The Horde had no space station near the collision and the Horde had discontinued their usual surveillance during the war. The Horde were not watching for a rogue sun that just happened to be passing near Turt's solar system.

Grol had sent Imperial Fortress ships to the collision area to renew their surveillance. The Imperial Fortresses couldn't see the collision with the same broad view that the Hika space station could see with their probes. The Imperial Fortress crews might miss the importance of the two rogue suns until it was too late or they might not see them at all.

Jeonk and Shok entered Grol's office with the Hika data, including the present positions and speeds of the two rogue suns. When they handed the data to Grol, he didn't look at it. He said, "Wait here," and immediately took the data to his team of geophysicists.

Grol returned after a few minutes and said, "My experts have already told me that Shok may be right. We have the planetary evacuation in progress, but most of the geophysicists think it is too late to save the majority of people on the planet. They think Shok's guts were right.

"They didn't all agree about the probability of the planet's crust shifting but they did agree with his opinion that the planet's surface is breaking up, for whatever reason. Maybe the data Shok received from his friend on the space station will give us some kind of time table for the break up."

Jeonk offered, "Will you accept our help? We have thirty-one cruisers in a holding pattern above Turt. We can crowd approximately seven hundred extra people in each cruiser with our crews. All we need is the coordinates for a planet that will not be affected by the two colliding suns. We'll pick up your people wherever they are assembling to leave."

Grol gratefully responded, "We have everything we can get into the sky from seventeen planets coming here for the evacuation. Our problem is, we don't know how many of them can be here before this planet is destroyed. I'll be happy to have any help you can give. It's difficult to tell if our other planets will be affected, but none are reporting the same problems we're having on Turt.

"Our nearest evacuation destination is ten light years from here. The planet's name is Niklak. I'll give you the coordinates and I'll inform our people that you are assisting in the evacuation.

"I want people from every part of the planet to be evacuated. I don't want to evacuate the capital first and everyone else second. I can assign navigators to each of your ships with instructions to assist you in the evacuation of thirty-one major cities. Your cruiser commanders can concentrate on those same cities for your return trips until everyone is gone or the planet is unsafe to land on. Will that be all right with you?"

Jeonk shook his head yes and said, "Any way we can help is all right with us. Shouldn't you transfer your command headquarters to one of your Imperial destroyers? When this place comes apart, no one will be able to leave and Shok still thinks Turt's crust is going to shift. We don't have an Admiral in the fleet that will bet against one of Shok's gut feelings. Neither will any of our seven kings."

Grol laughed and replied, "I'm not betting against anything Shok says, gut feeling or not. I'm using the Imperials and everything else we have for the evacuation. I have a fighter standing by for emergency use. If my geophysicists tell me I have to go, I'll go. Until then I'm taking my chances like everyone else.

"Your ships and your crews will be in the same danger we are every minute they are on the surface. I noticed, your Majesty, you didn't hold one of your cruisers off of our surface for a command post. You are using all of them and your commands will be given from Shok's flagship while you and your crews are evacuating my people."

18
PLANET TURT'S HORRIBLE DEATH

There was no time wasted in getting to the evacuation sites after the navigators boarded the cruisers. Jeonk and Shok chose to help with the evacuation of a city close to Tipa. They wanted to be near the flow of information when they were on Turt. They were also convinced that Grol intended to remain on the planet until everyone else was evacuated. Shok was afraid that plan would get him killed. Neither Jeonk nor Shok wanted another Horde Emperor to take over the rule of the Empire. They felt they had come to a friendly understanding with Grol, and they wanted him alive.

They descended on their target city, Sokra, at a spaceport near its center. Horrendous crowds of people were anxiously waiting for evacuation. There was a Horde spacecraft being filled with frightened evacuees as Shok's flagship landed. The city police quickly established exit avenues for the crowds to approach the waiting Argan cruiser but the panic to leave the city was obvious and overwhelming.

The crowds pushed the police and each other along the wavering lines of fearful evacuees. The exit lines were broken and the evacuees rushed toward the cruiser in their panic to leave. Stronger people knocked weaker ones down, and some were trampled in the mad dash for the cruiser. Jeonk ordered the ships Marines to maintain order at the cruiser's entrance hatches to keep the cruiser from being overrun by the fear-crazed citizens. Shok remarked, "It's like the last flight out of Hell."

"That's not too far from wrong," Jeonk agreed. "There are only minutes between strong earth tremors. I've felt several since we've been on the ground. Have your guts given you an updated schedule on the crust shift?"

"No," Shok replied, "but I think it will happen any time from right now until it happens and that will be real soon. I think we should tell our crews that they are to remain on their ships for all future rescues. We should take whoever makes it to the cruisers without considering how they got there, or who was hurt and couldn't make it.

"If the crust begins to shift while the cruisers are on the ground, they are to get into the air first and close the hatches second. If there is poor judgment in guessing the right time, the poor judgment will be automatically overlooked. The crews will only have a few seconds to get airborne. The crews are not to give consideration to anyone falling out of the hatches, or almost making it to the ship. Put each cruiser in the air before closing its hatches, slam the thrusters to one hundred percent, and clear the surface as quickly as possible.

"An area that is flat now can be a mountain before you can say spit. A dry plain can become an ocean in minutes. The wind may reach a thousand miles an hour. An ocean can become a tidal wave that washes over a continent. Everything will happen suddenly. Survivors will be rare."

"I know you're right,' Jeonk replied, "we've lost enough of our people to the Horde. Helping them is good. Dying for them is out. You stay on the command pedestal. I'll give the order to the fleet from the communications console right now."

The first of the panicked evacuees were loaded. The hatches had to be closed in the faces of those still trying to board the cruiser. The Argan cruiser commanders at the other evacuation cities reported the same experiences with their passengers.

As Shok's flagship gained altitude, the reasons for the desperation became apparent. Large rifts were forming in the planets crust. In some areas lava could be seen spewing out of the rifts. In others, ocean water flooded into the rifts and great plumes of steam rose thousands of feet in the air. Mountains were rising out of the oceans and coastal cities disappeared below the rising water. Millions of people were dying on the surface of Turt.

Shok ordered, "All cruisers, flank speed, maybe we can get back to rescues one more load before this planet blows its top."

Ten light years is just a short hop for the Argan cruisers. They reached the planet Niklak and descended to let the passengers debark. The debarkation was very orderly. The evacuees were met by friendly people waiting to give them help and congratulations for their lucky escape from Turt. The bedlam on the planet they had just escaped from was exchanged for the sanity of the untroubled planet they escaped to. The cruisers dropped their passengers and set a flank speed course for the bedlam of Turt, hoping to snatch one more load from the chaos of its seismic insanity.

The cruiser between the planet Turt and the Hika space station transmitted Admiral Nonazk's reported, "The two Hika planets are still evacuating. They have yet to suffer the extensive damage of Turt but the survival of the two planets is very much in doubt. We are moving our space station farther back from the galactic collision area. I hope the move will keep it from being destroyed by the double super nova I fear might occur when the two rogue suns collided."

As the cruisers approached within visual range of Turt, it became obvious they couldn't land. The planet Turt had become a death spewing open wound. The spacecraft with the last loads of survivors were fighting to get above the boiling debris that had become its atmosphere. Thick dust, smoke and rift ripping volcanic fire filled the air. Rescue ships of all sizes fought their way through the super heated air and horrendous winds to reach safe altitudes.

Shok ordered the cruisers' Commanders to use their tractor beams to help any ship they could locate in the tortured atmosphere to rise above the planet's death throes.

Jeonk and Shok set their course for where they thought Tipa might still be. Their scanners were useless. Everything on the surface of Turt was in motion. Mountain ranges were being sucked into chasms of fire. The oceans had become tidal waves of terror, sweeping everything alive and dead before them. Fiery rifts ripped the planet's surface from pole to pole. Mountain high waves of lava slithered across the planet's surface for thousands of miles, sped onward by the planet's crust rushing below in the opposite direction.

Out of that caldron of death rose one Horde fighter, desperately attempting to battle its way to safety through the twisting atmosphere. Jeonk yelled, "There he is Shok. Put a tractor beam on him. Maybe we can pull him out of there."

Shok reacted instantly, saying, "I've got him but we need to gain enough altitude to get us both out of here. We're pulling him sideways." They slowly gained altitude, towing the Horde fighter higher into clear space with the cruiser's tractor beam.

Jeonk grabbed the radio and asked, "You in the fighter; are you Emperor Grol?"

The pilot answered, "This is Grol, thanks for the lift. My wife and I will be in your debt for a long time. Can you tractor beam us on board? We were hit by something after we lifted off and my controls have stopped responding."

The fighter was quickly tractor-beamed on board. Jeonk and Shok went to the landing bay to greet the lucky couple. As Grol and his wife stepped out of the fighter, Grol asked, "How did you happen to be at the right place at the right time?"

"We thought you would be the last to leave," Jeonk replied. "When we returned and couldn't land, Shok ordered our cruisers to use their tractor beams to help anyone they could to lift off of the surface. We decided to make an effort to locate you and see if you were going to make it off the planet, and you told us you had a fighter waiting. Tipa wasn't where it used to be but we saw you working your way out of the atmosphere from its new location. Shok put a beam on you and that did it."

Grol's wife pointed at Shok and said, "This is the famous Shok?"

Shok answered, "That's right, I'm Shok."

She reached over, grabbed him around the shoulders and gave him a hug. She said, "That is for having smart guts. Our scientists almost got us killed. My husband said, 'Shok was right. This whole damn planet is shifting. We have to leave now or die.' He put hard hands on my arm and made me run to our fighter. Those scientists who said it wouldn't shift evacuated themselves before they could die from being wrong. I thought we were going to die in the fighter but you saved us again. Shok, if you ever ask anything of my husband and he says no, I will throw him out of our bedroom."

Jeonk rescued Shok from the necessity of a response. He said, "We have a rather nice galley on board. Can I offer you some refreshment? Shok and I like a cup of coffee after a close call. Coffee is a drink Shok gets from the planet Earth and you may not like it. Something else may be more suitable for you. We have some Turt wine you might like."

Grol and his wife insisted on having coffee with Jeonk and Shok. They showed no dislike for it but declined a second cup. Grol said, "I need to inform my people that we are safe. Can you do that?"

"It's been done," Jeonk answered. "Our Communications Officer contacted your people as soon as you were safely inside. I expect one of your destroyers will be here soon to take you on board."

Grol asked, "What are your plans now that you can't rescue any more of your former enemies? I would like, very much, to show you the hospitality of a grateful Empire and my personal gratitude for what you have done for me and my wife."

Jeonk explained the necessity of refusing his offer, "There are two planets in what we call the Hika group. They are on the other side of the collision in our galaxy and they are being evacuated now. We are going there to give them whatever assistance we can before their planets go through the same disaster Turt suffered. They began their evacuation before you did but it's unlikely they will be able to save all of their people.

"We have transports coming from Arga to help and our cruisers will also be used as transports. They think the most damaging part of their disaster will begin as the two suns close the distance between them just before they collide. They think they will lose both of their planets after the suns collide. We have three or four months before their major problems begin occurring but I don't know the time they have calculated for the collision of the two suns."

Grol was thoughtful for a moment. His wife reached over and pinched his arm. He looked at her and said, "All right, I'm just planning what to do."

She remarked, "While your planning, plan to tell these wonderful gentlemen my name."

Grol pulled his mind from the problem and said, "My wife's name is Aklee, and I think I can give you some help with the Hika group. Turt is the only planet on our side that will be in the danger area. We still had about four thousand spacecraft on the ground when the shift started and I think we lost most of them and most of the population of Turt. I don't want the same thing happening to your Hika friends. I'll have every spacecraft we can fly helping to move the Hika people wherever you want them. Is that plan all right with you Aklee?"

Without waiting for Aklee's answer, he continued. "In the next four months we can put a massive number of spacecraft to work on the evacuation. I wonder if we can save all of their people. I hope so. I'll take command of our part of the operation myself. I'll transfer Aklee to Niklak to keep her safe."

Aklee abandoned her quiet manner at Grol's last remark, "You will not transfer me to Niklak. You didn't get rid of that crazy Emperor when I told you to, and you were wrong. You didn't listen to me when I told you not to fight the war, and you were wrong. You didn't believe Shok about Turt, and you were wrong. I'm going with you but I promise not to interfere until Shok's guts say we have to leave; then, I'm going to interfere."

Grol was wise enough to know marital defeat when he heard it. He said, "You can stay by my side during the entire operation if you want to, but you will be the only woman on the command deck of the Imperial."

Aklee retorted, "I hate calling those big things Imperials or Imperial Fortresses. Jeonk and Shok call them destroyers and they look like destroyers. We should call them destroyers like they do. I don't care if I am the only woman on that destroyer. I will be doing something worth doing. There will be plenty of women leaving those planets and they should know another woman is helping."

19
RESCUE OF THE DYING HIKA PLANETS

Grol's destroyer arrived as Jeonk predicted. Grol left to make his arrangements. Shok turned the two Argan fleets toward the Hika planets to help rescue their people. Jeonk decided to make another visit to Admiral Nonazk's space station for a personal update on the rogue suns positions and conditions. The two fleets were going to need the latest information if they were to help with the evacuation.

Admiral Nonazk was glad to explain the situation. He related, "No one knows where the two suns came from originally. I think the larger came from the Attack Galaxy and the small one came from ours. The large one caused the destruction of Turt as it angled into the collision area. It seems to have a tremendous gravitational field, much larger than one would expect. Its gravity interacted with Turt's and flipped Turt's crust.

"I think it's a fluke for the two suns to be on a collision course. Neither began their journeys close enough together to draw one to the other. They just happen to be going in opposite directions and as they traveled closer to each other, the gravity of one began interacting with the gravity of the other. Now, nothing can stop them from colliding."

Jeonk asked, "Do you have a time table for the collision? I would also like to know when your planets will be so affected that evacuation efforts must stop."

The Admiral replied, "We don't have an accurate time for the collision. The suns' increasing collision speeds are controlled by their gravity and we have no way to accurately calculate the gravity of either. We have an idea from their size but neither is in the normal spectrum.

"They have no planets orbiting them. The two suns aren't in the orbit of either galaxy and they aren't going in the direction the galactic collision should be sending them. They are too high up to have been a part of the collision and both of them seem to be rogue travelers from God knows where.

"Their collision speed will be increased by an unknown rate as their gravitational attraction brings them closer together. We think the collision will occur no sooner than four months, but how much later would be a guess.

"The first problem will be when the smaller sun passes close to our two planets. They are in neighboring solar system and the affected planets will be closest to each other during the next three months. The smaller sun will pass between them but closer to the planet Ker.

"I thought at first the two planets could survive but I've changed my mind. The sun passing between them won't kill them but it can cause some severe problems with earthquakes and tidal waves.

"The killer will be the collision. The impact speed of the two suns will be fast enough to possibly force the smaller sun to pass through the larger. If it does or doesn't, there will be a killer debris field created, and both of our planets will be in the path of the debris. The only way they can survive is for a miracle to happen. The massive amount of debris will have to miss our planets.

"For a long time I was afraid the two suns might become supernovas. We would lose all of our planets if that happened. The mass of the two suns will be spread too far too quickly by the collision for them to explode like a supernova but explode they will and there is no stopping it. All we can do is try to get our people out of its way."

Shok asked, "How is the evacuation going. Does it look like everyone will make it off of the two planets?"

Admiral Nonazk shook his head and replied, "No, our spacecraft are too slow to get them all off. We haven't enough spacecraft to move that many people and we must supply those we move with food until they can grow their own on Nordic. We can't move them to another planet and then let them starve. We think we can get nineteen percent off and that's the upper limit of our transportation."

Jeonk recommended, "Stop using your transports for food. The planets on our side of the galaxy will supply the food until the evacuees become self-sufficient. If Nordic isn't big enough for the population of the two planets, we'll move some of them to Prssk. It has two continents that are nearly empty and most of Prssk's land is good farmland.

"You are going to receive help in your evacuation. We have fast transports coming from Arga and we can use our cruiser fleets as transports. The Horde has a new Emperor named Grol and he has promised to send every ship he can to help. He was on Turt when it was destroyed He said he didn't want to see the same thing happen to your people. You'll be seeing his ships coming very soon. Your nineteen percent can more than triple. I hope we can get them all off."

Shok, on hearing Jeonk's gift of Prssk to the Hika, remarked, "The Prsskians may be unhappy with the loss of two continents. Are you and I going to call on the Prsskians and explain the situation."

Jeonk replied, "No, I think Rakoup and my father will do the explaining. They fear Rakoup and my father more than they want to kill you and me. Prssk wont be a problem. They need decent people on Prssk, even if Prssk Command is suspicious of decency."

Shok turned to the Admiral and asked, "What are the evacuation plans? We need to know where to load the evacuees from your planets and we need the know where to land them on Nordic. We can begin immediately."

Admiral Nonazk picked up an astrological map from a nearby table and put it on his desk. He explained, "The two planets are here and here. There are places for debarkation in thirty major cities on each planet. The populations of both planets know they must leave. No matter where you land near people, they will fill your ships and leave without question.

"There is an Evacuation Communications Center on each planet. Both centers are operating on a receiver frequency of one hundred gigahertz. Their transmitting frequency is ninety-nine gigahertz. You can transmit and receive information about either planet on those two frequencies if you want to coordinate your efforts with them. You will not have a problem filling your ships, however you want to do it."

As a parting shot, Jeonk asked, "Where are your family? Are they on one of the planets we will be evacuating?"

The Admiral pointed to his map and said, "They are here on Ker."

Jeonk continued, "I'll send our fighters to pick your families up wherever they are. I can do that while we are loading other evacuees on the cruisers. The fighters can join us in space to prevent a delay in our cruisers' departures."

The Admiral said nothing. He reached for his pen and spent a moment writing instructions for the rescue of his family. He handed the information to Jeonk and said, "They will be in these two places and their names are listed. Thank you! My worry for them is ended. I still have many worries about some of the families of personnel on the station. Many of them have families on the two planets."

Jeonk suggested, "Have them inform their families to assemble at two locations, one on each planet, but not at one of the thirty pre-determined locations. I'll have cruisers take them to Nordic at the first opportunity. I'll contact you in two days for the pick up locations."

Shok asked, "Your opinion about the collision has changed since I last received information from you. You were going to move your space station back from the collision, but you can't move it very far. Do you still think the station can escape the effects of the colliding suns and, if not, what are your evacuation plans for the station crew?"

The Admiral replied, "We have a chance for survival here but not a very good one. The people you are evacuating have no other chance, except for evacuation. Our transports will be used for those with no chance."

Shok said, "You have, maybe, two thousand people here and they are some of your best technical people. We can get them off and we should. They will be needed later. Your job here is finished. One of our transports will take you off as soon as the first ones arrive, with your permission of course."

The Admiral shook his head and said, "Thank you one more time. I will move the station as far as I can. If it survives it will still be useful. We will be ready to leave when your transports arrives."

The Argan fleets were divided. One set its course for Ker to help the people there. The other was on a course for the planet Ast to aid in its evacuation. Shok and Jeonk took the planet Ker. It was the nearest and would be the first and worst hit. During their inbound descent on Ker, Jeonk ordered four fighters launched for the rescue of Admiral Nonazk's family.

The Hika evacuation wasn't as panic-driven as the one on Turt. There was more time and the planets' surfaces were still secure. It would be at least two more months before the people began to panic.

The cruiser fleets and transports from Arga began arriving before Shok's fleet made its first departure from Ker. The Royal Cruiser was among the cruiser fleets, with Jeonk and Shok's wives on board. There was no reunion of husbands and wives; everyone was too busy to bother with a reunion. They would have to see each other as time and circumstances permitted. The Royal Cruiser was immediately pressed into service as a transport and joined the other spacecraft in the flights from Ker to Nordic.

The evacuee encampments on Nordic were a pattern of chaos. People were landed quickly and left to their own ingenuity to find living quarters and to establish all of the necessary organizations required by a displaced population. The evacuees brought food with them but it wouldn't last long. It was apparent, to even a casual observer, that the food situation would become desperate in a very short time.

Shok ordered the fleet fighters to remain on Nordic to transport the excess food from the Nordic population to the Hika population. Two fighters would remain with each cruiser; the other thirteen fighters from each cruiser were ordered to remain on Nordic to be used for food transports and whatever other utility reasons they might serve. The empty fighter spaces on the cruisers would be used for more Hika passengers. Shok also ordered the fleet Marines to remain on Nordic to serve as police. The extra space that created would be used for additional Hika passengers. With the removal of the fighters and the Marines, each fleet could carry a much larger number of evacuees.

The wives, Aslain and Alice, joined their husbands in Shok's flagship when they reached Nordic. The Commander of the Royal Cruiser kept it in service as a fleet transport.

The return to Ker was uneventful until they were close enough to see the amount of traffic leaving Ker and Ast. Emperor Grol, once more, was true to his word. Every size and shape of Horde spacecraft was either landing on or taking off from the two planets. The massive amount of evacuees was staggering. Very large Horde cargo ships were bypassing the two planets to continue on a course for Nordic.

Grol and Aklee were on board Grol's Command destroyer stationed between Ker and Ast. Aslain and Alice were filled with curiosity about the Grols. They were adamant about making a, purely diplomatic, visit.

Shok said to Jeonk, privately, "If we don't go, they'll take one of the fighters and go by themselves. We should pay the Grol's a visit anyway. We need to know how Grol is controlling the Horde side of the evacuation. There may be some way we can cooperate to increase the number of evacuees. At any rate, it will be good for Aklee to know she isn't the only woman who is helping."

Grol and Aklee met them in the destroyers docking bay. Introductions were made and Aklee immediately reached out for Aslain and Alice's arms and said, "We must do some planning together. Men are good for the evacuation but they leave everything else to someone else. I had to force Yit to send things those people will need later."

Shok looked at Grol and said, "Your first name is Yit?"

Grol replied, "In your language, Yit means tender."

Jeonk and Shok tried not to laugh but they didn't quit make it. Grol saw the affect his name had on them and understood the reason they were laughing. He began laughing with them and said, "I had to live that name down after I became a military man. I never liked it but I'm stuck with it. Fortunately, I acquired enough rank to keep everyone but my wife from calling me Yit."

To change the subject, Jeonk asked, "We saw some very large cargo ships bypassing Ker on a heading for Nordic. Do you mind telling me what is in them?"

Grol answered, "Toilets, tents, water purification systems and food. Aklee insisted on the toilets and tents. She was right. They will be needed. She also insisted on nursing supplies for babies. I'm sure there will be babies born on Nordic but I assumed the mothers have most of the feeding supplies on their persons. Aklee pointed out that babies dying on Nordic are just as dead as anyone else dying on Ker or Ast. She was right again."

Shok asked, "Do you have an estimate of how many people will be evacuated by the ships you're bringing into the area?"

Grol replied, "The military spacecraft will be able to move about three million a day. I have asked for additional transports from every source in the Empire. How many more we can move depends on the responses to my request but I expect the civilian spacecraft to evacuate more than our military ships. I can't calculate the number until I see how we are doing.

"I have seen many non-military transports arriving since I've been here and I'm sure many others will be coming from the more distant planets. Moving billions of people in three or four months seems out of reach no matter what we do."

Jeonk suggested, "It might be a good idea to use your large cargo ships for transports after they make their delivery to Nordic. It was a good idea to send the initial supplies. They will be badly needed.

"I've contacted the Galactic Forum nations and told them of the problem and I asked them to send food and supplies to Nordic. More than eight hundred nations will be sending everything the Hika people can use on Nordic. Our Galactic Forum ships will be slower than your cargo ships. The supplies you sent will hold Nordic until ours arrive. Your faster and larger cargo ships may be able to lift more of the Hika people out of danger."

Aklee returned at that moment and said, "Yit, Aslain and Alice tell me they have plenty of supplies for Nordic coming from planets in their galaxy. We can stop using our cargo ships for food and other supplies. We can change them to people transports. What do you think about that?"

"We were just discussing that," Grol answered, "and it's a great suggestion; thank the ladies for me and tell them to consider it done."

He turned to Jeonk and said, "Stay with us for a while. Shok can tell his Vice Admiral to pick up a load of evacuees, take them to Nordic and pick you up on the next trip or you can stay here for the duration of the evacuation and help me keep it organized. We can contact the ships in both of our fleets with the equipment on board, and it is very powerful equipment, just as good as yours."

"We'll stay for a while," Jeonk replied. "When the action gets rough on the surface of Ker, Shok and I will leave. It's difficult to stay out of the action. There always seems to be something more we can do if we are at the center of it."

"I noticed that every time we've met. Especially the first time," remarked Grol. "I wouldn't think of keeping the two of you out of the action. Let's join our wives. Shok can contact his Vice from there."

The joint effort turned out to be a good idea. Each of them knew their different operations and was able to consolidate the evacuation effort. The thirty evacuation points on Ker and Ast were increased to forty. There were many times when spacecraft were ordered to use other cities for pickup stations because of the increased space traffic for the forty. At the end of two months, more Horde spacecraft were still arriving from the distant Horde planets and the Galactic Forum ships were beginning to arrive to evacuate even more.

Shok commented, "The space between Nordic, Ker and Ast is beginning to look like a people moving sidewalk. Keeping track of the number of people being evacuated is impossible. Every ship of every size is landing, being stuffed with people and taking off immediately. There is no time to do anything except make sure each ship is carrying as many as it can."

Grol added, "You know, the saddest fact is, the Hika people who are working the hardest to make sure everyone else escapes will be the people who are lost because they worked too long and too hard to be able to escape themselves. That's the way it was on Turt. The police, the military people, and most of those helping others to escape, were left behind, and died."

"We'll get them all out if it's possible," Jeonk stated, "but I never worry about those good people. They are God's heroes and God takes care of his own. Shok believes that too. One time I asked him why he believes in God and he said, 'I feel it in my guts. That's why I'm a Catholic. I know God in my guts.' Others call it faith, but Shok has his own way of saying things."

"Don't tell that to Aklee or she'll become a Catholic," Grol remarked, "whatever that is. She thinks Shok's gut feelings are as powerful as prophecy."

Jeonk continued, "Shok's wife is also a Catholic and she has probably already told Aklee. Our wives have been together for two months and I haven't seen them stop talking since they met. If I were you, I would begin looking forward to a trip to Shok's planet Earth for religious reasons."

"Are you a Catholic?" Grol asked.

"Well, almost," Jeonk replied. "Shok and I, a few years ago, with help from Aslain and Alice, arranged a merger between our religion and his Catholic religion. It's almost complete. We believe pretty much the same things and the differences are minor."

Grol remarked, "Shok changes everything around him without seeming to notice the changes himself. He deals with circumstances seen once in a lifetime as though he was in training to take care of them all of his life."

Jeonk laughed and said, "That's Shok, while everyone else is bogged down in details, he cuts to the heart of a problem in an instant.

"His wife is just like him. My wife and Alice have been very close friends for years. I haven't seen Alice and Aslain make such a quick deep friendship with anyone before they met Aklee. Its like they found a long lost sister."

Grol shook his head and said, "Good grief, I wonder what my wife will come up with after two months with them?"

The three ladies came into the compartment and the conversation stopped. Alice asked, "Jeonk, do you know where Shok is? I haven't seen him in two or three hours. I hope he didn't go to Ker. The Communications Officer said they are beginning to have strong earthquakes. Aslain and I are leaving with you and Shok when things get dangerous. We're going to be with you on Ker. Isn't that right Aslain?"

Aslain replied supportively, "That's right and we want you to fly the Royal Cruiser. It's the best cruiser we have. If things begin going crazy on Ker, and we need to leave in a hurry, I want to be sure we have our best chance to get off of the surface of Ker in one piece."

Jeonk replied, "Shok and I don't intend to do anything dangerous. This evacuation isn't like the one on Turt. Ker may shake for a while as the small sun passes it, but they will still have a month to evacuate before the two suns collide. After that, we don't know how much time they will have. The evacuation shouldn't be dangerous until then."

Aklee asked, "Yit, how many people have been evacuated as of now?"

Grol replied, "We have no count from the surface of Ker or Ast. There are more than five hundred thousand spacecraft from twenty-four planets lifting people off of the two planets and each is full when it leaves. The largest carries thirty thousand and the smallest can carry fifty people. I think about half of the population of both planets have been moved to Nordic.

"We can't get them all off and I'm sorry about that, but they won't die like the people of Turt. We lost more than ninety percent of the people on Turt because we didn't know what was coming until it was too late."

Aklee remarked, "The people are leaving everything behind, all of their personal possessions, extra clothing, family memorabilia and anything else that takes up the space needed by another person. I hope their planet isn't so devastated they can't come back later and salvage something of their lives here."

Shok came into the compartment with one of Grol's officer and heard Aklee's last remark. "If Admiral Nonazk is right," Shok stated, "Ker and Ast will be as thoroughly destroyed as Turt. Pieces of the big sun will hit them hard enough to turn them inside out. Your planets will be tracking the debris going the other way for years to come. Ours will be doing the same type of tracking to make sure the debris doesn't become dangerous to us. No one can be certain of the direction the debris will take after an impact like this."

Jeonk asked, "Shok, do you mind asking the Communications Officer to inform the Commander of the Royal Cruiser that we want it returned here. Aslain and Alice want us to use it instead of your flagship."

Shok laughed and answered, "Aslain and Alice did that two days ago. It will be here in a three hours and twenty seven minutes."

Alice gave Shok a disappointed look and said, "Kevin Kelly, Don't you ever miss anything. We wanted you and Jeonk to think we were getting your permission to use it."

"We intended to use it anyway," Jeonk informed the two ladies.

Shok stated, "I've gotten to know the destroyer's command deck personnel pretty well since we arrived, and I've spent a lot of time with the communications staff. The Communications Officer told me Aslain had radioed the Royal Cruiser Commander. That's why I didn't transmit to the cruiser myself. Jeonk told me you and Aslain would want us to use it."

The Royal Cruiser arrived on schedule. The Argans took their leave of the Grols, and their destroyer, to continue on in their own style. The Royal Cruiser was a mess. Every compartment had been stuffed with evacuees during its many trips to Nordic and it was easy to see the evidence of children among the passengers. There were sticky smudges everywhere and little fingerprints marred every shining surface. The crew did their best to straighten things up on the return trips but it was a fruitless effort. Each new trip brought new kids, new smears, and new sticky smudges.

The descent to the surface of Ker brought the Argans close to the desperation of the evacuees. The people of Ker were becoming more panicky with each passing day. They could see the oncoming sun in the sky and it appeared larger each day. The frequent earth tremors kept them aware of how little time they had before the doomsday sun would impact with its big brother and destroy their planet, and the homes they were now desperate to leave.

The Kerians were well organized for handling the volatile crowds of evacuees. Large stores of food had been brought to the evacuation points. The feeding areas were going night and day and available spaces on the outgoing spacecraft were given on a first come first to leave basis.

A color code system was in force for the departures. Each group of evacuees was given a different colored ticket. A colored light with the color of the group's tickets was shown when a spacecraft was available for that particular group and the tickets were handed out far in advance of the appearance of the spacecraft.

There was very little criminal activity. The only thing worth stealing was a ticket out, and anyone could have one free. There were some attempts to buy tickets for an earlier departure, but there were few sales. The ticket holders kept their tickets under close control to keep them from being stolen or misplaced.

The looting of property was virtually non-existent. Large areas of the planet were now emptied and anyone who wanted any part of what was left could have it. Those who might have been looters realized there was no place to take the loot that was waiting for anyone who wanted it.

The only official departure priority was for the farmers. Everyone knew the farmers would be essential to life on Nordic. There was no argument about the farm priority. Most of the people didn't know about the priority and the farmers had been lifted off of Ker on earlier flights leaving from evacuation points in the center of the farm areas.

Governments, being what they are, had supplied special spacecraft for high ranking officials and anyone else with a little clout. They had already been lifted out on Hika ships. The Argan and the Horde spacecraft weren't involved.

The Argans made an inspection tour of the planet and it showed a small number of people still remaining in almost all of the emptied areas of the planet. These were the people who refused to leave their homes and the lives they had there.

Jeonk brought the Royal Cruiser to a landing in one of the areas in an attempt to get some of them to leave. Most were adamant in there decision to stay. They were offered a tour of the Royal Cruiser to try to change their minds. All accepted the tour out of simple curiosity, and a few of them accepted the offer to be taken to Nordic on it. Most of them gave their thanks for the tour and returned to await their doom or deliverance. Many thought there would be some last minute miraculous salvation from certain doom, but they would accept whatever fortune fate brought with it in the place they called home.

The earthquakes became devastating as the rogue sun passed closer to Ker. The evacuation stations were hardest hit because they were near urban centers crowded with people. Buildings swayed in the quakes until their foundations crumbled and brought them down. Streets that had been passable before the quakes ended on cliffs rising from the torn earth. Every city became an obstacle course of fallen and burning buildings. Those waiting for rescue scattered in every direction in a vain hope of finding safety from the chaos that was everywhere.

Tidal waves rushed over coastal cities and spread inland, sometimes up to sixty miles. Volcanic eruptions occurred across the planet. Forests became uncontrolled blazing infernos spewing smoke across the land like a dirty blanket to cover the dead.

For four days the waiting spacecraft couldn't land. The rogue sun gouged the planet with its canon of lethal gravity, killing indiscriminately. The raging earth covered everyone in the wrong place at the wrong time. The rolling earthquakes could be seen from space as giant waves of land crossing the continents and tossing, or covering, everything in their paths. The waves of land forcing their passages in different directions met in explosive bursts of pure fury, hurling their dirty faces to the sky. The position of the rogue sun could be determined by the angle of any patch of water on the planet. The high edge of the water pointed toward the rogue sun, pulled by its gravity.

For the waiting space crews, the four days passed with great tension. They feared their job would be ended by the rogue sun's destruction of the people of Ker. When they could land once more, with some hope of getting their spacecraft airborne again, searches were made for the population. The crews knew the survivors would be scattered far from the usual pickup points by the devastation. The dead would never be counted but the survivors could be rescued, if they could be found.

Ships of every size scanned the planet for survivors. Some were found, but they weren't in large enough groups to fill even the smaller spacecraft. Jeonk and Grol made the decision to move the larger spacecraft to Ast. They would leave the smaller spacecraft on Ker and keep them scanning for one week. If they could locate survivors they would continue their searches. If the week passed and they could no longer find evacuees, they would transfer that rescue effort to Ast and save the most they could from the coming destruction.

Ast hadn't been hit as hard as Ker. Most of their pickup points were still in operation. The doom of the people on Ker was good fortune for the people of Ast. The number of transports on Ast nearly doubled. Ast lost hundreds of thousands in their earthquakes but most of the people survived, and Ast's evacuation system was still largely intact.

Ast used a similar system to the one used by Ker in its rescue effort. All ships left full and none of the waiting ships waited aloft for directions. If there wasn't an immediate pick up at one of the usual places, the spacecraft landed to load passengers wherever they found people. The Ker side of Shok's sidewalk to safety had collapsed but the Ast side was wider than ever.

The people of Ast had been told of the disaster on Ker and how much damage it did. There was no panic, but extreme urgency could be seen in the quick way they loaded into the waiting transports. People who had lived on the friendly planet all of their lives no longer trusted the land under their feet. Each of them wanted to be gone as soon as he could get gone. Each showed it with the quick movement toward the waiting spacecraft. Families clutched at each other fearing one of them would be lost. Mothers counted and recounted their children as they came closer to the departing spacecraft. Parents knew the loss of a child under these circumstances would undoubtedly be a permanent loss.

Young husbands and wives held hands tightly and remained very close to one another. The pregnant wives were especially fearful. When an Argan crewmember found a pregnant woman waiting to be loaded, he picked her up in his big arms and signaled her husband to follow. He moved her immediately to the interior of the ship and found her the most comfortable and private place to stay. Each cruiser carried a doctor, and pregnant women were sometimes taken directly to the infirmary for the delivery of a child.

The days of the evacuation passed in furious activity, always with an eye on the rogue suns speeding to their inevitable impact.

The Grol's contacted Jeonk, and asked him if he intended to make a close up inspection of the two suns. They wanted to make an inspection but their destroyer was too busy. If they used it, the destroyer crew would lose control of the evacuation process.

Jeonk hadn't considered an up close look but the ladies were all for it. They reasoned that a better time frame for the impact might add to the evacuation effort. After the ladies pressured him for a while, Jeonk decided to pick up the Grols in the Royal Cruiser and get a closer look at the two suns.

A close look at a sun isn't very close. The closest they got to the smaller of the suns was twenty million miles. Even then, the blast shields on the Royal Cruiser were closed and the look they got was from the command pedestal holograph. Every scan put more information on the holograph.

The doomsday suns didn't look more dangerous than any other sun. They were nothing more than two boiling spheres of fire slowly spinning on the command pedestal display. It was the knowledge of what was going to happen to them that gave the gut wrenching feeling in the pits of the viewers' stomachs.

Shok said, "If we clock the time from when the small sun passed between Ker and Ast to the time of the impact, we'll have the time it will take the debris from the impact to reach Ast. We need to make some allowances for the impact explosion to increase the speed of the debris but the clock time will give us an idea."

"After the impact," Grol added, "we can clock the debris' speed and be more accurate. I'll have some people on station to do that. I've already contacted our scientists and ordered them to track what's left of the two planet killers as their debris field works its way toward our planets.

"The Milky Way galaxy should get the heaviest load of debris," Shok remarked, "but Admiral Nonazk said he didn't' think it would endanger our home planets."

As the Royal Cruiser's command deck parties interest in the two suns began to lessen, Jeonk received important information from his cruisers that were taking off from Ast. Gamac and Prsskian spacecraft had been sighted at several locations on Ast.

The report said the Milky Way's most notorious pirates at first concentrated on deserted banks. The Hika had removed all of the precious metals from their banks and hid them in the safest places they could find. The Hika hoped to come back after the danger was over and retrieve their precious metal for use on Nordic.

The Gamacs and Prsskians had no luck with the banks. They couldn't find where the gold was hidden. They were now concentrating on the richer appearing mansions and anything else that looked profitable. They were steering clear of the evacuation effort, and didn't seem to be a danger to anything but deserted real estate.

Aklee said, "I can't believe anyone would loot a dying planet."

"Looting is the least of their crimes," Aslain responded. "The Prsskians and the Gamacs are involved in nearly every interplanetary crime in our galaxy. The Gamacs kidnapped Alice from Earth, took her to Prssk, and then sold her to the Mogs to work in a mine where they were digging for black hole metal. That's where Jeonk and Shok found her. She was almost dead when they rescued her."

Grol sat up at the mention of black hole metal. He looked at Shok and asked, "Is that where you found the pellets you used on us?"

"Yes," Shok replied, "but they weren't pellets when we found them. We used a small amount of the Mog metal to make the pellets. The chunk of black hole metal the pellets came from destroyed most of the life on the planet where we found Alice. The air was so foul on Mog-5 that the only ones who could breathe it, and live very long were the Mogs. One of the Mog's many Black Hole Mine problems was slaves dying before they could finish the Job. Alice was the last Earth slave left alive."

Alice asked, "Are we going to chase the Gamacs and Prsskians off of Ast, or just let them loot?"

"Let them loot," Jeonk replied. "They can't get anything important. They probably don't know when the suns will collide and they won't know when to leave the planet until they see the debris coming at them. If a few Gamacs and Prsskians don't make it off the planet on time, who will cry about that? The crime rate everywhere else will go down a little, that's all."

Alice still wanted to go after the thieves, "I think we should find out why they are on Ast. I think we should go after them just to be certain they aren't hurting anyone or anything. There are still people on Ast they could be killing. They could be taking slaves and no one will know. We cannot allow the Gamacs, or the Prsskians, to capture slaves and do nothing about it. "

Aslain joined Alice's campaign, "We can't let the galaxies worst criminals roam at will. Alice is right they could be taking slaves. It's our duty to make sure they aren't."

Jeonk answered, "You win ladies. We'll check it out." He turned to the Grol's and asked, "Do you want us to take you back to your ship or would you prefer to go Gamac and Prssk hunting with us? We can return before the two suns collide. I think a close look at the collision will be important."

Grol asked, " Aklee, what do you want to do? I would like to see if Aslain and Alice are right."

"I'm just as curious as you are," Aklee replied. "I want to see what this galaxy's worst criminals are doing on Ast."

Grol turned to Jeonk, and said, "My crew know they can contact me on your ship. We'll stay with you."

The return to Ast gave them a renewed confidence in the evacuation. The evacuation centers were running full blast but it was easy to see they were nearing the end of the evacuation. The outlying areas were nearly empty of space traffic and that made it easy to spot the Gamacs and the Prsskian spacecraft. Shok ordered four fighters from departing cruisers to join them on the search.

Each time they found a looters spacecraft on the ground, they scanned the area for whatever activities it was engaged in. Most of the looters were robbing expensive homes of abandoned possessions. Abandoned possessions may not have been their target when they arrived but pirates will take what they can get when they can't take what they want. Jeonk made no effort to stop the looting. Stopping it would take too much time and it was too unimportant to bother with. The only thing left for the Pirates was capturing slaves, and the entire party wanted that business stopped.

"There are dozens of Gamac and Prsskian ships on this planet," Shok guessed, "maybe hundreds. My scanner shows something happening on the top of a hill a few miles ahead. It looks like four Gamac corsairs surrounding a big house. The house has a landing pad with a small spacecraft at its rear and there is firing coming from inside the house. I'm ordering our fighters to hit the corsairs in the aft section to destroy their thrusters. We should be able to take a look inside the corsairs to see what the Gamacs are stealing.

The four fighters made short work of the grounded corsairs. One of the pilots reported, "The corsairs are finished and the Gamac crews are running. Do you want us to bring them down?"

"Let them run; they have nowhere to go," Shok replied. He turned to Jeonk and said, "I'll take one of the shuttles down and see how much damage they did. I think there are survivors in the house."

"I'm going with you, and you put on your pistols," Alice warned. There were a few repetitions of 'me too' after Alice made her announcement. All of the royal party left the command deck, well armed, to go to the mansion with Shok and Alice.

The mansion would have been quit a plum for the pirates to pick. The owners were obviously very rich. Everything inside the mansion looked expensive and there were many empty spaces where goods had been removed.

An older couple with a young man and woman were standing over another young man who had been killed by the Gamacs. The women were crying and the young man was trying to revive his dead brother. There was nothing Shok or the others with him could do to help. Except for the dead man, none of the others were injured.

Jeonk remarked, "We should take a look at the Gamac ships and the one on the pad. I'll tell these people to leave if the one on the pad will still fly. They have already taken at least one load of their possessions to Nordic. They came back once too often."

The four Gamac ships were partially loaded with loot of many different kinds from different places. There were no people on the first three corsairs. The fourth had a young Astian girl tied with metal straps to one of its seats.

Alice had been tied like that when the Gamacs kidnapped her. She rushed to the girl and began removing the straps to get her loose. Alice turned to Shok and said, "I told you they would be taking slaves. I'm sure they have a market for them on Prssk and Gamac. Most of our fighters are on Nordic; we can't stop all of them but we can stop some of them."

Aklee put her hand on Alice's shoulder and said, "Our fighters aren't on Nordic and they aren't very busy here anymore. Alice, Yit will take care of it for you."

Grol made his offer, "Our fighters will be searching every part of the planet for anyone not in the evacuation centers. As they make their searches, I will order them to shoot down or destroy on the ground, all of the Gamac or Prsskian ships they see. I'll and make sure they check for slaves before they do any shooting. I'll do that as soon as we get back to your cruiser."

"I and Shok carry radios with us all the time." Jeonk suggested, "You can use mine right now. The Royal Cruiser crew can patch you in to your commanders."

They returned to the mansion and started the grieving owners and their family toward the small spaceship. On the way, the young man asked Shok, "Why didn't they destroy our spaceship? We had no way to stop them."

Shok answered, "Because it is expensive and they wanted to steal it with everything else. They would have left you dead and flown it out themselves. There is a big market for personal spacecraft. You tell your parents not to come back. If they come back, they will die. You have no time to return. This planet and everything on it will be destroyed before you can complete a return trip."

The Royal Cruiser searched the planet for several days rescuing individuals and small groups of stranded people who couldn't make it to the evacuation centers. Grol's fighters were very effective against the looting pirates. The view of the planet from the Royal cruiser showed many crashed pirate corsairs and even more were caught and destroyed on the ground. The Gamacs and Prsskians apparently got the word after the Horde fighters went after them. No more pirate spacecraft were seen in working condition on the ground or in the sky as the days dwindled to Impact time.

The progress of the evacuation went better than they had hoped. After the shift of the spacecraft from Ker to Ast, it appeared all, or most, of the people on Ast would be rescued. The smaller spacecraft scoured the planet for those who couldn't make it to the evacuation center during the final days. Most of those making a final desperate effort to reach safety were from desolate areas where travel wasn't easy, or communication systems weren't the best.

Jeonk and his guests on the Royal Cruiser decided to watch the rogue suns impact. They would return to Ast ahead of the debris to make sure the interplanetary rescuers made their escapes before the planet was destroyed.

The small talk on the Royal Cruiser was about the possible affects of the galactic collision. It seemed to have brought every society in two galaxies into its focus. Aklee asked, "Shok, what do the people on the planet your from, you said its name is Earth, think of the collision? Are they as worried about it as we are?"

Shok answered, "The people on Earth can't see the collision as well as we do. Earth astronomers do see your galaxy. They call yours the Magellanic Cloud, and see it as a galaxy traveling in the same direction as ours. They think the collision is the result of the two galaxies touching, sort of rubbing shoulders as they travel together. They are very much interested in the collision but it doesn't worry them. They don't think the two galaxies are going to destroy each other."

"What do they think about the war?" Grol asked. "Or do they know about it?"

"They don't know about it," Shok replied. "Earth is an isolated planet on one of the spiral arms near the outer edge of the galaxy. The only inner galaxy news they hear is from us, and we haven't had an opportunity to tell them. They don't have manned interplanetary spacecraft yet but they are building fast. It won't be very long before they can go where they please and inform themselves."

Aklee asked, "If they are all by themselves on the edge of the galaxy, are they all like you and Alice?"

"No," Shok replied, "We have white, brown, black, red, yellow and mixtures of each. How we happen to have so many races on an isolated planet is something for the theorists to speculate about, but I don't think anyone really knows. Other than the color of our skin, we Earth people look pretty much the same."

"They must be friendly with each other," Grol remarked. "They wouldn't have outside problems pushing them into war."

"Inside problems cause as many wars as outside problems," Shok responded. "There is always a war of some kind in progress on Earth, but most of us are friendly when we're not fighting each other."

Jeonk interrupted the conversation, "If you want to see the collision of the suns, now is the time to look. The two are so close together the view is staggering. This is truly a once in a lifetime occurrence."

The cruiser's blast shields covered the viewports for protection. The two suns appeared as glowing orbs of light on the command pedestal holograph and they were within minutes of the collision. The small sun was lined up to impact the large one dead center.

The two rogues had been lining each other up for months and their moment was approaching. Huge lances of super heated gaseous discharges spread between the two. Each sun seared the other in a final locking of fiery horns. The flames on the outer rim of the small sun leaned toward the larger, pulled by the large sun's more intense gravity. The smaller sun developed a large fissure, the beginning of its breakup, as its lesser gravity fought a losing battle to the power of the greater.

The smaller sun began to rip apart even before it ground into the center of the larger. The noise of the impact couldn't be heard on the command deck, but everyone there was well aware of the colossal display of unbridled power being watched on the holographic display, within the quiet security of the command deck.

The small sun sank into the death-dealing heart of the large sun, splitting the larger into pieces, pushing its ruptured surface in all directions. Planet sized chunks of the larger sun careened outward in a fury of flame twisting, turning, churning paths. The careening smaller pieces followed the larger pieces to form their own reign of burning horror on whatever got in their way.

Hot debris exited from the rear of the large sun as the smaller sun thrust its shattered, twisted remains through the larger sun's boiling center on its journey in the opposite direction. Millions of small burning shards strung themselves out behind the large sun like a dagger from hell that had penetrated its body and ripped out its flaming heart.

The colliding suns' Goliath explosions forced their shattered parts into the flame battered space, grinding the smaller parts into even smaller parts, and slamming the larger one's together; crushing them, and forming more burning asteroid challenges to the lives in their paths. Planet sized chunks of sun impacted with other planet sized chunks of sun, spreading the burning debris in all directions around the deadly burning suns, forming clouds of searing rubble to speed the astral cadavers to their final destructive rest.

Grol remarked, "It will take at least one day for our scientists to collect enough data for an accurate picture of where the debris is going. They will be able to tell us if or how much of it will hit Ast."

Jeonk noted, "There is a large cloud of the stuff on the other side of the suns' collision. The cloud seems to be heading in the direction of Ast. If we get in front of it and stay ahead of its course, we'll know within a day if it's going to hit Ast. The cloud of solar debris is spread out and very thick. I don't see how it can miss. Most to the stuff in it looks big enough to kill a planet.

"Shok, tell the pilot to bring us in front of that large mass of asteroids."

"All right," Shok replied, "and I'll tell him to set a course for Ast as soon as he is in the center. If it travels away from us, it will miss. If it doesn't, it will hit Ast."

The cruiser's rear scanners locked onto the careening mess of metallic fire. The field of rubble spread quickly outward on the unstable course forced on it by the explosions. There were constant collisions within the hot mass of debris. The massive collisions spread the debris cloud into an even wider path. Holes appeared in the mass of burning asteroids. The crashing remains of the suns once again filled the gaping holes. The field of hot rubble was in constant motion but its main path kept it on a constant course for Ast. Hopes for a miss dwindled with each hour until it was obvious; Ast was targeted for death by the hot roiling debris.

Shok reported, "The course of the cloud of asteroids set. All we have left to do is take a look at the leading edge of the part that will hit Ast, and what is following it. We may be able to see how much will hit early and when Ast can expect the death blow."

The mass of rubble they were in front of had become cone shaped. The pieces first blown out by the explosion were leading with the later following. The leading chunks of rubble would miss Ast but they would be visible from the planet. Anything on the planet after the leaders passed would need a lot of luck to get off the planet. Shok made his calculations for the speed of the leaders and then ordered flank speed to Ast.

"How much time do we have after we reach Ast?" Alice asked.

Shok gave her his best, calculated, guess; "We'll be on Ast for ninety seven hours before the stuff behind us arrives. I suggest we leave early. Some parts of that boiling rubble pile seem to be accelerating. There are pieces back in the pack that appear to be catching the leaders. Maybe they received an extra hard push from one of the bigger pieces when the suns broke apart or maybe a secondary explosion pushed them off later and faster. The field of debris is strung out far enough to cover the whole surface of the planet. Nothing will be alive after that mess hits Ast."

Shok Contacted the Argan Cruiser Commanders, "Be off the planet in ninety five hours after we arrive and I will signal my arrival time to the fleet. Take everyone you can get on board before that time and go immediately to flank speed. Ast is finished after that time. Keep your scanners pointed toward the collision just in case you must leave before then." He turned to Jeonk and said, "I gave them two hours grace time. We'll have constant updates on the progress of the debris to make sure two hours is enough?"

Grol was just as emphatic to the Horde crews, "Get your crews off the planet in ninety five hours after my arrival or on my signal. Don't expect to survive on the planet surface that is away from the first hits. There are burning asteroids coming at you that are big enough to go through the planet. If I say get off, I--mean--right now! Leave with what you have."

The next hours were hectic on Ast. The spacecraft crews boarded the frightened evacuees with intense urgency. Those leaving late were crowding each other as though being closer might be safer. They knew there would be no return trip and nothing to return to. The evacuees were grim faced and quick to comply with the urgent orders of the crews who were determined to lift the last person off of Ast. As the final hour approached, there were few spacecraft waiting to be loaded. Most had cleared the planet and escaped the approaching cloud of death.

Grol and Aklee were delivered to Grol's destroyer so he could protect his crews in the evacuation. Jeonk, Shok, Alice and Aslain went immediately to the Ast's surface. They were on the ground inside the last evacuation center in operation. They watched as the last of the evacuees from the center boarded the last cruisers to leave.

Just as the last ones were leaving, they received an urgent message that one hundred and seventeen evacuees were waiting in a center they thought had already been emptied of evacuees. The evacuation center was thirteen hundred miles away. The only ship left that could pick them up was the Royal Cruiser.

All four of them rushed to the ship and put it in the air on a heading to pick up the last people on Ast. Shok put the scanners on the incoming asteroid cloud and said, "We don't have a lot of time. The first of the asteroids will hit in less than half an hour and they will hit right on the pickup point. Those people couldn't have picked a worse place to be late. After landing, we'll have eighteen minutes to find them and get them loaded before the nastiest storm we've ever seen comes down on us."

Jeonk informed the crew, "Fifteen minutes after we land, everyone is to be back on board and the hatches closed. There are no last minutes to use. Anyone outside after that time will die here.

Shok took his place at the command pedestal and did the fastest short-range cruiser flying he had ever done. He wheeled the cruiser as it approached the Evacuation Center, spun it to the ground, popped the hatches and jumped out of the command seat, motioning the pilot to take his position and be ready to leave in a hurry. Jeonk, Aslain and Alice made it outside ahead of him, running toward the evacuees. Jeonk yelled at the first one's he saw, "Where are the others?"

The evacuees were stunned by the urgency of the three people coming at them. They hadn't been informed that they were minutes from death. Shok ran hard, passed the group, entered the building and shouted, "Everybody out and on the cruiser. You have two minutes. He grabbed the nearest arm, spun the girl to face him and said, "Where are the others? There are one hundred seventeen of you. Where are they?"

The girl answered, "They're in the next room. What's the matter with you?"

Shok barked, "Get going! Now! He shoved the girl toward Jeonk and the exit.

Ten of the cruisers crewmembers had exited behind Shok and were hurrying to the Center. Other crewmembers stayed by the hatches and pushed the evacuees inside the cruiser as fast as they arrived. The evacuees were angry about the brutal way they were told to get going and the poor treatment by the strangers pushing them outside but there was nothing they could do but complain to each other. The cruiser crew was too busy to bother listening to them. The fastest moving death any of the crew could experience was coming at them with the certainty of sunlight.

Jeonk, Aslain and Alice cleared the first room of confused evacuees by pushing and shoving them through the exit to the waiting crewmembers. Shok rushed into the next room and found the missing evacuees lounging, talking and reading books. He went to the far end of the room, drew his pistols, fired a few rounds into the air and shouted, "Get off of your butts and get out!"

The evacuees allowed themselves two seconds of stunned disbelief before Shok lasered a few more rounds into the air, adding to the number of fires already burning on the ceiling. Their stunned disbelief turned to panic as they got off of their butts and ran for the door to avoid the crazy man setting the place on fire.

Jeonk was waiting for them on the other side of the door. The evacuees entered in a hurry but the people in the room they had just entered seemed more reasonable. They slowed down to ask what was going on and began milling around instead of leaving. Jeonk drew his pistol and fired into the ceiling at the same time Shok entered the room. Shok joined Jeonk in the pistol fire. The burning ceiling caused the evacuees to renew their run for freedom from the shooters. The cruiser crew shoved, pushed and kept them hurrying to the cruiser.

The Argans quickly manhandled the evacuees into the cruiser. They had them loaded within Jeonk's fifteen minutes deadline but Shok's estimate of the worst storm they would ever see was a little off. The Argans could see the first of the hot meteors hit as they entered the cruiser.

The hatches were being closed as the pilot punched his thrusters to lift off. The Royal Cruiser left the ground with meteors hitting around it. The pilot quickly pushed the Cruiser's thrusters to one hundred percent to get away from the cloud of asteroids thickening above them. The pilot held a low course to keep ahead of the cone shaped cloud of burning debris and lifted as he maneuvered to safer space.

A small meteor hit one of the Royal Cruisers center thrusters as it climbed out of the storm of fire. The Royal Cruiser's thruster began to overheat. The pilot shut down the damaged thruster to keep it from exploding. He tried to compensate for his loss of speed by using his Light Accelerators, but the same asteroid had damaged the Light Accelerators. The loss of the thruster caused the cruiser to begin slowing and slow meant they wouldn't make it. The cloud was widening above them and they needed more speed than the damaged cruiser could give them to keep ahead of it.

The tractor beam that grabbed them was the most welcomed thing any of them had felt for days. Its heat made them a little uncomfortable, but it gave them the added speed they needed to get out from under the cloud of death. They watched the planet Ast being ground into its destructive funeral march as the tractor beam pulled them free of the hot asteroid cloud and into open space.

Grol had been told of their plan to rescue the last evacuees and he was afraid they didn't have enough time. If they cut their timing too fine, they would die on the ground. He positioned his destroyer to get them out if he could. Grol watched the Royal Cruiser's lifted off, and he thought they would make it until the Royal Cruiser began to slow down. He put his tractor beam on them and pulled for all the beam was worth.

After Grol's destroyer pulled the Royal Cruiser to safety, he radioed and said, "I'm glad you made it. Unless you want a slow trip to Nordic, dock with me and we'll finish the trip together. I have plenty of space for your crew and passengers."

Jeonk and Shok were the last to leave the Royal Cruiser. Shok asked just before they made their exit, "Are you going to give it to him?"

As Jeonk picked up the brief, he answered, "I've intended to do that for the last few days but I wanted to give it to him as a parting gesture. I almost waited too long. I'll give it to him first thing."

Grol and Aklee were waiting with Aslain and Alice as Jeonk and Shok left the cruiser. Jeonk walked directly to Grol and handed him the brief, saying, "This brief explains what we call Light Infusion Thrust Technology. It has the design specifications for our Full Spectrum Accelerators, the technology that gives us intergalactic speed.

I wanted to give this to you as a final gesture. Thanks to you, the gesture is still possible and it isn't that final. I'm sure your scientists will figure it out but this will make it much quicker for them. If you find you need more help to develop it, we'll be glad to give you the help you need. Thanks for pulling us out from under that rain of death."

Grol was surprised by the unexpected gift. While he was finding his voice, Aklee remarked, "It was no more than you did for us on Turt. We don't meet people like you very often. When we do, we like to be friends with them with us as long as we can."

Grol found his voice, saying, "Jeonk this will save the billions of people we formed the Empire to save. I want the gratitude of this Empire to have some substance. If there are any tyrants that try to take over you or your galaxy, we will take them on together. I will be proud to fight beside people like you, Shok, your tough Argan friends and your Galactic Forum people. I wish we didn't have to go galaxy hunting. It's a tough job and we have found good friends in yours."

Grol's last statement gave Shok an opportunity to say something that had been on his mind since Turt was destroyed, "I don't think our two galaxies are doing what the Hika and your late Emperor's scientific buddies say they are doing. I think the astronomers on Earth are right. The galaxies are just rubbing shoulders as they travel together. They are causing big problems around their edges, but the two galaxies aren't killing each other.

While you are developing the technology to leave, I think it would be a good idea for your 'scientific' astronomers and our Argan astronomers to get together. We should get rid of the late Emperor's scientific sycophants and take an actual scientific look at the situation. We may be able to plot the real course of the two galaxies, and determine the actual danger the two galaxies are to all of us. I would like to have a better opinion than the one we now have before I believe something as far reaching as the destruction of our two galaxies. I like to know the people who actually have their hands on a crisis have the expertise to understand, evaluate, and solve the crisis. If the Hika space station survived, we can buy it from them, or use it with them to get that opinion."

"Shok! Is this another one of your gut feelings?" Alice asked.

"If this is one of your gut feelings," Grol remarked, "we'll just tell the two galaxies to stop bothering us and get back where they belong."

Shok laughed and replied, "It's not a gut feeling but I'm having a lot of trouble believing what I've heard so far. There is just something about it that doesn't fit. I can understand the Hika. They are so close to the shoulder rubbing that their planets are in immediate danger and they have to leave no matter what.

"I can understand the dead Emperor's point. He took over an Empire in crisis and wanted to hang on to the crisis to amplify his Imperial ambitions. He could, and may have, manipulated his scientists and their information for his own purposes. He may have used scientifically false information to increase his imperial stature by attempting to take control of two galaxies instead of one.

"What bothers me is this. The two galaxies have been bosom buddies for millions of years. Suddenly, your galaxy, according to your, and the Hikan astronomical teams, decided to slip under ours, take a new direction and even go so far as destroying each other by banging their nucleuses together.

"All of this new galactic activity is supposed to happen in a very short time. Where does the energy come from to force a change in direction? No one has pointed to a new source of energy to make the two galaxies do anything they haven't done in the past. We must all accept that they are colliding but what new event has happened to make anyone think the collision pattern has changed?

"I don't believe what I've heard. We need a cold, calculating, scientific look at this collision business. We need some of our best physicists with the astronomers."

Grol and Jeonk looked at Shok for a long time, not knowing how to answer him. Alice walked over to Shok and put her arm around his waist. Grol spoke first, "Shok, if you will make periodic checks of the teams progress and take command of the team while you are on site, I'll put the very best scientific team I can put together to work on what is actually occurring.

"The Hika space station survived and we can use it. I'll also give you whatever you need from the Empire to prove a nearly gut feeling about the collision. I have a great personal respect for your opinions. I think they are seldom wrong. Besides that, I don't want to listen to Aklee, daily punching my eardrums, telling me how wrong I am if I don't do it."

Jeonk added, "Shok can make two trips each year until the project is finished. We'll put the best team we have with yours and Shok will do the hiring. I'll do my best to return with Shok, and while we are in your neighborhood, we can do some visiting together. Aslain and Alice will want to come with us to visit Aklee. Maybe we'll be able to do some things together that have, absolutely, nothing to do with disasters.

Shok remarked, "If the two galaxies are actually going to destroy each other, we can hire Jarl Gast to pull them apart. He may need three cables for a job that big."

There were some chuckles after Shok's remark and the good mood they were in gave Aslain an opportunity to put in her word of hope, "Our galaxies may be at war, but the people in them are not. Our many different people have given each other intergalactic support under very dangerous circumstances. Only good people who respect each other can give that depth of support. Now, we know each other. There is peace between us and it appears to be a widespread, friendly peace. I hope our people will always be peaceful and friendly."

THE END

MARVIN E. FOX

www.ingramcontent.com/pod-product-compliance
Lightning Source LLC
Chambersburg PA
CBHW080902120626
46555CB00008B/2920